FOR THE WIN

D.C. Knights Book 7

JUNO CHASE

I pretend to look around, but I was actually looking at you.

anonymous

Chapter 1

Congressman Lincoln Pierce shuffled the papers on his desk, as if moving them around might bring some order to his mind. He needed a break from all the legalese he'd been reviewing for hours. At this point, simple three letter words were beginning to look odd.

His stomach growled and churned. *Hangry. That's what he was.* Hungry and Angry. How could he be so hungry at only eleven in the morning? He'd take a break for food and come back to this.

On his way out of the office, he paused at Opal Meyer's desk. Her purse was gone and her computer turned off. The last two weeks had been intense—nonstop drama unfolding with some of his top employees. The way Opal had handled each situation spoke volumes. Empathetic yet to the point. She unravelled dilemmas and acted quickly. The admiration he had felt for her ever since they met had blossomed into something more for him.

These were difficult times politically when it came to dating. To being attracted to someone. *Anyone.* How in the hell was he supposed to deal with genuine affection in a climate where so much could be taken out of context? Lincoln could practically see a neon light flashing before him—PROCEED WITH CAUTION.

Being the boss made things ten times harder. Even he wasn't that dense. If he wanted to pursue a relationship with Opal, either she'd have to quit, which he would never ask her to do, or he would have to fire her. That would be a great way to start a relationship. *No.* He'd continue to rein in his feelings. He'd have lunch alone.

However, as he passed by the staff bathrooms, Opal emerged as if on cue.

"I'm so glad I caught you. I'm off to lunch. Have you eaten?" he asked. "I'd be happy for some company." *So much for distancing himself from her.*

"I'd love to. I was going to grab a quick bite downstairs, but lunch with you beats that any day." She smiled brightly at him.

They walked through the building construction and out the front door, both talking about how inconvenient the construction was but how nice it would be to not have dripping ceilings. The walk from his office to the food truck assemblage was only five minutes. Every day, six food trucks parked along the street.

The aptly named DC Taco Truck was parked at its usual space in the line-up. The line was fairly long, but it would be worth it. The stuff coming out of this little mobile kitchen was as good as at any restaurant in the area, if not better. The lingua tacos were to die for, and the churros were always super fresh. The caldo de mariscos called to him as well.

"I've been meaning to get down here to try some of the food. I've heard people rave about it," Opal said as they passed by the statuesque buildings that lined the streets near the Capital.

"I can't eat fancy all the time. I come here at least once a week for lunch. You like adventurous food?"

"I do, actually. Any recommendations? It all looks good."

"I was thinking the fish soup. Also a suite of street tacos: pork back, carne asada, and lingua. If you like tongue, this is the best there is."

"Tongue? That is adventurous. I've never had it, but I'm willing to try."

"Great! Grab a seat over there," he said pointing to the tin tables. "They go fast and one just opened up. I'll order for us."

"How much will it be?" Opal opened her purse and dug around inside.

"Let this be my treat," he said as he turned to the truck to order for both of them and she moved quickly to nab one of the rare open seats.

When Lincoln walked towards the table, he paused to take in Opal's distinct beauty. There was a classical elegance about her. Her features weren't unusual or exotic. It was more about how she moved, how her lips curled up into a smile and how her eyes twinkled when she got on a ranting roll. She tucked a loose strand of hair long brown behind her ear and smiled as he approached. He sat down and their shoulders brushed against hers. Purely by accident, and the touch left a lingering warmth.

"Why, thank you. You are a fine gentleman." She looked at the tacos on her plate using a dainty finger to open them a little wider for her inspection. "I'm going to guess this is the lingua."

Lincoln picked up his own lingua taco. "I'll go first." He bit into it with relish. The flavor was similar to brisket, the meat rich and fatty on his tongue. *Damn, it was the best.*

Opal looked back and forth between Link and the taco several times while holding hers at the ready. "Okay. Here goes." She took a tentative bite and chewed thoughtfully.

Link took another bite, watching her with great interest. "Well?"

"That is good. Really good. It's much better than I thought it would be."

"It's funny how food truck food always seems better than in a restaurant. I don't know if it's the water or being outside. It's just better."

"I agree. And it's nice to be here with you. We're usually working so hard; this is a nice change of pace."

"My sentiments exactly. I notice you're not devouring that taco."

"It's good. Not my favorite thing I've ever eaten, though. I'd probably never order it again." She held it up to him, half eaten. "You want to finish mine?"

Lincoln looked in her eyes. *Would it really be crazy for us to date?* But they were in public. And it sounded so corny in his mind, the last thing he wanted to do was to drive her away. He took the unfinished taco from her. "Happy to help a lady out."

Opal laughed a little, and put her hand on his arm briefly. It was all he could do to not ask her out then and there, in spite of the mess it would cause. Before he could say anything she spoke.

"I always wanted to ask you. Why did you join the Navy?"

"I wanted to see the world. Thought it'd be better

if someone else paid for it. That and to serve my country, of course."

"Good answer. But that's what you have on the website. That can't be the only reason?"

"Part of me thought I'd look dashing in Naval whites. A surefire way to get the girls."

She lifted her delicate eyebrow and Lincoln's heart skipped a beat. She could read him pretty well and wasn't afraid to show it.

He held up his hands as if he was giving up. "The real reason? I wanted to be a hero. Save the world." It sounded corny, but it was true. He was more than a little relieved when she didn't tease him about it.

"And now? You still want to be a hero? You're not jaded?"

"It's hard not to be jaded in politics. But I don't like that word. I do like to be realistic."

Opal rubbed her hand under her chin. "That is the god's honest truth there."

"But the hero part? I don't know if I believe it. I mean, I like the idea of being a hero, but they are so one note. Brave. Period. People are complex. My friendships aren't about that. But in front of my constituents? Damn straight I want to be the hero."

"I love that answer. I've never heard anyone say it quite like that before," Opal said, picking up her second taco and taking a much more confident bite of it. "I knew that about you, having worked with you, but I've never heard you say it."

He shrugged. It didn't feel like they were in the middle of a lunch crowd. Somehow she had a way of making the conversation feel intimate, like it was just the two of them. "I'm a man for the people. So, Madeline tells me that you teach ballet on the weekends?"

"Yeah. I have ten sweet little girls and two boys. My studio's in Anacostia. The neighborhood isn't too bad. Fairly safe, during the day, anyway. The kids are low income, and it's my way to give back. One of the girls has Down syndrome. I used to be scared of that—I didn't know how to deal with it at first, but then I got to know her. And we adapt things for her all the time. She's the sweetest, most innocent, person on the planet. The happiest, too. I just love her."

Lincoln loved the way her eyes softened, the way her expression changed. "How long have you been teaching them?"

"Not long, only two years. When we started they were a handful. A bunch of wiggly bratty kids at first. The lip I got? Oh Lincoln. You should have heard them. Sounded like New Jersey truck drivers. But this year, they've really changed. Grown so much. They've come out of their shell. Nice kids. We're doing a production of Giselle this year."

"The blunt truth with you. You know, Opal, I have

to say, joking aside, I admire you. It's incredible, actually."

A little heat rose to her cheeks. She was blushing. "I'm much nicer there than I am on the job."

Lincoln shrugged his shoulders. "You get the job done and done right. Can't always be worried about what toes you're stepping on."

"I'm glad you have my back, Lincoln. It's great working for you."

"I hope you plan to stay with me," he said,."Our current project will launch me into the national cycle. And I need you there. But you've been here for a number of years now. I hope you're not burning out or looking elsewhere." The fact that she was one of the most capable people in his office made it all that much harder to not be attracted to her. Link had always liked strong women. If she did leave, the only benefit would be that dating her would no longer be an issue. It would cause a whole host of problems for his office otherwise. It was Opal who held everything together.

"I'm not going anywhere."

"Kat will be moving into Carleen's position. Transitioning over the next few months. Would you be interested in her job? Senior Legislative Assistant. It's a move in the right direction."

"You're really going for the presidency? You're serious?"

"Yes, ma'am. That's why this project is so important to me."

"Why do you want to be president? I mean, I know your background, and I know you, but I don't think I've ever heard you say why. The real reason why, not the sound bite."

"It's probably because I never told anyone."

"Is it a secret?"

"No. I just, it's not something I talk about. Remember we were talking about heroes earlier? Well, the reason I want to be in politics is centered around that."

Opal paused in her eating, watching him with her serious blue eyes tinged with a bit of gray.

"When I was little, like the fifth grade, we had to move. I got beat up as the new kid. A lot. And really, nasty things. Bugs in my school bag. This one kid had it in for me. He'd hide around a corner and jump me for my lunch money. Classic bullying stuff. I guess I was different. I was in a speech and debate club, and I used to be in art, too."

"Speech and debate? As a fifth grader?"

"Well, I liked to talk and I liked to argue, so my teacher set up the club just for me. Only a few kids came, but my teacher was pretty awesome."

"Yeah, she was."

"And, one day, I talked that kid out of beating me

up. Pretty soon, we started playing baseball together, and became... well, not friends, but not enemies, either. I know now, looking back as an adult, he was just lonely. His dad was high up in a tech company, they'd moved twice already that year. He'd had to move to six different elementary schools. And I liked the feeling that it gave me, being able to talk my way out of a situation. Make change through words first. Actions came later, sure."

"It's harder now."

"In some ways, yes, that's true. But in some ways, it's never changed. Most people have the same goals, they just can't agree on how to get there."

"But the presidency? How do you make that leap?"

"I want to be a force of change in people's lives. Help them live in a safe place, make our world better with more education, those sorts of things. I like being the complex hero there. And I'm good at it."

"You're not in it for the fame and glory?"

"I'd be lying if I said I wasn't. It's an awesome power, but let it get to your head, and everything goes south. I've seen too many go that way. It's a hard drug to fight."

"I've always believed that you're one of the good guys."

She said it without irony, and a hopeful warmth sparked in his chest.

"There's something I wanted to ask you about the Service Dogs of America. The organization helps provide dogs for PTSD veterans. But right now, the armed forces are sort of turning a blind eye to the organization. Do you think you could talk to someone in the Naval forces to help put their stamp of approval on it?"

"See, Opal, now here's where the realistic part of politics come into play. I can certainly ask, but don't hope for anything so spectacular."

"All right, thought I would try. If you don't ask, the answer's always no, right?"

"True. You ready to head back?"

"Sure. I'm glad we went to lunch. It's nice seeing this other level of you. I mean we work together, and we work hard, but I like getting to know you too."

Link wasn't sure what to do, so he sat there staring.

"You okay?"

"Oh yeah. I'm fine." This wasn't the right time to pursue a relationship with Opal. And now that he had offered Opal Kat's job, the opportunity seemed even further away.

Chapter 2

Lincoln was back in his office, trying to plow through piles of legislation. He took his glasses off and rubbed at the pain on the bridge of his nose. He made a mental note to get a new pair. Carleen Bigalow put a gentle hand on his shoulder. They'd worked together for twenty years, and he trusted her like family.

"Only a few more things to sign," she said. She flipped through a stack of papers, placed it in front of him, and dropped her perfectly manicured finger on the next line.

He put the glasses back on, wincing. Maybe it was time for progressive lenses. He lightly pushed her hand away. While they were good friends, he didn't particularly want a sisterly touch at the moment. He put his finger where hers had been to backtrack through the pages. He didn't have time to read every page, but he skimmed the salient parts and prayed he didn't miss something hidden deep within all the 'whereas' and 'where-to-fors'; he had to trust his staff to check the details.

"Kat looked this over, right?" he asked.

Katherine O'Malley was the Senior Legislative Assistant who initially reviewed all documents that crossed his desk. "Yes sir. She would have flagged anything worrisome."

He flipped back to where Carleen had originally been pointing and signed with a flourish. They repeated the process with four more documents, except he didn't bother to read through anything else. It was sad, but a reality of politics. Half the bills they passed, he didn't have time to read himself, and he relied on his staff to have done due diligence. He signed where Carleen pointed. She stepped away and neatly tapped the pile of papers into a neat stack.

"All right, Carleen," he said, putting his pen back in the holder on the desk. "Why don't you tell me what's up with the whole Vegas meeting. Who is coming with me?"

Carleen dropped into the chair across from him, crossing her legs neatly at the ankles. "Sir?"

Carleen was like everyone he hired—smart, dedicated, resourceful, and willing to do whatever it took to survive in DC. He trusted her with every aspect of his office, but the mood in the office had shifted over the last few weeks. Ever since he'd announced SUNFLOWER to the small group of women he felt most qualified to handle the situation.

"Don't play coy with me. Something is going on around here. I haven't pushed because I trust you all, but things are getting down to the wire." He put his hands together. "Out with it, Carleen. I can't deal with much more bullshit when it comes to my staff."

"Sir..."

He'd never seen her look so uncomfortable before. After all these years working together, he expected her to be able to speak frankly without fear.

"Carleen, this week has been screwed beyond all measure. And you know more about it than you are letting on. I can tell by looking at you. I'd beat you at poker, and you know it." As he spoke, he stood and looked out his window, turning his back on her. The view wasn't all that great, but he figured not looking directly at her might help her open up. "First the thing with Lizbeth goes haywire and I have to get her out of that huge mess. I'm telling you, untangling that cost us an arm and a leg and a good deal of personal capital with the intelligence community."

He glanced over his shoulder. Carleen was looking up at the ceiling, not quite ready to talk. "Then, the

Cheyenne debacle with the sex tape. I have no idea how that is even going to pan out, and I am putting a huge amount of trust into Kenny and Dallas. And the funny thing about all of this, it sure seems coincidental. It has to do with the timing around SUNFLOWER."

Lincoln spun around to face her, leaning palms flat against his desk. "What the fuck is going on around here?"

Carleen looked a little startled by the sudden change in conversation tactics. "Sir. When you told them about SUNFLOWER, that they had to decide who was going...?"

He narrowed his eyes waiting for her to continue. It was unlike her to prevaricate on anything.

"Well, sir...they are all equally qualified. You didn't seem to care who might go with you. Instead of pulling out their resumés and deciding, they chose to have some fun and play a game to determine who would go to Vegas."

Lincoln wasn't opposed to a little competition. He encouraged it most of the time, but Carleen's demeanor told him they weren't playing a simple game of five card stud. "Out with it."

Carleen breathed in, obviously not thrilled with where this was going.

"They are playing something called Monument

Bingo. Or, were. I put a stop to it, but there have been some obvious repercussions."

Carleen went on to describe one of the most insipid games he'd ever come across. A *kissing* game? The notion that these women—these strong, independent, intelligent women—were stooping to the level of what amounted to something he expected from a thoughtless frat boy, flooded him with anger. Disappointment, more like. And for what? Why go to such outrageous lengths to decide who would go?

"When I asked them to figure it out who was going with me, you know what I expected, Carleen?"

"That they would do a pro-con check-list for each and every person?" Carleen asked.

"Exactly. Not this. Not an insipid game."

"No, sir. Not this. I told them to stop, but I suspect they continued anyway."

He put his hands on his hips. "How long have you known about this little game of theirs?"

"Since last week."

"They *all* agreed to this? That the winner of this... this...stupid game...is going with me to Vegas?"

"I insisted that they stop. Unfortunately, I did not stay on top of them to verify they had. I should have picked one of them myself at that time. I am sorry, sir."

Lincoln dropped back into his chair. He'd played his share of games, but he'd never done anything that toyed with the human heart. When he was in college, he'd dared friends to do physically reckless things. Sure, tossing a piano off the roof of a ten-story building had been crazy. At least no one had been hurt with that one. The piano was crushed, but it had sounded totally cool on impact. Filling his buddy's dorm room with a thousand balloons had been time consuming, but it had taken the other guy's mind off a particularly frustrating lab experiment. The way he and his ship-mates let off steam while overseas, blowing off the angst and anxiety while at war, had included pranks on other guys that made everyone laugh. Mostly, anyway.

Sure, the everyday work life at the office could get a little boring, but what excuse did his employees have for playing this particular game? Was their work not exciting enough for them?

"It's too late for that now, Carleen. Do you know who's going yet?"

"We have a meeting this afternoon to finalize things. I've been assured we will have a name by the end of the day. If not, I *will* pick someone myself."

"But you basically gave it your tacit approval by not squashing it like a bug?"

"Sir? I put the kibosh on it as soon as I knew. Immediately."

"I suppose there's nothing more we can do right

now. Be sure to schedule a meeting with Eleanor in IT to clean and remove all offending pictures." Lincoln rubbed his temples. "Wait, Cheyenne was with those men as part of this game? That's how she met them?"

"Coincidence, sir. The men were unaware of the game. It just so happened to be at the same time."

Lincoln rolled his neck. If it wasn't so early, he'd consider breaking open the Scotch. It was that kind of day. The blackmail threat of a sex tape that involved Cheyenne LeFleur, one of his staffers, was still on the table. He had every confidence that Kenny Marshall and Dallas LeFleur would be able to clear the mess up, but he wouldn't rest easy until their plan was in place and the threat was finally over. Link hated unfinished business of any kind, and this was of the worse political sort he'd encountered in a while.

He waved his hand, dismissing her.

She paused at the door. "I am sorry, sir."

"Don't be sorry, Carleen. You did your part. I'll have a talk with appropriate staff members individually."

Lincoln closed his eyes. To think that all of them had agreed to this Bingo game blew his mind. He pulled up Instagram on his desktop. He had an official account that Madeline was in charge of, and he knew how to use it, unlike some of his esteemed colleagues in Congress.

He started with Chloe Cassell. Her account showed a picture of her at the Jefferson Memorial. Lincoln shook his head. Just the one #monument posted. She was young and an intern, so he'd give her a pass.

And what about Katherine O'Malley? He pulled up her account. There was a picture of her at the Washington Monument. *You too, Katherine?* Her disregard for respect felt almost like deceit. Could he trust her not to do something so stupid in the future? Especially if she was about to take over Carleen's position? She should know better than to get embroiled in adolescent games.

Next, he looked up Madeline Asher. They would have to talk too, but he wasn't sure if it would amount to anything. He had a feeling she wouldn't be staying long, anyway. She went all in with work, spending long hours as necessary, but Link got the impression she would do what she wanted, no matter where she worked or who she worked for. Her loyalty was to her ethic and her work, not her employer or current brand.

He pulled up Lizbeth Crandall next. No pictures of her. He breathed a sigh of relief. She already had her hands full with the events at the Chinese Gala. He couldn't talk to her, anyway; she was no longer working for him. He'd miss her skills, but glad that she had the opportunity to further her career.

How was it that Eleanor Winslow had four pictures? *Unbelievable.* Her IT knowledge was high quality, but she didn't care about social norms. It was impossible to tell what she was thinking at any point. The way she'd helped figure out the blackmail scheme over the last couple of days was phenomenal. Even though he didn't want to, he'd have to talk with her as well. He was not looking forward to the awkward and uncomfortable reaction, but his team needed to be held accountable. He had to make sure nothing like this ever happened again, especially once he officially announced a bid to the press.

He didn't really want to look at Cheyenne's account. Good lord. She was the one that had the sex tape which ended up being used to try and blackmail him. On the tape was someone who looked exactly like him. Watching him do things Lincoln would never even dream of had made him lose sleep. Lincoln was a one-woman-one-man kind of guy. He girded his loins and clicked on Cheyenne's account. There were twelve #monument photos. *What in the...?*

He scrolled through, looking for the men who had sent the blackmail tape, but he couldn't find them. There were photos of food more than anything. That was her passion, after all, and thankfully she would get to explore that professionally. The fact that she was leaving was the best decision for everyone.

Now. Who else was in that group? Right. Opal. *No way.* Disappointment flooded through him. How could Opal be involved in this too? Just as he clicked on her account, she entered the office after a warning knock.

"Sorry to trouble you, sir, but I wanted to confirm a couple of the details for the Vegas set-up."

It was like being caught with his hand in the proverbial cookie jar. Half-annoyed, half-chagrined, he closed the window before it had fully loaded. He didn't really want to see Opal's proof. Or imagine her kissing other men at various monuments around the city.

Link wanted to ask Opal about the game, but decided not to. Carleen had assured him the game was over, but he wasn't sure if that was correct by the looks of Instagram. The most recent update had been just a couple days ago.

Opal glided into the room, quiet as ever, the hint of rose or gardenia or something that would be cloying on anyone else was fresh on her. Enticing. *Damn it.* Every time she got near him, he noticed something about her that he shouldn't be noticing.

Employee, Pierce, off limits.

"Lunch was nice. Thanks again," Opal said before she opened her ever-present notebook—the one he joked once was her work bible because he'd never seen her without it—and listed off the things he needed to know. "Any questions before we begin, sir?"

I do have one question. Are you playing the game?

He wasn't ready to confront Opal over it. The less he knew of her involvement, the better. He felt, if he was honest, jealous. Aside from the game being an incredibly stupid risk from a professional point of view, he was actually jealous. He was her boss, not her lover. He could never be that to her. Unless she quit. Or he fired her. But he couldn't do either of those. He needed her here, in his office keeping everything together. Hell, he just offered her Kat's job.

"Let's get started, then. First up, seating chart logistics. I'm planning to have you sit next to the governor of Nevada."

He shoved aside the judgments and focused on the task at hand. "Why would you do that? She's about to be my primary opponent in my presidential bid."

Opal tilted her head toward him as if he should know. "The best way to overcome an opponent would be to make them your ally, sir. If you convince her to be your running mate, you'd have a strong ticket."

"You think I don't know that? It comes across more like you're trying to set me up personally, not professionally."

"You don't know for sure if she is going to run and besides, she *would* make an amazing VP. She's smart and connected." Opal pressed her lips together. "If not VP, consider her as a First Lady?"

You, Opal, YOU, would make a good First Lady, not the governor of Nevada. How could you even suggest it?

"My being single is not your problem." He tried to say it kindly, without exasperation. "Please stop delving into my personal life. Look at political affiliations all you want, but do not, I repeat, do not set me up with anyone again."

Opal was completely unreadable. "Of course, sir."

He should have asked her out at lunch. Made his feelings for her known to pre-empt any more of this nonsense.

"I'm serious. I do not want a political marriage to facilitate my rise to the top." He would not be that guy.

"Of course, sir," Opal said. "Consider it a politically motivated seating chart, then."

"Fine. Anything else about Vegas?"

She had a couple of details to finalize. After covering them, she stood up as if to leave.

"Hold on a second."

Opal dropped back into her seat. "Sir?"

"At the afternoon meeting, I'll be announcing both Liz and Cheyenne's departures from this office. Your help with both situations has been most welcome, but please keep the details private, even after the general announcement. Loose lips sink ships."

"Duly noted. Others have asked about their absence. It was a bit of a shock to see Cheyenne's cubicle completely empty this morning. I've been telling people that she had a sudden career opportunity. With cooking. The office was excited for her, but upset they couldn't throw her a goodbye party. Same as Liz' sudden departure earlier in the week."

As she spoke, he couldn't take his eyes off her lips. Their sweet bow shape were perfectly kissable. The more he told himself she was off limits, the more he wanted her. Was it fair for her to be kissing everyone else? *No. She couldn't be playing this game.* Not Opal. Of all the staffers in his office, the one most definitely not playing the game was Opal.

She closed her notebook and set it on her lap, hands clasped together on top. She was the best. She was able to get shit done and look good doing it. Lincoln tried picturing Opal going out on five dates with five different men and smiled. Not that she couldn't get the dates, but he just couldn't believe that she would play a game like that. Unfortunately, that meant she wouldn't be going with him to Las Vegas. It would be someone else accompanying him. *Damn.* Why had he left the decision up to them? He needed someone competent at his side. He wanted Opal.

Chapter 3

Opal glanced at Senior Legislative Assistant Katherine O'Malley's meeting reminder as it popped up on her monitor. It simply said 'Vegas Appointee' as if it were any ordinary meeting. There were no notes included that explained the last two weeks of the game taking place privately amongst the women working fort he honorable Congressman Lincoln Ulysses Pierce. In fifteen minutes, they'd be making the final decision of who would be going to a top-secret meeting in Las Vegas.

Opal had been working for Lincoln for nearly four years now. Even though he could have practically any woman in DC, even though he was on one of the top committees, and even though he was powerful in DC, he was still a nice man. He was conscientious of his staff. He was kind to his constituents. But he was strong as nails when it came to political wheeling and dealing, and he was known for his no-nonsense negotiating. There was something sweet about him underneath all that political strength. *He was realistic.*

And so incredibly handsome. Opal sighed and chided herself. It was much better if she didn't think about his classic good looks. His salt and pepper hair. His sweet, sweet smile. Those lips she wished she could trace with her finger. *Stop it. The boss. He's the boss, girl!*

He was one of those truly good guys. He'd make an amazing husband for some lucky girl. *Someone like her.* She shook her head. *Stop being ridiculous.* She was an employee. Besides, it would be a fun ride to the presidency, and Opal wanted to be there, right next to him, his right-hand woman.

If no one ever found out about the game, that is. *It has to be over.* She opened up Instagram and perused through the accounts. No one had gotten to five kisses yet, so the Bingo game was still in limbo. They didn't have time to extend the game, thank God. She should have followed Carleen's advice and nipped it in the bud then, but she got sidetracked with the Liz and Cheyenne drama. Now, Kat would make the decision. Which was what they should have done in the beginning.

Link should have assigned someone to go with

him. *But no.* He asked the team to pick the right person. Instead of a boring and mundane but logical decision to send the most qualified staffer to the meeting, the team went to a bar to discuss their options. While there, Madeline Asher, the Communications Director, jumped in with her own twist on things and suggested they play a kissing game—Monument Bingo.

"It'll be fun," she'd said.

The thought of kissing that many random guys did not excite her in any way, shape, or form. *Five guys, five kisses, five monuments.* Ugh, gross. That was not how she operated. She only said she'd go along with it at the bar almost two weeks ago because she didn't want to be a spoilsport.

Pinching her bottom lip, she regretted not speaking up. Lamely, she had suggested drawing straws, but no one had paid her any attention. She should have just stopped it there, but everyone seemed excited. Then there was agreement amongst the team. She honestly thought between Madeline and Cheyenne that the game would be over in a few days. Except it wasn't. Unfinished business—especially due to frivolous reasons—made her want to scream.

She scanned the office and saw her officemates were busy on other projects, which unofficially made her the lead on organizing the big SUNFLOWER meet-up in Las Vegas. She and Andrew Donohoe were working together to make sure the agenda was settled, along with any other generic questions and concerns. Donohoe Industries was the primary backer on the project. Their political clout and flush cash reserves would make sure the project found widespread bi-partisan support. Without them, there would be no SUNFLOWER. She had spoken with Yukika Math-ews, the technical genius behind the basis of SUNFLOWER, several times via email as well as on the phone.

Opal unhooked her laptop from the monitor and picked up a pen, her notebook, and her cell phone. Chloe and Eleanor were gathering up their things for the meeting as well. She caught Chloe's eyes and she shrugged. Even though Chloe wasn't going to Las Vegas, she was beaming. She met the hunky environ-mental attorney Harrison Rousseau while playing the game, and now she was in love.

It was as if all of the other women who were playing had fallen for someone hard and fast. For a brief moment, Opal wished she had played too. Maybe she would have found someone of her own to love, but she shook off the regret. *Fickle Friday feelings,* she murmured to herself. She knew she didn't need a kissing game to meet the love of her life.

The three women headed towards the conference room. Kat and Madeline were already ahead of them down the hall. Madeline wasn't anywhere her normal self these days, either. In fact, this kissing game was wreaking havoc on the normal day to day running of the office. If this meeting didn't get things in line and straighten the office back up, Opal was going to have to take the reins and make sure it happened.

Opal followed Chloe and Eleanor into the conference room. Eleanor opened up her laptop and started to answer an email. Chloe was on her smartphone. Opal couldn't tell if she was working or texting. The slight smile at the corner of her lips indicated she was probably texting. Madeline sat down and didn't do anything but take a sip of her coffee. Kat sat at the head of the table. After she got her laptop set up, she tapped her metal to-go coffee container three times.

"Good afternoon, ladies," Kat said. "I'll get straight to the point. It's been a long two weeks and as you know, we have no clear winner in our little endeavor."

The room was quiet; no one wanted to respond. Chloe and Eleanor smiled, Madeline looked miserable, but at least she was trying to seem vested, and Kat had on her poker face. It was all Opal could do to not take over.

"Madeline and I discussed the possibilities before us. We briefly considered extending the game over the weekend or looking at who *was closest to winning...*"

Opal's eyes widened in disbelief. *You can't be seri-*

ous. The game stood at Madeline and Cheyenne tied. Cheyenne was out, so that would leave Madeline. *No way.* Opal's hands clenched at her side. Madeline had set this up to win all along.

"...but neither of those are great options. Madeline and I reviewed all the pros and cons of each individual here. After a careful review of the scenario and all the actual job-related qualifications, it became clear the person who should go is Opal."

Everyone turned to look at her as she sat back in her chair. She was still flustered that Kat and Madeline had considered extending the Bingo game or a tie-breaker, and now she was in shock. This had been almost too easy. She had known all along she should be the one to go but had given up the notion when she refused to actually play along with the Bingo game. And now?

"Really?" Now that she was going, she pursed her lips together, irritated at all this pomp and circumstance which could have been avoided had they simply chosen her to go in the first place.

"Yes. You're the liaison between all the different individual components. You're working with me and Chloe on the creation of the bill. You have a relationship established with the Donohoe family. You and Eleanor are collaborating on the technical aspects of the events. It makes the most sense. It's you. You're the perfect choice," Katherine said.

The door opened, and Carleen walked in. "Who is the perfect choice?"

Kat, looking startled at first, collected herself quickly. "Opal. She is going to be Link's working partner in Vegas."

"I'm glad that you all finally made a decision. I saw this meeting invite on the group calendar and wondered why I wasn't invited. Is there a reason?"

"No," said Kat. "We...I... The truth is, I was going to invite you, but your calendar showed that you already had a meeting."

"Still, you should have sent an invite. I had a last-minute cancellation and was able to make it. Just to be sure, the decision was based on the appropriate person to go, right? Not on some silly game?" Carleen said, meeting eyes with every woman as she looked around the table.

"We didn't decide who was going based on the Bingo game," Kat said, her face a perfect oval of innocence. Carleen looked around the room and squinted her eyes at Chloe. Chloe responded with a healthy nod that felt so naïve, Opal almost laughed out loud.

She twirled the diamond tennis bracelet on her wrist around, still looking at Kat as if she didn't believe her.

"It's Opal," Kat said. "Madeline and I needed time to review the information, to make sure we sent the right person."

"Why Opal?" Carleen asked, keeping a steady gaze on Kat.

As Kat repeated why, Opal knew the line of questioning wasn't asked due to her lack of skills, but to make sure that nothing else was amiss. Had something happened to spook her? The distinct absence of Liz and Cheyenne had everyone on edge before, and now Carleen's extra scrutiny sent her pulse up a few points. Was there something else going on that she didn't know about? Hadn't Lincoln brought her in on everything that was going on in the office?

"Opal, we are so glad it's you." Madeline clapped first, then Chloe, and the rest of the girls joined in.

"You're perfect for the job."

"I knew it would be you!"

Opal, surprised by the generosity, smiled broadly. Part of her wanted to be exasperated about them playing this dumb Bingo game, but at the moment, she reveled in the praise. They had no idea how much she understood and knew about the underbelly of the entire office.

Carleen finally took her eyes off Kat and gave Opal a warm look, mouthing, 'You deserve it.'

Opal swallowed hard, thinking about the alternative. What if they had insisted on settling this with continuing the Bingo game? What if Carleen had walked in on that conversation? Heads would be rolling. Thankfully, better sense prevailed. An individual was chosen based on merit. And that individual was her.

When the clapping died down, Madeline tapped the table to bring everyone's attention back to her. "From the PR and marketing angle, I wanted to let you know that Gretchen Hughes of DCBlogAboutTown has contacted me. She has a few pictures she sent over." Madeline turned to look pointedly at Opal. "Since you know her, I thought you might have a meet and greet with her."

"Sure. I'll meet up with her. I've known her a long time now. Send me the pictures."

Madeline nodded and gathered her things, ready to head off to the next meeting. "I'm going to miss the staff meeting. Let me know what happens."

"Sure. I'll also send you the fundraising information for a press release."

"With that, we can call the meeting to a close. Unless anyone has any further announcements or anything they'd like to share?" said Kat.

"Should we have a celebratory happy hour for Opal?" asked Chloe.

"Sure. Work with Madeline on getting that set up," Kat said.

"What about Liz and Cheyenne? Are we going to get to say goodbye to them?" asked Chloe.

"Link will announce that in his staff meeting, coming up later today."

"Why is Cheyenne really leaving?" Chloe asked.

Opal met Katherine and Carleen's gaze for a moment. They were not allowed to tell anyone about either situation. Lizbeth was preparing to be part of a covert operation over in China. Cheyenne was going to Hollywood to be part of a reality television show and they had signed a non-disclosure agreement.

"Liz is leaving due to physical and emotional stress. And Cheyenne is leaving to pursue her cooking goals."

"Opal, you look like the cat that ate the canary," Eleanor said, her eyes narrowing on her.

Opal tried to control the blush creeping up her cheeks. She had been warned against playing poker with Eleanor. It was as if the woman were reading her mind.

"Yeah, dish, girl. You've been in Lincoln's office a lot lately," Madeline said, crossing her arms.

Opal considered her answer carefully. She could almost feel Carleen holding her breath as she waited for an answer. Didn't they trust her to say the right thing? "Their departures are unrelated to each other and it is coincidental that they are leaving in the same week. Both would have been gone regardless, and all I know is that they both got amazing job opportunities."

The way she said it made it clear the subject was closed.

"Whatever," Madeline said, clearly annoyed she wasn't in on something. She threw a glance at Katherine, but got no support there. "So, Opal is going to Vegas. Carleen, do you need anything else from the rest of us?"

"No. Carleen, do you have a moment?" Opal asked. She motioned for her to have a seat if she wanted and Carleen sat down. They waited until the room was empty.

"Do you need me to help with the papers for tonight?"

"No. I've got them ready to go. Nice job deflecting on the questions about Liz and Cheyenne."

"Eleanor must be killer at poker," Opal said.

"Yeah, I've heard she is, but you handled it well."

"Thanks. So, I wanted your opinion on something. I'm seating Link next to Governor Gilroy at the benefit."

Carleen looked at her sidewise. "You're not thinking of setting them up romantically, are you? The governor will be a better political ally, not a romantic relationship." Carleen pursed her lips together.

Opal wasn't about to admit that had been at the back of her mind. Lincoln had set her straight on that score, and the last time she'd set him up with someone had been a disaster. Apparently the woman had drunk herself practically under the table at the Chinese Gala the previous week. After Lincoln's stern words, she was ready to go all hands off. Or mostly, anyway.

"I think Governor Gilroy and Lincoln would make a phenomenal power ticket. She's young enough to be veep for a couple of terms and roll into a presidential spot after that, if she wants it. But, you know, Link cannot go into a presidential bid as a single man. He is already being watched, but as a single president? His dating life will be under a microscope. An electron microscope at that."

"Not your problem. It's his. And any woman he ends up dating. Your name isn't DatingHotCongress-men, so please give him some space."

"Is this coming from you or him?"

"From me. He'd never ask me to do something like this. You are going to Vegas, so that means a whole lot of busy just piled onto your plate, as Link might say. When we get back, let's discuss this further."

"You know I only have the best for him at heart. I want him to be happy."

"Me too," said Carleen, "but I don't think this is the best use of your time. I heard you got a call from Andrew Donohoe. Anything new to report?"

"Nothing new." Opal almost shared that Andrew had gotten pretty flirty on the phone lately, but he hadn't actually asked her out. Dating Donohoe could cause all sorts of thorny problems. Besides, she wasn't dating him, and if that changed, she would find a way to make things work. She always did.

Chapter 4

Opal had set up her computer on the kitchen table and worked through emails. With all the changes in the office of late, she had picked up more work than she could reasonably handle during regular hours. She was always the one to fix everything and put it back right. Most days, she didn't mind. *Take one for the team* was a recurring mantra. But on this beautiful and sunny Saturday morning, she was inside, working. She could be out riding her bike or hanging out with friends at brunch.

Life had a natural order to it, and should be acted upon accordingly. There was nothing worse than indecision. But people were odd ducks; they liked to muck with things. Boring and mundane ways that work had to be tampered with. Except finally, the decision was made. Opal smiled as she examined her spreadsheet with an unmarked task: purchase ticket to Las Vegas to attend the Service Dogs of America fundraiser. Her name was next to the task.

The fundraiser was a cover for Operation SUNFLOWER, which would take place in Las Vegas and was guaranteed to change the face of automotive manufacturing. It was Link's ticket to the big leagues. This secret meeting between the congressman and three top entrepreneurs in the automotive, battery, and manufacturing arenas would boost him onto the national spotlight. The groundbreaking deal would bring together old school manufacturing with new technologies to modernize the industry and had been in the works for months. He planned to secure a presidential nomination with it.

She got up from the table and went into the kitchen to make a cup of coffee before starting to work down the final to-do list required before the meeting. The big items were Madeline's email with Gretchen's pictures and booking a flight. Opal could have given Chloe, the intern, more to do. Even though she was smart, she was new. Which meant a lot of Opal's time was spent showing her the ropes. Eleanor was great—she always performed at the top of her game, but she was stiff. Eleanor never smiled at her jokes. But honestly, they worked together, they didn't need to be best friends.

Monument Bingo was over, but the possibility of Monument Bingo becoming a headline made adrenaline race through her system. She had to make sure the fiasco didn't adversely impact Lincoln's office. The silly game could derail the Congressman's career. If the knowledge fell into the opponents' hand—lobbyists, a PR rep, a journalist, a social blog, any senator or congressman who didn't like Lincoln—they would be done for. His career would be finished.

She didn't have time to play offense and defense, and do her actual job all at the same damn time. She thought about calling Kenny, the office's go-to fixer, to create a plan ready just in case somebody found out about it and the story broke on CNN or Fox. But she dismissed the idea. The less people that knew, the better. Her body was agitated just thinking about the last two weeks; with her heart still racing, she felt on the verge of a panic attack. Instead of capitulating to the adrenaline, she practiced a few yogic breaths to calm her body down.

Once her body calmed, she sat down at her desk and crafted an email to the congressional travel services. There was a bit of a sting for Opal, though, that she wasn't chosen initially, as she entered her name into the online travel form. She had a masters from Harvard in business with dual bachelor's in political science and American history.

As a child, she had dreamed of being a ballerina. Unlike many girls who go to ballet classes for a couple of years and move on to other things, Opal had stuck with it until high school. She could have gone professional. And, i fit weren't for her mother's meddling, she might have. Opal shook her head to clear it. The last thing she needed was to think about her mom while trying to get work done.

Opal had discovered politics. She got her first taste of it while walking in a women's march and working on a local campaign with her favorite aunt. She was voted class president for her junior *and* senior year. That was enough experience to know she wanted to be involved in the work, but not be the face of it. The popularity aspect of it made her want to burrow under a blanket and hide.

It was mid-morning already; she wanted to finish up her work so she could go outside for a walk. The Bingo game could have been averted had the congressman simply made a decision. She surmised that he wanted everyone to feel like it was a team decision. But to what end? She wished the congressman would be more direct. She wished he would be more vocal about what he needed.

But what did he need?

He needs me.

Opal shook her head. Where did that come from?

They worked together; now was not the time to get all doe-eyed over her boss. There was work to do and a lot of it. A sudden yawn escaped and she reached for her giant cup of decaffeinated coffee with a splash of half and half.

Her next item was to finalize the seating chart for the fundraiser. She wanted to optimize the chart for the congressman's benefit, and placed Lincoln next to the governor of Nevada. She was his intellectual equal and ruthless in politics. Hopefully, she would get along with her as well. *Done.* She added herself to the table, and a few other notables that Link would appreciate having the opportunity to hobnob with. She placed the Donohoe family on the other end of the room. Service Dogs of America (SDA) had no special requests other than their director be at the head table with Link and the governor. The rest of the tables were assigned at random. That was it. She clicked the save button.

She checked Madeline's email from Gretchen that contained photos. These were pictures of Chloe, one of the interns, in the middle of a fistfight between Gordy—the lobbyist from Levin and Associates—and Harrison, the environmental lawyer. Gretchen had invited Opal out to coffee to give her a chance to comment before publishing the post. *Oh, for the love of Pete. More drama?* The pictures were pretty damning, but she knew Gretchen was hoping to parley the pictures into something more substantial.

She managed to get Madeline on the phone, a miracle in and of itself, and her advice was to offer Gretchen an exclusive on Las Vegas. If she was going to turn Gretchen away from the social side of DC, she'd have to provide more political stories. Gretchen was dying to be taken seriously as a political journalist, so grooming her now made sense. Opal really wished Madeline, the PR director, would attend to these things, but since Opal knew Gretchen personally, they decided she was the better candidate.

The picture, by itself, had no value. If Gretchen published it, and then started a new series focused on the single women in Lincoln's office, that could be a problem. That could even lead to uncovering the Bingo game. Gordy was a mighty pain in the ass in so many ways. And he always seemed to get away with the most egregious things. Somehow, he came out of gigantic messes smelling like roses. But at least Gretchen had nothing on any of the business with Cheyenne or Liz. The last thing they needed was for Gretchen to go digging around Gordy.

If Gretchen chose to go to Vegas, she might capture a moment between Opal and Andrew and make up a headline. Opal personally didn't like that idea. Gretchen might figure out why they were all meeting and unveil SUNFLOWER to the public before they had a chance to and without their input and ability to control the message.

But it was a risk. Not a certainty. The real reason to invite her to Vegas was to get press for Lincoln. Those pictures of him shaking hands with the governor of Nevada and Jack Donohoe would become important after he announced his bid for the presidency. She shot off an email to Gretchen to see if she wanted to meet Monday morning.

Her cell phone rang with a video call from Andrew Donohoe. She glanced at her reflection in her monitor and realized she had no makeup on. She smoothed her hair back, pinched her cheeks and put on her glasses. She mashed her lips together, hoping to bring a little pink to them before sliding to accept the call.

"Well hello, Mr. Donohoe. Fancy seeing you on a Saturday morning. I thought you'd be out sailing around Cape Horn."

"Ms. Opal, Cape Horn doesn't hold anywhere the excitement I feel when I get to talk to you."

"Oh you jest. Such a funny guy. What's up?" She smiled tightly, hiding a twinge of anxiety. There was no reason for him to be calling. They'd discussed everything they needed to during their session.

"I'm looking forward to finally getting to meet you after all this time."

"Me too," she said, searching for something to say. "Things are mostly wrapped up here. I'm about to send the seating chart over to the Service Dogs of America."

"Am I sitting next to you?" Andrew asked.

"'Fraid not. You're going to be a few tables over, up front and center."

"Not next to you? I'm disappointed."

Opal blushed. She had gotten to know Andrew well over the last few weeks while working with him to set the agenda. He was a legend in the automotive world, leading the multinational company and new ventures. He was a bit of an adrenaline freak. She'd seen celebrity shots of him racing Formula-1 cars in Italy, he drove a few vanity rounds—top speed—around the Talladega Super-speedway in the company sponsored race car. And according to the blogs, he had skydived, drove sled dogs across Alaska, and was a climbing addict, having already scaled eight difficult mountain peaks. Red Bull wanted to sponsor him, but he didn't need the money. A woman was always on his arm, usually a model or actress. And the man was in shape. She'd seen several pictures of him without a shirt on.

And now, he was pouting about not sitting next to

her? His expression shifted and Opal tensed. He was getting to the real reason he'd called. She braced herself.

"There are a few things that popped up, and I'm concerned," he said, his face expressing a level of seriousness beyond mere concern.

"Oh?" Opal held her breath. *Did he know about the game? Did he know about Katherine and the lobbyist? Had he heard anything about what happened at the Chinese Embassy with Liz?*

"Gordy called. Wanted to know why I was going to Vegas the same time the congressman was."

Opal let out a sigh of relief. Of all the scenarios running through her head, this was the least problematic. "He probably got a hold of the guest list at the SDA luncheon; it is public. He's trying to see if anything triggers. Testing the waters, so to speak. Don't give him any reasons to." They could handle him if everyone played it cool and didn't tip him off.

"I'm concerned. He's an oil and gas lobbyist. He's only got one thing on his mind, and it's killing renewables. He could really mess up our deal."

The man was direct. He had to be, given that he was in charge of Donohoe Industries. "I've known Gordy for three years. Trust me. He's fishing. I'll bet he came up with a list of names and is calling to see if anyone panics on the phone. So please. Don't panic."

"Okay, okay, okay. I know office politics, but this kind of politics? I don't know how this works." He relaxed a little bit. "I'll trust your judgment on this one, Opal. If you're sure."

"I am." She chose a tone intending to close the subject.

"I'm not finished yet," he said, swallowing. "Yukika called me as well. Says she might have a deal-breaker."

"And?" Opal made sure to keep her face neutral.

"She's heard a few rumors about a graphic three-way sex tape. Her contact said Link may or may not be involved."

Opal was ready for this. She and Kenny had talked privately about how she should handle any inquiries that would come up.

"There's nothing to it. It was a blackmail attempt. The tape was Photoshopped, any expert can attest to it."

"Experts don't matter when a video is viral. That image will stay in people's minds. I haven't been able to get a copy, but the word is out. People are talking. Rumors might be worse."

"Does Yukika have a copy?" Opal watched to see how he would react.

Andrew tried to remain neutral, but she could tell he was trying to bluff her. "All right, fine. There's no tape. There are no digital copies. There are no hard copies. Zip. Zilch. Nada. Not that we can find, anyway. So well done. I wanted to see how you'd handle it."

"That's what I thought."

"How much will it take to have you quit Lincoln and come work for me?"

Opal wasn't sure what kind of expression she had, but Andrew responded right away.

"I know. You'll never leave Link. Anyway, I'll let Yukika know."

"Have her call me if she has any questions. I'd be happy to address them for her. Do you, by any chance, know how she knows? I'd like to track it down." Opal could take a good guess about how Yukika had heard about the tape. Gordy was playing hard and dirty. If he'd called Andrew to leak the info, then he wouldn't have hesitated to call Yukika as well.

"You'll have to ask her. I didn't ask any further detail."

"Tell me the truth, Andrew. Were you attempting to squash this deal on a dumb rumor?"

"No. Nothing like that. I want this deal for the company. Wave of the future, but I don't want to go down the road in flames of bad publicity. Figured it was more efficient to come to the source."

Opal smiled, but kept her opinion on the matter quiet.

"Look, I'm actually in town for a meeting with one of my vendors. And, well, I've heard you talk about teaching ballet before, so I thought I would see if you're interested in going with me. To the ballet, I mean."

"Um. Sure. What show?"

"As luck would have it, I have tickets to the Washington Ballet."

"Oh? I thought the season closed in March?"

"This is a private showing, something called The Mélange? A friend got them at a fundraiser and doesn't even want to go. Gave me the tickets after I beat him at golf the other day. They perform a few scenes from a number of ballets. The Land of the Sweets from Nutcracker, the dance with the prince in Swan Lake, something from Snow White, a bit from Romeo and Juliet. It's like a dance-buffet, I guess. Since you told me that you liked ballet, I thought you might want the tickets?"

It was all she could do to not cut him off. The Mélange was a high-profile event, but it was always out of her league financially. "Are you kidding? I would love them!" She immediately thought to invite her neighbor, Mrs. Borges, who lived down the hall from her. She was in her seventies and living alone. They had become friends over the course of seeing each other in the hall, and found they both had a passion for Shakespeare and Alfred Hitchcock. They visited once or twice a month to have coffee together.

"Great. The show is tonight. I wish I could have given you more notice, but I just got the tickets an hour ago."

"Thanks," Opal said as she glanced at a framed picture on her desk. She was young, maybe seven or eight, and dressed in a light pink tutu, posed in first position. Her mom was right behind her, her hair perfectly done and in a black dress. Even then, Opal had been noted as a rising star. Until she wasn't. But she couldn't invite Mrs. Borges to the show because her mother always had a way of finding things out. Her mother had taken a distinct dislike of Mrs. Borges–with good reason. Opal loved her mom, but she was so judgy and always had an agenda all her own. Mrs. Borges had a way of listening and helping Opal find her own answers to things. She had taken to confiding in Mrs. Borges on important things in a way she didn't feel safe with her mother.

Taking her mother to the show would mean spending more than half an hour together. Opal couldn't handle that kind of stress at the moment. Besides, what man casually gave tickets like this away without expecting an invitation? Andrew had bought the tickets, likely at some huge expense, knowing that offering them up hours before hand would get him an invitation. Opal wasn't sure how she felt about such a move, so she decided to be flattered by it.

"That show is legend. I've always wanted to go. Would you want to go with me? I'm not sure I can find someone at such short notice."

"I'd love to. Want to have dinner first? I can pick you up about seven?"

The fact he was ready with a dinner invite made it clear she'd called it. Andrew had been expecting her to invite him. "I love it. Can I meet you at the restaurant? I have errands to run first."

"I'll text you the address. In a few hours, the best-looking girl in DC will be on my arm. Which reminds me, be prepared for some paparazzi. It can be unnerving the first time."

"I've already experienced it working for Lincoln," she said.

"That's good. So you know how it works. Dress your best. Gotta look good for the camera."

Opal smiled so she didn't look so harsh. The way Andrew said it annoyed her, implying she didn't know how to handle herself.

Andrew cleared his throat. "Just so you know, I'm not calling Lincoln while I'm in town. He doesn't know I'm here. I could call, but I just didn't think it was prudent. If the two of us went out for coffee, I don't want the news picking it up, or those pesky lobbyists, or anyone else, for that matter."

"Okay." Opal wasn't sure what to say. Link and Andrew should not be seen together, but didn't the same philosophy extend to her and Andrew as well? She wasn't as high profile as Andrew. She wondered if Link would be offended if he knew Andrew was in town and no one told him. Both men had pretty large egos, and she was loathe to incite either one of them this close to the secret meetings they had all worked so hard on.

It would be fine, she was overthinking the scenario.

They finished the conversation with some pleasantries and Opal ended the call. She leaned back in her chair. *Hot damn.* A wealthy man. A fine-looking wealthy man. After saying goodbye to Andrew, she decided to keep her date with him to herself. This was her private life, after all.

Opal loved the art of ballet, the strength it took to be *en pointe*, the graceful leaps across stage. Opal leaned forward and ran a finger across the top of the old photo of her and her mother, smiling across the years to a different time. She still treasured ballet, but the simple beauty of dancing hadn't been destroyed for her yet in that picture. Her mom had retained a youthful appearance, and anyone would be hard put to not think they were sisters.

Usually, Opal passed along the extra freebies to her mom. Concert tickets in the skybox from the lobbyist groups. Fundraising parties. Exclusive soirees. Free food. Free booze. But not this time. Nope. She was going on a bona fide date with *the* Andrew Donohoe.

Her mom would kill for these tickets. The Mélange event was the holy grail of ballet shows in DC. Not only would she be able to be seen and heard, which was what she loved to do, she'd turn green with jealousy hearing her daughter had a date with *the* Andrew Donohoe.

With a deep breath, she moistened her lips and cast a wistful glance at Link's profile picture on the office email directory. Shaking her head, she ignored the sentiment. They worked together, after all. She was slated to be one of his top aides. No way would she risk that for a flitting feeling of attraction.

*L*incoln blinked away the stinging tears the onion had produced. He stared at the little pile of white bits. No dates lined up for the weekend meant he could consume as much garlic and onion as he wanted. He added a few more cloves of garlic and finely minced it before tossing them into the pot. Time to fry the onions, let the meat soak up all the flavors, and give the food time to let it mellow together. Fresh ingredients made excellent spaghetti sauce—Bolognese sauce, to be precise—but his mother taught him the real secret was time. It would taste fine tonight, but it would be amazing as leftovers.

It was great to be cooking again. It had been a few weeks since he'd had the chance. After a super-high stress evening the night before, Link was ready to settle in and have a relaxing evening. Dallas and Kenny had reported back late last night that their plan had worked and they had destroyed every possible copy of the sex tapes. He'd spent most of the day Saturday preparing for the barbecue he was holding the next day.

His mom would chastise him for not adding in the carrots and celery she always did, but he had to put his own twist on things. After the meat was browned, he added a cup of milk and let it absorb completely. He grated a bit of nutmeg over that and added a cup of white wine. Finally, he added crushed red pepper, black pepper, dried basil, some oregano and a healthy bit of salt. This was all way more spices than a traditional Bolognese, but he didn't care. He liked the end result. Finally, he put in the cans of crushed tomatoes. Maybe he should get one of those Instant Pot things everyone was talking about. The pressure cooking would make this part faster, and he wouldn't have to worry about the bottom scorching.

He laughed at himself. Here he was, a congressman in charge of introducing new bills to the United States of America, and actually worried about improving his mother's spaghetti sauce. A glass of Scotch ought to make it interesting, and he poured himself a glass. Most of the time, he liked the quiet being alone gave him. But it was kind of sad to be sitting at home alone on a Saturday night thinking about domestic appliances.

Reducing the heat to simmer on a back burner, he set a timer. Three hours would be perfect, but he'd dip into it at an hour for tonight's meal. He picked up one of his guitars and slumped back into his sofa. His fingers glided over the strings, picking out a couple of chords before settling into *Beautiful* by Gordon Light-foot. He had learned to play in college during a misguided adventure to form a band with some frat brothers. Six of them had gone to a Depeche Mode concert and decided they could do better.

Their band was a hare-brained scheme that fell apart after six months. Link was the only one who already knew how to play the guitar, and for the band, he'd improved while playing an acoustic one. He'd gone on to learn songs he thought would impress the guys or have the girls swooning all over him. Later, the music had saved his sanity during his deployments. The doorbell interrupted him just as he got to the chorus. He continued humming the tune it as he set the guitar down and jumped up to answer it.

The security camera at the door only showed him a woman with her back to the camera, looking away from the entrance of his apartment building. He paused to admire the delicate upsweep of hair, her long, elegant neck. She was dressed to the nines in a perfectly fitting black dress with a low scooped back.

He hadn't forgotten a date, had he? And from the looks of her dress, an important date.

"Yes?" he asked.

She turned to look up at the camera and waved, holding up a sheaf of papers. It was Opal. Opal looking like he'd never imagined her before. He buzzed her in immediately, though he couldn't imagine what she was doing at his apartment early on a Saturday night looking like that. *Beautiful.* He'd seen her dressed up before, but never glowing. What, or rather *who,* made her look like that?

Link shoved the prickle of jealousy aside. He had no right to it. He was her boss. He took in a great breath of air and opened the door to the hallway, waiting for her to emerge from the elevator. She stepped off the elevator with a grace he had grown accustomed to.

"Opal? What are you doing here?" He tried to keep his voice nonchalant, but he was unnerved by her appearance.

"Sorry I didn't call first. I meant to, but got busy." She peered over his shoulder and toward the interior of his apartment. "Hope I'm not interrupting anything?"

Was she looking to see if he was alone? Link backed away from the door so she could come in. He couldn't remember when the last time she'd been there had been. His annual BBQ last year? "Just cooking dinner. Come on in."

"I have papers for you to sign. For SUNFLOWER." She sniffed at the air. "Mmm... smells delicious. Something Italian, right?"

"My mom's sauce."

"I like the new furniture. It's classier than what you had before. And definitely more...erm...bachelor pad?"

Link patted the soft brown leather sofa. "It's brand new and very comfortable." Link's biggest secret from the world was his four-month liaison with a woman he kept from the world. Even his office staff didn't know he'd been seeing her. He'd lived with her for six months without a single photo of them together. They never went out, and hiding his relationship from the world was unnatural to both of them. Resentment from her end grew into a festering wound. What good was dating him if no one knew they were together?

The reason they split? She left wet towels on his side of the bed as a passive aggressive action to protest his limited available time. He left dishes in the sink all the time and didn't care if she wanted the kitchen spotless. They didn't work together. He needed someone who understood the pressure of constant media and dedication it took to be a public servant. A relationship where both parties acted peevish from the start was not a good one. He broke up with her. She was upset. When she left, she took the furniture with her, a ploy to get him into another argument. Instead, he had picked up a Restoration Hardware catalogue, measured out his rooms and ordered a completely new living and dining room online in an hour. Everything was leather and antiqued bronze with shades of blue mixed in.

Opal had walked into the room. "A man's man kind of place."

Lincoln agreed. His foray with the Restoration Hardware catalogue had created a very industrial look. And he'd admit to no one that he missed the scented candles and pretty pillows that came with a woman's touch.

Opal examined the oil painting above the fireplace. "Yosemite, right?"

"Yes."

"It's so romantic looking. Ethereal." Opal stopped short of touching the misty water on the painting and leaned in close to read the signature on the painting. "Albert Beirstadt? Don't think I've ever heard of him, but I feel like I've seen this painting before. The light, coming from behind the rocks, looks absolutely real. It's stunning."

Lincoln had a weakness for quality art, but he didn't like to brag about the things he owned. This was his most prized painting. It showed the natural beauty of this great country in a romanticized splendor. "It was my grandmother's. Beirstadt was a pretty famous artist a hundred years ago. Apparently, my grandfather and grandmother met Beirstadt on a train back to New York on the way home from their honeymoon. Beirstadt and my grandfather hit it off, and Beirstadt felt bad about a drinking incident on the train, so he gave my grandmother this painting as a way of apology."

"That is so cool," Opal said. She reached out but didn't actually touch the painting, her hand stopping several inches shy. "Sorry I've never heard of him, but his work does feel familiar."

"He's part of the Hudson River school. The art was a major reason for westward expansion, Manifest Destiny, Westward Ho! thing."

Except right now, Lincoln wasn't interested in the painting. He couldn't take his eyes off Opal, watching her gaze into the mists of Yosemite, a dreamy expression on her face. He hadn't seen her dressed up like this before. Had she ever attended one of the many galas or events requiring black tie? He chided himself. Opal was attractive as always, but now he was acutely aware of how perfectly tailored the dress was and exquisite her body was. A body to match the mind within. *Beautiful.*

He might have to fire her if he kept up this train of thought. Chiding himself, he told himself to get control and not go down the asshat route. It would be so easy to come on to her right now.

"You look nice, Opal. Are you headed out with your mom?" he asked, hoping she wasn't actually going out with another man.

A tiny hint of a smile surfaced on her lips and disappeared as quickly.

Amused? Annoyed? Flattered he'd asked?

"No. As a matter of fact, I'm on my way out to the ballet with Andrew Donohoe."

Feigning a sudden interest in his spaghetti sauce, he stepped into the kitchen to lift the lid and check it. She looked at him with a slight concern. Her arms were crossed and her eyes darkened. He shouldn't say anything. His relationship with Opal was completely professional. It wasn't like she could ever be anything more to him than an employee. Lincoln Pierce didn't date the women who worked for him. That way led to ruination and confusion. And yet, he had a right to be annoyed.

Andrew Fucking Donohoe? Why the fuck was she going out with him? And why was he upset about this? He had no rights over Opal. *But Donohoe? Really?* He banged the lid back down on the pot and turned to face her.

"What the hell, Opal? You're going out with Donohoe? A week before SUNFLOWER?" He made damn sure his angst was about putting the operation in jeopardy, not jealousy over her looking so magnificent for one of the richest men in the world.

"It's no big deal," she said. "Andrew comes to DC on a regular basis. No one will make any undue connections."

Link put his hands on the counter and leaned across it toward her. "How can you say that with certainty? You are going to the ballet with one of the most eligible bachelors on the planet. That is going to make someone's headline. You'll be all over the web tomorrow. You shouldn't go out with him. Not this close to the meeting."

Opal laughed and her cheeks flushed.

Link couldn't tell if it was a nervous laugh or an angry laugh. The only thing he knew was that she was dismissing his concerns.

"Chill out. It's not a date. And, even if it were, I shouldn't have to answer to you about it. I need your signature at the two flags on these papers. I'll drop them at FedEx on my way to dinner with Andrew."

Link grabbed the papers and signed them. He wanted to tear through the papers with his pen, but he kept his feelings in check. Appealing to Opal with logic was a better approach. "People seeing you with

Donohoe is going to raise flags after the bill is announced. Come on, Opal. You're smarter than that."

"Sir, my private life is none of your business. If anyone sees us, we are two people enjoying the evening. Nothing more. Nothing less."

Even though the papers were signed, he skimmed them. He'd been too caught up in other things at the office to find out who was going to Vegas with him. There, in front of him, was her name in black and white. She'd won their ridiculous game?

"You're going with me to Vegas?"

"Are you disappointed?"

No. Yes. Oh, hell. No, he wasn't disappointed, because he wanted her at his side during the meetings. And *yes*, he was disappointed because this meant she had played that ridiculous game. And won. Kissing all those guys. *Why did he even care?* Was his anger about her date with Donohoe simple jealousy or was there really concern about SUNFLOWER?

"How did you decide who was going? I'm curious about what took you all so long," he said as casually as he possibly could. "I'm not understanding the long process you all went through."

She blinked at him a few times before finally speaking, her face a calm mask. "The team just wanted to be sure the right person went." She reached for the papers, but he held them up, pretending that he was still reading them. "The papers? I need to be going. I don't want to be late."

"Going out with Donohoe is a really bad idea, especially with you going to Vegas."

Don't go. Please. Was there anything he could say that would keep her from going out with Donohoe? Probably not.

"Duly noted. The papers, please?" She held her hand out.

I can't possibly tell you how incredibly stunning you look right now without stepping across all those boundaries I've established. And Donohoe is the lucky guy who gets to take you by the arm and sit next to you all night long, breathing in that sweet scent.

"Don't suppose you have time for a drink?" *Careful, Pierce, this is bordering on badgering. If she says no, drop it and let her go, don't be that guy.*

"No." She held out her hand and wiggled her fingers in an impatient 'gimme' gesture. "Papers. Now."

He gave them to her. Pushing her to stay would put him firmly in the wrong at this point. She said no, so he accepted her answer.

"I'm sorry, Opal. It's not my place to dictate who you see. I'm concerned with the optics of you having a date in DC with the very man who is helping us develop SUNFLOWER. When we announce it to the public, someone's going to connect the dots."

Opal slid the papers into a waiting cardboard envelope and gave him a reassuring smile. "That's not likely going to happen. I'm not a high level employee. We'll spin it. Don't worry."

"You will be if you take Kat's job. Spin only goes so far, Opal," Link said, running a hand over his face. His whole world was spinning. Right now, he wanted to entice this incredibly intelligent gorgeous young woman to stay with him, but he couldn't.

Opal's lips parted slightly in surprise. "Oh. By the way. When Andrew called today, he told me that Gordy had called him, but I don't think he was tipped off. If oil and gas shows up at the fundraiser, we'll know. And also he said that Yukika had heard about the sex tape. But no one has proof, so it's moot as far as it goes. If everything goes as planned tonight."

"No reason to think it shouldn't." Link checked his watch. It would be hours yet before the whole fiasco was over, but he trusted Cheyenne's brother, Dallas, and Kenny to fix the situation. The plan they'd concocted just hours before wasn't perfect, but they had a reasonable chance of success. He resigned himself to the fact that he couldn't persuade Opal to not go on the date. "We're getting closer to being able to present this bill to the House. Let's hope nothing derails it, all right?"

"Everything will work out fine. Text me later, maybe a thumbs up when things go well tonight. Maybe a 911 if you need my help with anything." She smiled sweetly before leaving, almost as if she knew what effect she was having on him.

As soon as she was gone, Link opened Instagram to look at her account. He'd been interrupted before, and never actually checked, but now he needed proof. He wanted to draw up whatever disappointment and ire he could so it would be easier to distance his heart from hers. Her account was marked private, however, and she hadn't given his official account access to hers. Only her allowed followers, or whatever they were called, were able to see her photos.

Damn. He put on water for the pasta and picked up his guitar again. Singing usually made him feel better, and, right now, he had to focus on anything, on anyone, other than Opal. Only the wrong songs came to mind, so he hung up his guitar and focused on dinner. Once his plate was piled high with spaghetti, he plopped onto his man-sofa and clicked on his man-TV. He browsed through his Netflix list until he hit on an oldie but a goodie, *Casablanca.* That would fit his mood for the evening.

Chapter 6

Opal walked to the nearest FedEx office and mailed the paperwork. From there, she caught a cab to Marcel's, a high-end French restaurant in close proximity to the Kennedy Center. The kind of place people went for special occasions like an anniversary or milestone birthday, or before a big date at the Kennedy Center.

She was finally meeting Andrew Donohoe, the famed son of Jack Donohoe, for dinner and then the ballet. Andrew had been featured on the cover of magazines as the most eligible bachelor in the country. The outing might even qualify as a date-date. She knew he liked her, but she wasn't sure if he *really* liked her. She wasn't sure if she liked him either, to be fair. She'd only talked to him over the phone and Skype. In-person chemistry was important to her.

Either way, Andrew Donohoe was famous, and as she arrived, she scouted out the area to see if any reporters or bloggers were staked out, but saw no one. The last thing she wanted to do was appear on the paper or in the internet. But in DC, dinner was never just dinner. She was sure Gretchen Hughes, the social blogger who always covered Andrew Donohoe's activities while in town, had probably hired a photographer or would show up in person. She seemed to have a second sense when it came to celebrities in DC, but more than likely she had a web of bribed restaurant and hotel workers.

Opal got out of the cab and walked into Marcel's. Well-dressed patrons filled the outside patio. Once inside, she was surprised by how small and intimate the location was. The host was pleasant and professional, taking her coat and leading her to the best table in the house. Dark wood around the windows contrasted against the modern arches and light fixtures, the remaining details designed a palette of light colors. She had never eaten here before but had assumed some day she would, though she'd always imagined it would be with someone she loved for an anniversary. Something special. Still, she was excited to be there nonetheless.

Andrew stood as Opal approached the table. She came in for a cheek kiss and when she stepped back, he cocked his head to the side and grinned. "Opal, you are beautiful."

With a flirty shrug, she lifted the hem of her dress slightly. "Thanks, Andrew. You look handsome yourself."

"Since this is the first time we've met in person, I'm going to expect you in evening wear from now on." Both eyebrows were raised, an exaggerated caricature of sincerity.

"Very funny, Mr. Donohoe," she said drawing out the name formally and intentionally.

"Seriously, if you get any more beautiful than this, I might go into early heart failure. Please sit," he said. The maître d' pulled out her chair, then handed them menus. "The show is starting in an hour and a half." He looked pointedly at the maître d'. "Well, get to it then, find me a waiter," Andrew said, lightly smacking the menu.

"Yes sir." The maître d' did not seem perturbed. "Henri will be along shortly. He'll be able to tell you the best courses."

"What the hell kind of shit show are you running here? Get the waiter here now. I just told you we're on a tight schedule."

Opal was a bit taken aback. She wasn't used to people who treated the staff so rudely.

The maître d' excused himself with a bow. The

waiter was at the table within a minute or so. "Hello, Mr. Donohoe. I apologize for the delay. Chef highly recommends the Scottish salmon and pairing it with a Washington wine. But of course, if you'd like to see the sommelier for a wine choice?"

"That's more like it. No sommelier just yet. Opal, what would you like?" he asked. She read through the menu, and found everything looked delicious: pan seared Hudson Valley foie gras with beef and bramble essence, Scottish smoked salmon carpaccio, Maine scallops. She sucked in her lower lip, trying to decide.

"May I order for you? This is really my favorite thing to do."

Opal agreed. She wasn't picky, and her taste in food was fairly varied and on occasion she could be quite adventurous. He ordered three courses and then he asked the waiter to instruct the sommelier to pair each course with an appropriate wine. The maître d' clicked his pen and gave a short bow. His behavior was not commendable towards the maître d, but she did like that he wanted to order for her. She got the sense that he wanted to impress her with his palate. In contrast, when Link had ordered for her at the food truck, it was as though he wanted to make sure she loved the food. A subtle difference.

The meal was going to be exquisite: Marcel's was known for its fine French food. She could certainly get used to this amazing array of delicacies and two hundred dollar glasses of wine, but what she was really wanted was something Italian. Spaghetti, to be precise. It'd be nice to be in her yoga pants, snuggling up to Link watching a movie while having a plate of delicious, spicy noodles.

Get real. Stop thinking about your boss.

If she ever engaged in a more personal relationship with the honorable congressman and it didn't work out, her chance to rise with the team to the presidential level would be toast. Instead of letting herself further elaborate on that fantasy, she straightened the silverware on the table and made sure everything was in perfect place according to Miss Manners. She was pleased to note that there were no spots on the glassware or the silverware, either.

"A day without laughter is a day wasted," Opal said, only having thought of the saying, but not having a reason to say it.

"Shakespeare?"

"Charlie Chaplin."

The sommelier stopped by with a bottle of wine. He presented it to Andrew, who nodded in response. The white wine was uncorked and a sample poured. Andrew pushed the glass in front of Opal. "Would you like to taste?"

She took a sip. "It's perfect."

The sommelier poured two full glasses.

"I really like you, Opal. I've had fun getting to know you. Serious too, of course, but you have a wicked sense of humor."

"I've refined it over the years. What brings you out to DC?"

"The yacht was getting a tad boring. Like being stuck in the middle of nowhere. I like more adventure."

Opal didn't say anything, but instead took a small sip from her wine. She wouldn't get bored on a yacht in the middle of the ocean.

"That sounds terrible, doesn't it?" he asked, rubbing a streak of condensation from his water glass.

She'd been around enough wealthy people to understand that sometimes one man's dream was another's monotony. Since she had moved to DC, she'd been invited to be on yachts, motor boats, and sailboats. On the Fourth of July, a friend invited her out to a boat to watch the fireworks from the Potomac river. She and a group of friends ended up swimming from boat party to boat party and landed on a pontoon boat with a dance floor complete with a disco ball and strobe lights. So, surprisingly, she understood where Andrew was coming from even if she didn't agree with him.

"No deep-sea fishing available? No runaway marlin?"

"I wish. This was more like a floating Motel 6."

"That bad?"

"I exaggerate. Motel 6 is better. You have the option of leaving. I prefer memories rather than materialism."

Andrew was quick and witty. She raised her glass to him. "To memories."

He clinked his glass against hers. "To making new ones."

The first course came and went. She enjoyed the food as well as the company. She and Andrew talked about the way they grew up—she came from a middle-class family who moved to the big city. They had to help around the house. Andrew's family had money, but his dad wouldn't allow the housekeeper to clean his room or do his laundry. He had to do chores and work in the factory if he wanted a weekly allowance in high school. He hated it when he was a teenager, but now, he said, it gave him a whole true appreciation for work.

"What got you into ballet?" he asked. "I love that you're teaching a class for kids."

"I grew up dancing. One of those little girls enchanted by pink fluffy tutus. Then it became my thing. I practiced ballet every day for two to three hours. Weekends too. Did some hip-hop and jazz for fun, but it was never better than ballet. In the summers, I'd apply for intensive studies at the major ballet companies. You have to audition. When I was twelve, I was accepted into the Chicago Ballet's advanced program. That was amazing."

"Why didn't you go professional?"

"And give up the allure of politics? Ballet dancing is beautiful, but its hard work and extremely competitive. And I had a dance mom." It was as close to the real reason why she'd quit ballet, but she didn't want to elaborate. None of that mattered now, she tried to tell herself. She fulfilled her passion by teaching ballet to underprivileged kids.

What did matter was that she was a Harvard graduate working for a presidential-bound congressman, having dinner with a very wealthy, very handsome man. And she did it all on her own. What on earth more could she possibly want?

Spaghetti dinner and a movie.

No. No. No.

Wanting *that* would get in the way of everything she had aspired for. She straightened out the setting on her table yet again, making sure the fork was set straight and aligning the knife and spoon together. Andrew was perfectly fine. Better than fine.

"I get the dance mom thing. My dad was overbearing, but then totally aloof, never coming to any of my games. He was a hard guy. I used to hate him for it, but I guess it's good?"

"My mom was the same," Opal said laughing.

"What about your dad? What's he like?"

"He died when I was thirteen. Cancer."

"I'm sorry to hear that."

"Don't be. It was a long time ago. My mom and I made it through."

"That's what I like about you, Opal. You know the ones with brains always win."

She smiled back. When she first accepted the date, she had known he always had beautiful women on his arm. She was worried that maybe she wouldn't be able to compete with that kind of beauty, so it was nice to hear Andrew compliment her intelligence too. After they finished dinner, Andrew didn't bother to wait for the bill, he gave his credit card to the waiter who promptly whisked it away. "Consider it my treat. We talked about work, so I can write it off."

"Oh, okay." They hadn't talked about work, so the comment threw her off. Was this a work date for him? Or was it a real date? Or were they just friends? Modern dating could be confusing, at least in the beginning.

She picked up her light jacket at coat check, and they headed outside to wait for the private car. Once inside the black town car, Opal rubbed the back of her neck.

"What's the matter?" asked Andrew.

"Just tired. Work was busy."

He agreed and patted her knee. "Don't worry, sweetheart, I've never had anything I can't fix."

Opal bit her lip at the comment. It wasn't his job to fix. She wasn't a car or a problem to fix, and she didn't like being referred to as such. Or being called sweetheart in that way. He just complimented her on her intelligence and then he made a jab like that? Her *job* was to worry about the little things. The reason she was paid the big bucks, well, metaphorically, anyway. It was just a little irritation, and she brushed it away.

The car drove up to the Kennedy Center. The signature 1970s squarish building was lit up, beaming white against the dark sky. Once there, the driver opened the door for them. Andrew got out first and held out his hand to help her out of the car. He tucked her arm into his as they walked up the stairs. She didn't need to lean on him for balance, but there was something about the warmth of his companionship that made her cling to him more than she needed to. Inside was decadent—red velvet carpets, crystal chandeliers. From the ceiling hung flags from countries around the world. Everyone famous, from U2's Bono to Queen Elizabeth, had been here to attend one show or another. They asked one of the patrons to take a picture with Andrew's phone, then Opal's phone. She silently wished she would have brought one of her real cameras, but it wouldn't have fit in the tiny evening purse.

She was excited for this private event only given to board members and high-end donors. Her mom would be so jealous. Andrew took her hand as they walked up the stairs. She had never felt so glamorous. Her outfit was perfect, her hair done just right, her shoes were even comfortable. They walked down the famous hallway, and she saw that it was, indeed, a veritable who's who of DC in attendance, and then some.

After they took their seats, the lights dimmed. Tchaikovsky reverberated through the room, literally setting the hairs on her arm straight up. According to the program, the first half would be excerpts from Swan Lake, and when the curtains rose, she couldn't believe the lavish set. The show really was above and beyond.

At intermission, Andrew was approached by various men in well-tailored suits who wanted to shake his hands. He introduced Opal, but with no preceding information—no "my friend" or "my date"— just her name.

"Would you like a glass of wine?" he asked. "I'll go get you one."

"Oh, thank you, I would. White, please."

Andrew excused himself and disappeared. Opal glanced around, wondering what it would be like to have this life. It was nice, but after watching years of her mother's social climbing, she had no desire to do it for herself. She wanted her name to be on the invitation. She had no desire to be the plus one.

Andrew returned with two glasses of wine. They did a little clink, a private cheer.

"What a fantastic show so far," Andrew said. "I mean, I have heard before that this is over the top, but I thought it was hyperbole."

"I had heard, and thought the same," replied Opal. "Usually these events are way overstated, but I do have to say, it is undoubtedly the best performance I've ever been to. Thank you for the tickets."

"Aw shucks, darlin'," he said, affecting a Southern accent, "weren't nothin'. I oughta thank you for inviting me. I was half afraid you had a boyfriend you could call on."

"No. I'm not seeing anyone at the moment."

He smiled and lifted his glass in salute. "Lucky me."

After the show, all the dancers came out and each set received a standing ovation, roses thrown onto the stage—the whole kit and caboodle. Opal closed her eyes for a moment and imagined herself as a young girl on the stage. The dusty smell of chalk. The stench of body odor. The slightly cold air. She loved it, but she didn't miss it; she was glad to be where she was. They attended the special after party for the really high rollers, and Opal was sure to get pictures of all the dancers to show her students the next morning.

Andrew walked out with her to the front where the driver and town car were waiting. "Are you sure you have to go home? I'm having a really nice time with you."

"My ballet class is tomorrow morning. I'd love to, but then I won't be at my best for the girls."

"Just one more drink?"

"I really can't, Andrew."

"I love a woman with her priorities straight." He pulled her close and gave her a kiss on the lips; chaste, but the intention was certainly not.

Opal placed her hand on his upper arm and kissed him back. The kiss was nice, even pleasing, but she didn't feel the need to lift her foot with the proverbial air of love or to twirl around after in a pirouette. Frankly, she didn't even feel a zing. These things took time, didn't they?

Chapter 7

Once she got home to her apartment in Dupont, Opal's shoes started to pinch and the glamorous dress was suddenly constricting. Right in the living room, she kicked off her shoes and took off the dress, dropping it on the living room floor. To her, it felt deliciously scandalous since she was such a neat freak. In her bedroom, she changed into a pair of cotton shorts and a T-shirt, then headed into the kitchen, undecided between ice cream or another glass of wine.

She opened her fridge and scanned the options. Mrs. Borges, her neighbor, had made her a homemade flan from an old Spanish recipe that came from her grandmother. Tonight, she needed something light and opted for ice cream.

Another glass of wine wouldn't make her

hungover, but she would have a headache. If she had a headache, she wouldn't have the patience necessary to teach the class. Often, there were high-pitched squeals of joy along with constant questions that demanded all her patience. The kids' lives were already difficult, the least she could do for them was show up as her full self and not be a cranky old lady.

The class was made up of ten girls and two boys aged five to seven. She couldn't wait to share her pictures with the class, especially those of the private after-party where she got to meet the ballerinas who were still dressed in costume. Opal made a mental note that she should get in touch with the principal ballerina and have the class meet her.

Even though she could have, she never went professional. What she'd told Andrew was only part of the story. When Opal was thirteen, her mother had set up an elaborate scheme to make sure that she was cast as Clara in the Washington Ballet Company's Nutcracker. She got the role, but the other dancers taunted her afterwards. She never knew if she got Clara because of her skills or because of her mother's back-room machinations. Opal dropped out of ballet and joined the prep school dance team that was all hip-hop, more to annoy her mother than for any other reason.

With a bowl of berry chocolate cherry in hand, she

sat down on the couch. She picked up the remote and was about to turn on the TV when one of her pictures caught her attention. It was of her when she had just started photography in high school, a school issued DSLR in hand. Her hair was super long; she remembered that she wouldn't cut it until she found a new passion after she quit ballet.

Her mom tried to get involved but had no way of doing so. Opal took no classes for her to join. She took most of her photos during the school day, as she was on the yearbook team, and if she did go out on an excursion, she made sure to do it when her mom had some important social event to attend. Photography was the art of individuality.

She put the picture back and looked up across the room. On top of a glass cabinet, she had all her old cameras: Leica M3 Double Stroke with Summicron 5c, a Rollieflex 3.5e Zeiss Planar, a Polaroid, and a Canon F1, which she used the most. Her mom begged her to take up ballet again, but she would not. Not until after she was done with college. She had missed ballet deeply. And, after settling into her job with the congressman had started teaching ballet at a school serving kids who wouldn't normally have access to it. Her mom chided her for the decision, but Opal paid her no mind. She was back in tights and a leotard, moving. Dancing. And no pressure.

Her resolve was firm as her muscled thighs. Opal was grateful for it, and her memories before the Nutcracker debacle were good, but she couldn't help but feel like she had missed out on childhood, just the ability to go play outside or do nothing or read a book by herself. Every minute had been scheduled, so it seemed. The pro was it taught her discipline and focus, even though she didn't really know how to relax. Maybe she ought to try out tai chi, like Lizbeth, who promised it was calming.

Maybe. But right now, she wanted to watch a movie. She found the remote and chose Netflix. She started one that she'd put on her watchlist, a classic: *Casablanca*.

Before she pushed play, the need to get up and at least put away her dress and shoes, and to do something besides sit there and be lazy was overpowering. Instead of ignoring the feeling, she jumped up. She picked up the shoes and dress and put them in her closet.

When she returned to the couch, she curled up and wrapped a blanket over her bare legs. *I am relaxed.* To help convince herself, she took a deep breath and exhaled out her mouth. She squeezed her eyes shut and shook her head. *Relax.* She felt better. Not great, but better. She pointed the remote at the TV and pushed play. She'd relax if it killed her.

The phone rang. The special ringtone indicated it was her mom.

Great.

She pushed pause on the remote, got up and grabbed her phone. She didn't want to answer it, but usually she didn't call so late at night and was curious. "Hi, Mom."

"A little birdie told me that you went to the Mélange this evening."

She knew her mother would find out; there were plenty of people there that might have told her. "No way. Are you serious?"

"Stop that. You know it drives me crazy. I've been wanting to go forever. And my little birdie told me that you went with the one and only Andrew Donohoe."

Opal didn't answer right away. Instead, she opened her computer, entered her password and clicked to all the DC society webpages. She started to scour social media for any Andrew Donohoe hashtags and the ballet, but nothing came up. She dodged a bullet there.

"It's kind of cool, the people I meet at some of the fundraisers. But really, Mom, it's not a big deal," Opal said. She had learned the art of conversation with her mom. Too much excitement egged her on, not enough and she would combust with questions.

"What fundraiser did you meet him at? I'd

remember one you attended that Andrew Donohoe had gone to. And what was he like? What did he wear? Did he smell as good as he looks?"

"Ugh. Mom! He came as a plus one, if you can believe that. Please don't comment if anyone asks you. Try not to say anything. Not to your friends, not to a reporter. Not even for the good of my career."

"Opal darling, really? It's the talk of town, or at least to those that matter." She knew her mom well enough to know that she was contemplating the risk of dropping an anonymous comment to Gretchen's DC Blog or any place that might report on her daughter's date.

"Please, Mom. If this mysteriously shows up on a blog somewhere, then he might not want to see me again."

Opal knew from the quiet response that her mother wouldn't say a word.

"It would ruin my chances with Andrew. Even though he's always being photographed, he can be quite vocal about his privacy."

"Oh fine. I won't, darling, I promise."

"I should get off the phone. It's been a long day. And I've got a trip next week I need to prepare for."

"That's nice, dear," her mother said in that tone she used when she wasn't really listening. "So, tell me, what is going on with Andrew? Has he called you since the date?"

"Mom. We just went out *tonight*. He dropped me off less than an hour ago. No. He hasn't called."

"If I was on that date, trust me, Andrew would have texted by now. Is it possible that he's not into you, then? What about Link? What's going on with you two?"

"We have a trip to Las Vegas next week. I'll be out." Opal took a bite of her ice cream. Why did her mom think she'd want to date her boss? He was handsome. He was a total gentleman. He was funny. They had a lot in common. They had good chemistry. *Stop!* If she kept going down this line of thinking, she'd have to quit work just to date him.

"Well, if you're not interested in him, maybe I should see if he wants to go on a date with me. This is the twenty-first century. A woman can ask a man out."

Opal felt a jealous surge run down her spine. "Mother! He is my boss. You'll do no such thing."

"Retract your claws, darling. I didn't ask him to marry me."

"Don't you dare do anything like that."

"I actually had no intention of doing that. While he is a handsome fox, I'm intrigued by the way you are reacting. A bit strong for someone who *just* works with him."

"Come on, Mom. Knock it off. You know as much as I do how important the social events can be."

"That I do, darling, that I do. It's important no matter where you go. It was how I got your spot on the Nutcracker ball all those years ago. I do wish you wouldn't have quit right after; you were at the top of your game."

Opal's mouth dropped a little. She couldn't believe that she would bring that up, and that she would be proud of it, or that she didn't make the connection between the Nutcracker affair and why she quit. It had happened right after Dad died, and she didn't have the heart to say anything. She still didn't. Best thing to do in this situation was divert her mother's attention.

"Do you have any plans for the weekend? Any big parties going on?"

"It looks to be a dull weekend. Which will be fine; it will give me a chance to catch up on all those little things that pile up around the house. And there's a sale at Neiman Marcus. Georgie called me and wants to show me some of the arrivals. Want to go?"

"Thanks, Mom, but no thanks." Opal yawned and exhaled purposefully. "It's almost midnight. Time for Cinderella to get to bed."

"Who else will be going besides you and Lincoln?" her mom asked, ignoring the request to end the conversation. She asked in the same exact conspiratorial gossip mongering voice Gretchen had earlier that day.

Opal's stomach clenched. "It will be a whole range of people. All work."

"It's too bad Andrew can't meet you there. That would at least make it fun."

"Actually, he will be there."

"Oh? Why is he going to be there? He doesn't seem interested in...what was it? Dogs? Service dogs?"

"In fact, yes, he's going to be at the same luncheon with Lincoln."

"Isn't that interesting. Do you think Lincoln will be jealous, having him there? I've seen how he looks at you."

She couldn't believe the conclusions her mom was jumping to. But to be honest, she had thought the same thing. What bothered her was that it was so obvious.

"Don't say or do anything stupid, especially to your friends. I know how fast word travels in your circles."

"I am still your mother, Opal Marie. Now go to bed. And have a good sleep, little princess."

After she hung up the phone, Opal's back tensed. There was a strong desire to have another glass of wine. Instead of letting the need build up in her, she forced herself to change focus. Kids ballet. The pictures to share.

Is there anything I'm forgetting?

She had purchased a bolt of tulle and elastic for simple tutus for most of the girls. The only elaborate costume would be for Giselle. She'd paid out of her own pocket for an experienced seamstress to make that one. One of the moms had promised to sew the others for her. She placed the materials in a canvas bag and set it near the door.

She rubbed her eyes and yawned for real. She was more tired than she had realized. Instead of indulging, she turned off the TV, took the last bite of her ice cream and put the bowl in the sink, lifting her back leg into an elegant arabesque as she did so. She brought her leg down and spun gracefully on her toe toward her soft but lonely bed.

*L*incoln checked the news, as he always did, before going to bed. Nothing showed up. He half-heartedly wanted to see a picture of Opal and Andrew, only to be able to say that this publicity was going to ruin SUNFLOWER and that she needed to do him a personal favor and stop dating Andrew until after the bill was released. He might do that anyway, but cringed at the idea of butting into her personal life.

Publicity was the part of his job that he hated, having to work with all eyes on him and his team. One moment he was relieved that Kenny and Dallas had succeeded in neutralizing the blackmail scheme. The next, he was confronted by the possibility of dirtying the name of SUNFLOWER by his staff member dating one of the main supporters.

Once in bed, he tossed and turned, searching for comfort in vain. He slept fitfully. Unbidden images of Opal clouded his dreams. He'd seen her dressed up before, but there was something different about her tonight. And he really didn't like that she had been on a date with Andrew Donohoe. Forget how comfortable she probably was in his arms. Like they'd been seeing each other for a while. Had she gone home with them? Were they already sleeping together? Lincoln shook his head, trying to clear his thoughts.

He had no right to be jealous, of course. It wasn't jealousy. *No.* It was that Opal being seen in public with Andrew Donohoe could raise a whole slew of questions. That was the real problem here, not some unfulfillable crush he had on one of his employees. Opal being seen in public with Donohoe threatened the entire project. That was what bugged him the most. How could Opal put SUNFLOWER in jeopardy?

Sunday morning, Link forced himself awake to prepare for his biggest summer BBQ. One thing he could do well was throw a party. His apartment building had an upper floor that tenants could reserve for larger gatherings. A couple times each summer, he invited over a bunch of people and spent most of the time cooking. The first of the season usually included a mix of people from his office, a few lobbyists he couldn't snub for political reasons, and some old friends. Whatever family that happened to be in town was always welcome, too. It was kind of funny that his parents had ended up coming to town the same weekend every year for the last three years.

He hired a couple of teenage neighbors to act as helpers so that he wouldn't have to do everything on his own, but the grill was his domain. It was amusing to see which men came over to grab his tongs or dispense advice. More amusing, though, was that the women were happy to abdicate the cooking entirely and be waited upon.

He spent the morning forming a hundred perfect hamburgers. He had read a food lab cookbook explaining the best way to cook a burger. The trick was freshly ground meat—store-ground meat just didn't compare. His mixer had the requisite grinder attachments, so why not? Unfortunately, scaling the recipe up to twenty-five pounds of meat resulted in twenty-five times the mess and time.

It was worth it, though. First, it was important to keep the meat cold and not let the electric grinder get too hot. Even though he was a rookie, he was efficient. The burgers were made and chilling in the refrigerator before noon. In past years, he'd followed various recipes, adding all sorts of things to the meat, but this year, the version was simple. Nothing but meat until it hit the grill. Once on the heat, a generous sprinkle of sea salt and grinding of pepper was all the recipe called for.

His guests were invited to drop in anytime between three and ten o'clock. Usually it was just his office staff who stayed that late, and they often stayed to help him clean up. By four o'clock the rooftop was buzzing with conversation and laughter. The teenagers he'd hired were in charge of making sure the coolers were well stocked and the side dishes kept full. People grouped themselves around the various tables spread across the rooftop. There were about a dozen other congressmen there with their wives. None of them would dare bring a mistress to one of his functions, though he'd seen a few of them with other women in the last couple of years at places around towns. Here, though, they had to keep things straight.

What was wrong with them? When he married, it was going to be for keeps. One hundred percent forever. If he could only find *The One.*

Congressman Martin White approached him as Link flipped a set of burgers.

"You better not flip them until you see the blood on the top," the other man said.

"How're you doing, Martin?" Lincoln asked, ignoring the other man's directions. "Tonya is looking lovely as ever today."

The Honorable Martin White looked over toward his wife and held up his beer in a salute. She tilted her head and smiled at him, bright-eyed and cheery. He blew a kiss at her, and she caught it.

"She's as good as they get, Lincoln. When are you going to find someone and settle down? You're getting a bit long in the tooth to be single. You know what people are saying about you, don't you?"

"I'm only forty-seven; that's hardly doddering these days," Lincoln said, his eyes on the burgers. He laid out cheese slices on half of them, leaving the others plain. "And I'm not particularly worried about what people are saying about me."

"Yeah, you think that now," Martin said, leaning in close. "But when you go for that presidential bid? You're going to want a fine woman on your arm and no question about your manhood. I saw that exposé online. People are already wonderin'. There was that article on the Internet too, from that Gretchen woman insinuatin'..."

"You're suggesting someone being gay would be a disqualifier for being president, Martin? I would have thought better of you," Lincoln said.

Martin laughed. "Well, you and I both know that ain't gonna happen 'til a few old people in this country die off or stop voting. We've come a long way, Lincoln, but we ain't come that far. You'll be too old to run when this country is ready for an openly gay president. We'll have a woman in office before that happens."

Martin clapped Lincoln on the back good-naturedly and went off to schmooze elsewhere.

Lincoln moved the cooked burgers to a platter and set them next to the pile of buns and fixings on a table.

"Come and get 'em, folks!"

His staff turnout was disappointingly low this year. Opal, Eleanor, Carleen and Chloe were the only ones who could make it. Chloe had brought an attorney he recognized by face as her date, but the others were solo as far as he could tell.

They had filtered in while he was paying attention to other guests. All of them but Opal had gathered around one of the standup tables in the far corner of the rooftop rather than mix in with the rest of the party. He approached the small group, intending to break them up and get them mingling.

"Afternoon, everyone, thank you for coming. I trust you are having a good weekend so far?"

Chloe bounced onto her toes and back down on her heels, obviously excited. "Thank you so much for including me, sir. You remember Harrison Rousseau?"

Bless you, Chloe. "Of course. Tulane. Environmental law, helped us out with that review hearing last week, right?"

Harrison shook his offered hand. "That's right. It was a lot of fun working with y'all."

From the look of it, he'd done more than work on the legislation. His arm was around Chloe's shoulders, claiming her in front of everyone. Harrison had to be a good ten years older than Chloe. But Chloe didn't work for Harrison. There was no power dynamic there, not really.

"There's beer in the cooler and wine over on the table. Make yourselves at home, as usual," he said. "And make sure you try the burgers; I ground the meat myself this year. Trying something new. And you all should circulate. Get to know some of the other people here. That's an order."

Carleen sighed and saluted him a weary salute. She didn't look like she wanted to be here. Not one bit. Before he could check in with her about it, she slipped her arm through Eleanor's and dragged the other woman over to a group of senators and jumped into their conversation.

"Come on, Chloe, I think I see a friend of mine," Harrison said, dragging her away. "Let me introduce you."

Lincoln nodded a goodbye as he scanned the party. Everywhere he looked were people he liked and trusted. So far, none of the more annoying busybodies or lobbyists he invited had shown up. Maybe they'd stay away this year. Sammy Hewes, his best friend since his Annapolis days, and his fiancée Lauren Barnes were chatting with Opal at the drinks table.

"Sammy," Link said, opening his arms wide. "I didn't see you get here, buddy. How are you?"

"We snuck in when you were busy at the grill," he said raising his glass of wine at Opal. "We're well taken care of." The two men hugged briefly. Lincoln leaned in to give Lauren a kiss on the cheek.

"I see you met Opal," Lincoln said. "My office would fall apart without her." *Me, too, probably.*

"You're just charmingly beautiful, dear," Lauren said. "How old are you, anyway? Lincoln, why are you hiring teenagers to work for you?"

She was saying it with a smile and teasing tone, but Lincoln found it hard to smile back. It wasn't *that* funny. Opal was one hundred percent woman. She might look young for her age, but she was probably— no, she *was* the smartest one at the party.

Opal worked the bottle of Chablis back into the ice bucket and grinned. "Don't judge an album by one song."

Lauren laughed. "Really, Link, you do surround yourself with charm, don't you?"

Link didn't want to let on how he really felt about Opal so he shrugged. "In my office, resumés come first, the other traits are a coincidence."

Sammy clapped Link on the shoulder and squeezed. "Brains and beauty are a lethal combination."

Link met Opal's eyes briefly. She didn't seem to be upset by this conversation, but wondered what she must be thinking. Was it the same thing he was? There was seventeen years difference between them. Was it an unimaginable gulf? How old was Andrew Donohoe? Thirty-five? Thirty-seven, at most. *Crap.* Why would Opal be interested in him when Donohoe had youth *and* money on his side?

Opal poured him a glass of beer and held it out for him. She had an uncanny ability to know exactly what it was he wanted without him having to ask. Their fingers touched as he took it and he let his linger a moment longer than he should have, little blips of happiness darting through him when she didn't shrug him off.

"Thank you, Opal." Their eyes met and his breath caught in his lungs. He could look at her all day long.

Carleen waved at him, pointing at the empty burger platter. "Time to get grilling again."

"Thanks, Carleen. I'm on the job. Please excuse me." He squeezed Sammy's shoulder as he left the trio to tend to the grill.

He put on another dozen burgers. As he worked, his mind rushed through these distinctly new emotions around Opal, rejecting the realization that they weren't actually new, but deeply buried. He'd been attracted to Opal from the moment he met her. She was an employee so he'd forced that attraction aside. As a man, he was, in truth, attracted to a lot of women. But, more and more recently, his thoughts kept coming back to her. Every time he turned around in the office, she was solving some new thorny issue with integrity and thoughtfulness.

"There you are, Lincoln," said a smooth silky voice right next to him.

He turned to see who it was. "Oh, hello, Erica." He had invited Ms. Mitchum before their failed date at the Chinese Gala and completely forgot she might be coming. "How are you?"

"You weren't expecting me, were you?"

"I'm sorry about last week. Crazy things happening and all that."

"I was there, Lincoln. I saw that man after he was shot. I get why you had to be on it right away," she said putting a hand on his shoulder. "But I don't see why you haven't called."

He sidestepped, not enough to be obvious, but enough for Erica to know that she should move her hand. The date with Erica at the Chinese Gala the previous weekend had been nothing short of excruciating. She had drunk at least three glasses of wine before they sat down and another three during dinner. She was well on her way to being a sloppy drunk before the clock hit ten. By the time things fell apart and they were evacuating the embassy, she could barely stand on her own. He'd gotten her into a cab and sent her on her way before turning his attention on the catastrophe within the embassy.

"Sorry to disappoint," he said. "How about I make it up to you with a delicious burger?" He held up a fresh one on his spatula.

"I already had one. It was delicious. You are a good cook, Link. But, honestly? If you're not interested, just say so, and I'll move on."

Link lowered the burger back to the grill as he looked around the deck for someone to introduce her to. She wasn't a bad person, but she had none of his interests. He pointed to Sammy and Lauren. They were in a group of four other shipmates laughing. "I've got to finish the burgers, but I'd like to introduce you to some friends of mine. See the guy with the buzz cut wearing the Annapolis shirt? We call him Pepe. Just ask him why and you'll get to know him well."

"Not interested and setting me up in the same breath. Wow. And my feelings aren't even hurt," she kissed him lightly on the cheek as she headed toward Sammy, Lauren, and Pepe.

He caught Sammy's eye and he nodded in understanding. His best friend was a great wingman and knew exactly the kind of help Lincoln needed. He glanced towards Pepe and Lincoln nodded. As Erica approached, he introduced himself to Erica and Sammy made sure that she was introduced to Pepe. It wasn't long before the two of them were alone, leaning on the rooftop railing and chatting, both with huge smiles on their faces.

Another wave of people came onto the roof as a few others left. Lincoln buzzed around the roof making sure there was plenty of food coming off the grill while people had a good time. Around seven, his parents finally showed up.

"Lincoln Log," said his mom as she grasped his cheeks in both hands and kissed him squarely on the lips.

"Mom, please, not in public."

"Nonsense. You are and always will be my baby. Now, where is the wine?"

He gave his dad an open-armed hug and led them over to the drink table. "Come on, you two, let's get you taken care of."

His mother took the glass of chardonnay he offered her and held up her other hand as if she had just remembered something. "Oh, and look at this! I finally got your great-great-grandmother's engagement ring fixed. It's been cleaned and restored."

She waggled her hand at him. The ring belonged to his great-great-grandmother and had been left in his mother's care when he was a young boy, to be kept until he married. The ring was rather simple and elegant, particularly for a Victorian era piece of jewelry. Eight tines of rose gold held a simple, single diamond in the center. Lincoln had always thought it was beautiful, and now it was even more so.

"Why are you wearing it?"

"I can't wait for you to find the right woman any longer, Link. Jewelry like this needs to be touched. It's all yours when you find the right person."

Lincoln watched his parents settle into the party, greeting people they knew and introducing themselves with ease to everyone they didn't know. As they moved around the rooftop, his father occasionally reached out to touch his mom. Little, sweet, comfortable pats to emphasize something he was saying or to encourage her to continue with what she was talking about. They were about to celebrate their fiftieth wedding anniversary later in the year and were adept at finishing each other's sentences.

Opal was still manning the drink table like a bartender and eased into conversation with his parents like a pro. She had brought along Mrs. Borges, her neighbor, and introduced her to the couple. Opal had a knack for always introducing the right people at a party too. He made a mental note to ask for her help to organize a big anniversary party for his parents. Fifty years together was an achievement. And, as much as he hated to politicize the personal, making a big deal about his parent's long marriage publicly would play well for his own success.

"Your parents are amazing."

Lincoln started. He hadn't even noticed Opal at his side until she had spoken. "They are. Fifty years this fall."

"They must have married young."

"Really young, especially by today's standards," Lincoln said. They stood alone, close to the grill. He dropped his voice so only Opal could hear him and looked around to make sure no one else was close enough to eavesdrop. "Mom was pregnant with my older brother at eighteen. In those days, you pretty much got married if you got pregnant. But, I think they would have anyway, just a couple years later."

Opal nodded thoughtfully. "Still, fifty years is a long time."

"If fifty seems like an eternity, forty-seven can't seem far behind." At forty-seven, Lincoln doubted he'd make it to fifty years in any relationship. "At this stage in my life, I'll be happy for twenty-five good years with someone."

"We're in the same boat. Given that I'm already

over thirty, I doubt I'll ever have that long a relationship. Kind of makes me sad."

Link didn't say anything in return; he wasn't sure
what to say.

Opal chuckled. "Awkward. Hey, I'll stay late and
help clean up. Chloe and Harrison are off to a show
somewhere. Even Carleen has something going on."

"You don't have plans later?" he asked. "I wouldn't
want to interrupt anything with...anyone."

He turned to look at her when she didn't answer
right away.

She was looking at him, her eminently kissable lips
grinning. "Nope. Tonight, I'm all yours."

All yours? Did she have any idea exactly what
image that brought to mind? Lincoln searched her for a
double entendre, his body zinging into life, wishing he
could pull her into his arms and make her all his for
real. He shifted his feet around, hoping his sudden
erection wasn't visible to the entire planet.

Damn it all to hell.

He'd put so much effort into ensuring no one he
employed would feel harassed, and now, here he was,
teetering on the edge. When was it okay to jump? The
last thing he would do was to come on to Opal with
unwanted advances.

But what if she was doing the inviting? He
searched her face for a clue. And his conclusion was

that there was no open invitation on her face, no new obvious longing on her part. Just a friendly offer. An employee offering her boss a helping hand. Nothing more.

She nudged him with her elbow. "Hey, look who just showed up." She grinned and waved at Kenny Marshall. On his arm was one of Cheyenne's roommates, Zach. He carried a plate of cookies stacked high with chocolate chips, oatmeal, and snickerdoodles.

He held them out to the congressman. "Cheyenne says hi, but she's not able to make it today. She sent these instead."

Lincoln took the plate. "Definitely going to miss her treats around the office."

"Me too," Opal said, pulling a snickerdoodle off the top. "O.M.G. She must use some special kind of cinnamon on these things. So. Good."

"Hey, sweetie, can you do me a quick favor and grab me a glass of wine?" Kenny asked, tilting his head toward the drink table.

As soon as Zach was out of earshot, Kenny leaned in close to Lincoln and Opal. "As far as I know, we're good. I haven't heard any reports of *any* leaks whatsoever."

Link shook his hand. "Good work, Kenny. You and Dallas make a good team."

"I see you made a new friend, too," Opal said, tilting her head toward Zach.

"Yeah. And, thank you for calling me in on this, sir. I'm at your service."

Kenny headed over to a group of senators. It was not a surprise when half of them pretended not to recognize him. Admitting you knew Kenny Marshall was tantamount to having had some scandal to deal with. But Link was proud to have him at his party. He was a good man, and great to have as part of his extended team.

At some point Link's parents appeared with Mrs. Borges between them. "We're going to take this dear lady home. She's completely tuckered out."

"Oh, thank you, Mr. and Mrs. Pierce," Opal said. "That way I can help your son clean up after the party."

Mrs. Borges hugged Opal goodbye and went off happily with Link's parents.

"Kind of funny you brought her instead of your mom," Link said cautiously.

"Well, I brought my mom two years ago, and she hit on half the congressmen in attendance, married or not. It's hard to know if she'll behave."

"I hadn't realized," Link said. It was amazing how different the two women were. The few times he had met Opal's mother had been fine, and he'd been completely unaware of her schmoozing at his BBQ in the past. Whatever. She'd raised an amazing woman, so she couldn't be all that bad.

After everyone left, Lincoln and Opal cleared away the last of the dishes. The teenage helpers had brought everything down from the rooftop and left. Opal washed as Link rinsed, dried, and put things away.

It was easy work, enjoyable even, with Opal at his side helping. To help them along, he put on his iPod to shuffle. When a Tchaikovsky piece came on, Opal brightened. She spun away from the sink, doing a fancy and athletic ballet movement. Link watched, jaw open. He'd never seen Opal move like that before.

"I didn't know you danced." She was a graceful swan in his own kitchen, dancing, spinning, turning. Her long neck so kissable.

Opal plunged her hands back into the soapy water. "You know I teach dancing, right? That means I know how to dance." Her tone was light, almost teasing.

Lincoln winced at his choice of words. They were so lame. What was wrong with him? Something about Opal smooshed aside his calm and usually steely nerve and turned him into a gibbering idiot. He was almost fishing for her to jump in and assure him he was the still the hottest most eligible man in DC. Jesus. He wanted to be a hero to the world, and he was too worried about the political repercussions of asking Opal out.

OPAL HAD her hands in the soapy water when she heard thunder. She'd missed the lightning, but where there was one rumble, there was likely to be more—and more lightning with it. After a moment, there was a bright flash off to the side. She counted one Mississippi, two Mississippi, three Mississippi, four...*Boom!* Opal loved thunderstorms, and this one was shaping up to be a doozy.

They both paused at the sink waiting for the next round, dishes forgotten. She barely counted to three before the thunder boomed like a timpani roll, long and low, building into a dramatic roar.

"It's getting closer. I'm getting my camera." She grabbed a towel and ran for her purse. She always had a camera with her, but this was the first time she'd wanted to take pictures in a long time. Mostly, she'd been too busy for it but there was a good chance she'd be able to catch the lightning from the roof.

"What are you doing?"

"Just follow me." She led him out of the apartment and up to the rooftop deck. It wasn't raining here, not yet at least. The wind had picked up and the clouds to the north east churned and billowed in dark puffy waves. "Wait for it," she said.

From this height, the entire arc of lightning was visible, spreading wildly from the ground to the sky. With the next big flash, he smiled like a boy excited at finding his first frog or catching his first fish. The booming rumble reverberated over the deck after only two seconds.

It looked like the storm was going to pass them by. If she was lucky, she'd be able to get some great photos.

"Here come some good ones," he said.

Electric streaks stretched out over the sky, sometimes dipping down to the earth. Or did they start at the ground and span upwards? It was as though she could almost see the energy buzzing in each flash.

Opal steadied her camera on the railing and took shot after shot, hoping to catch a bolt of lightning at just the right moment.

Lincoln stood mesmerized by the flashes of light, a sweet and innocent delight that brightened his usually serious expression. She turned the camera toward him and took his picture just as the sky brightened in an almost blue arc. The thunder crashed loudly almost instantly—not even a single Mississippi.

"We better go inside before that lightning strikes us," he said. "There are way too many metal poles out here for my comfort."

Opal hadn't noticed the antennas and metal framework to keep the birds off the deck until he pointed them out. "Oh yeah, way too much metal. Let's not pretend we're Ben Franklin and play in the rain."

Both of them walked through the door leading back to the apartment at the same time. Their shoulders squished together, and they both turned toward each other to let the other one pass. They were within kissing distance. Opal looked into Link's eyes, then down at his lips, and back up to his eyes. Link met her gaze. A beat or two passed.

Could he read her mind? Kiss me. Kiss me now. Her heart hammered in her chest. *They were so close, and yet...*

"Oh excuse me," he said.

"No, excuse me..."

"I didn't mean to..."

They escaped from the tight spot and made their way back to his apartment. The awkward moment turned into an even more awkward moment as they went.

"I should go," Opal said as they got back. He didn't argue, and her heart ached a little at how easy he acquiesced.

"Thanks for helping with the clean-up," Lincoln said as he held the door open for her, not quite shoving her out the door.

Opal rushed out of the building and sat in her car wondering why she was so upset. She reviewed the photos to calm herself. She had taken about a hundred photos, most of which were pretty sucky. They were blurry or framed poorly. A handful were worth keeping.

The most spectacular one was the photo of Lincoln framed by the dark stormy sky and lit up by a streak of lightning. He was looking off into the distance, the delight at the spectacle before him obvious on his face, yet he was dignified and calm. Intent. Was this what Lincoln Pierce looked like when his guard was down? Opal traced a finger along his lips wondering what they might feel like on hers.

Chapter 9

*M*onday morning at Tryst, a coffee shop in Adams Morgan, did not disappoint. Opal purchased a short medium-roast drip and found a seat at a small round table near the front. She loved this place—the eclectic furniture, coffee that didn't taste burnt. The crowd was a range of diversity from tall Ethiopian women wearing colorful headdresses to men with purple streaks in their hair. She was meeting Gretchen Hughes, the same social blogger who had posted the pictures of her and Andrew without bothering to contact her for a statement.

Gretchen had emailed back agreeing to a Monday morning meet. Opal checked her watch. Gretchen was late. She was always late; something always took precedence over being on time. When they met five years ago at a photography class, her lateness ranged from traffic to unexpected phone calls. These days, her busy blog was the reason. Over the years, the excuses had changed, but her lateness remained constant.

When they first met, they had hung out a lot and even went on a few photography weekends together. Their friendship grew over time as they bonded over their art, but ever since Gretchen's exposé on the congressman's office, Opal had declined invitations and backed off their relationship. Gretchen had titled it "Link's Strong Women," and featured all the women in the office. Gretchen *had* included their bona fides and featured the consistently high level of education each woman had. Everyone who worked for Lincoln Pierce was highly qualified and came with impressive resumés. She'd even managed to feature photos of each woman in professional dress.

The article would have been great, except for the general undercurrent questioning Link's sexuality. He'd never been married and his office was full of strong, successful, single women so...the reader was left with a feeling of uncertainty regarding Lincoln. Uncertainty didn't bode well in market tests. It was part and parcel why Opal had tried to set Lincoln up in the past, but she was done with that now.

Those kinds of stories, if they got picked up in the national news cycle, could make or break careers. Opal didn't begrudge her, though; people had to make a living, and if it wasn't Gretchen, there would be someone else. *Better the enemy you know.* She couldn't help but be wary.

Opal rubbed her forehead and took a sip of her coffee. She opened her phone and started to read Gretchen's blog. There were pictures of Donohoe in DC, waving his hands to the audience. She was surprised that she hadn't shown up at Marcel's.

While they were cleaning up after the barbecue, Link hadn't asked her any questions about her date with Andrew. They had a great time, and she'd taken some amazing photos. She kept returning to the photo of him. The expression on his face was serene. Underlying that was something else. Gumption? Mettle? Courage? Those words were close, but they weren't the right ones either. *That* look in his eyes. She loved it. It was like she really saw who he was in that moment and her instinct to take a picture had taken over.

"Hi, Opal," Gretchen said as she came in the door.

Then there's the real world.

Opal waved to her as Gretchen headed to the counter to place her order. If she and the congressman ever did decide to date, it would be a nightmare. The press would go crazy. Gretchen would probably stalk her. That kind of life didn't appeal to her. But Link? So many complications there.

Opal closed the blog and opened the Service Dogs of America website. She reviewed the seating chart of the luncheon. Donohoe would be across the room from her table. She'd be next to Lincoln, and on his other side would be Kendra Gilroy, the governor of Nevada. Lincoln would be speaking during the lunch. Where was she going to seat Gretchen? Definitely not with the Donohoe's, but maybe a table in between?

"Sorry to be so late," said Gretchen. "The blog keeps me busy."

Opal didn't even bother to nod. "Where's your drink?"

"They'll call my name when it's ready," Gretchen said, sitting down. "Sooo, did you see Andrew Donohoe is in town?" she asked in a conspiratorial voice that made it sound like they were best friends. It probably got others talking, but, to Opal, the gossipy tone only annoyed her. What Opal wanted was a resolution to the photos she had. If she had to go back and forth for a whole hour with Gretchen, she'd lose her mind.

"Interesting." Opal remained aloof.

"Off the record?" Gretchen asked. "I heard that you were his date at the fancy ballet event. Tell me as your friend. I'm genuinely curious. He's a great catch."

Opal didn't say anything, but in this business 'qui tacet consentire videtur,' Latin for 'he who is silent is taken to agree,' so she made something up on the spot about work and free tickets.

"He's about as private as a goose flying south in the winter, so your date must have been something special, right?"

Opal gritted her teeth. She hated dealing with the society column. The reporting felt like bottom feeding, high school style judgements of who was in and who was out. She had to make it through the next hour without letting her emotions get the best of her. She needed to maintain a calm, collected demeanor that didn't betray her anxiety or her anger over Gretchen's blog.

Gretchen's name was called, and she jumped up to grab her drink.

Upon her return, Opal tried to smile naturally. "Do you need a comment from our office for the blog?"

Gretchen took a seat and sipped at her coffee. "This picture I have is decent," she said, retrieving her phone from her purse and entering a password. She handed it to Opal. On the screen was a picture of Harrison about to deck Gordy and Chloe standing right in the middle of it, looking like she was either going to cry or deck Gordy, maybe both. She liked Chloe; naïve as she was, she was feisty.

"'Lincoln's staff is out of control,'" Gretchen said,

adding air quotes. "Or do you think maybe 'Link's Intern in Hot Water'? Meh. That's not as catchy."

Opal sighed. Gretchen was smart, but she hadn't caught on that Gordy was an oil lobbyist and that Harrison was an environmental lawyer. Gretchen also didn't know that Gordy and Harrison had been roommates in Tulane. If she dug around just a little bit more, Gretchen would have a real story. But when it came down to it, she didn't want to do the real journalism, she wanted quick and dirty, and lots of hits on her website. If Gretchen really wanted to make it as a political journalist, she'd have to change her ways.

"Well," Gretchen said, taking a sip first of her coffee before answering, "Congressman Lincoln's intern, that good looking lawyer from Tulane, and a lobbyist. It's almost too easy..."

"Too easy to what?"

"To write a headline that suggests the wrong story," Gretchen said. She took another sip of her coffee and didn't break eye contact.

Opal was surprised. Gretchen *had* done some research. *Dammit.* Now she would have to appease Gretchen to get the outcome she wanted. Fortunately, Opal was aware of almost everything that went on in the office as well as most of what went on outside it. And in the case of Chloe and Harrison, she knew the important details.

It was also true that shiny objects drew Gretchen's attention. A nice shiny object was professional journalism. Gretchen had been complaining that no one took her seriously. Recently, she'd become very vocal about finding a way out of social blogging and her desire to move upward professionally.

Opal thought it would do Gretchen's career wonders if she started working a system based on favors rather than threats, but she couldn't say so directly. "Let's say, instead of writing about some intern and a bar brawl, which frankly might be grasping at straws, you could write an article about..."

"What really happened at the Chinese Embassy?"

"You didn't get the statement?" Opal didn't like being interrupted, and she especially didn't like the Embassy line of questioning. Lincoln had told her everything and she was glad for it now. Instead of looking shocked, she was able to easily maneuver past her question.

"Yes, but that's not what I heard," Gretchen said.

"Maybe your headline could read 'Is Congressman Pierce looking to run for President?'"

"Maybe. I'm listening."

"There's an upcoming event in Las Vegas. A fundraiser. Even though it's small, lots of big players are going."

Gretchen did not look convinced. "Instead of the

Chloe article? Hmm...And digging into the Chinese story? I have a few pictures of the gala."

"You can run whatever article you like and we can end this conversation. Or we can talk about Vegas."

"I could do both. What's to stop me?"

"An interview with Lincoln?" The words flew out. Opal smiled to cover up her look of concern. *Shit.* Lincoln would not be happy with this. Deep down, she knew he would do the interview for her. Maybe they could have a phone interview so he wouldn't have to spend much time with Gretchen in person. "And frankly," she said in a gossipy tone that matched Gretchen's, "with the Chinese story, you know as much as I do."

Gretchen sat back in her chair and sized her up. "The rumor is a Chinese diplomat had a planned US defection. Liz was involved, maybe even helped to plan it."

"That sounds a little woo-woo conspiratorial, Gretchen. That doesn't seem your style."

"The other rumor I heard is the CIA agent and Liz fell in love. My friend is a nurse at DC General and Liz is practically living there. He's guarded, but all the nurses know he's CIA. She happened to read a story in the Post and saw a picture of Liz in the background."

"You know more than I do, then." Opal breathed in a calming breath. It was amazing how impossible it was to hide anything these days. The level of accuracy, especially from Gretchen, was astonishing. People really did love to talk. All of that was supposed to be secret, and the nurses went blabbing. Loose lips really did sink ships.

Liz had been working with the Chinese embassy staff for months organizing a gala event that went haywire the previous week. The congressman had spent a lot of energy and political capital keeping the whole affair from the press. It didn't seem like the details had gotten out, though. Gretchen was obviously fishing for more.

"Don't you know everything that goes on in the office, Opal? Are you losing your touch?"

"My touch is fine. There's no story."

"Right. Why are you are trying to shut down the Chloe story? It's not that big of a deal. It's just a little romantic fun. *Two hot guys fight over gorgeous young intern.* Classic DC drama."

"Look. Lincoln's going for the presidency. The rest of it, it's playing in the weeds, it's child play. I'm giving you an opportunity. Do you want it?"

"Would you pay for my ticket?"

"Only for your seat at the banquet. Play this the right way, and maybe we can get you on the campaign trail as part of the press junket."

As Opal watched Gretchen's eyes light up, she knew she had her.

"That sounds very interesting." She set her coffee down and twirled the base of it. "Would I get an exclusive interview with the congressman?"

"Yes. I can't guarantee the interview will be longer than fifteen minutes, but you'll have one."

"Guarantee thirty minutes and I'll go." Gretchen got her phone out of her purse. "What are the dates?"

"The banquet takes place on Saturday," Opal said. "Will that be a problem?"

"No problem. I'll just get a last-minute cheap flight from a website."

Opal put her phone back in her purse. "We're good? I'll send you an invite later today."

"Is your offer a Hail Mary?" Gretchen eyed her suspiciously, then shrugged her shoulders. "Never mind. It works for me. For now. How's stuff with your mom? Is she still hovering close? Mine flies so low she is driving me bonkers."

"She's fine." Opal didn't want to sit around with Gretchen and talk, but appearances of friendship sometimes meant more than actually being friends. "She's still getting invited to all the parties."

"Is she going to be there?"

"In Vegas? Why would she be?"

"Your mom always shows up at these things."

"What? Do you want to interview her too?" Opal said. She had to physically hold back from wincing. What was she doing? What was with her and all the interview offers today?

"No thanks. There are a hundred women like your mom. No offense."

"None taken." Opal relaxed. It was hard enough already just having her show up at nearly every event in DC.

Gretchen's phone dinged. She made a show of checking it. "My calendar reminder is telling me I'm late. Gotta run."

Like clockwork. Opal sat quietly as Gretchen gathered her things, tossed back the dregs of her drink, and left. The last thing Opal wanted to do, after this crazy week, was to tell Lincoln that he had to do an interview with Gretchen, but that was the way of politics. If you wanted to avoid the shitstorm, sometimes you had to play in the mud.

Chapter 10

The direct flight from DC to Las Vegas was calm and uneventful. Lincoln, Opal and Carleen shared a row in the main cabin. First class would have been nice, but Lincoln didn't believe in wasting money on such luxuries. Plus, riding coach guaranteed that someone would take his photo and tag him, generating free publicity. If they'd been on a longer flight, maybe, but anything under ten hours was regular seating for anyone on his staff, including him.

Opal happily took the middle seat to give Carleen the aisle and him the window, their preferred arrangement. He didn't recognize anyone on the plane. Once they were midair, Carleen put on headphones and started a movie on her iPad. Link saw that Opal got a text from Andrew Donohoe with a photo of him in his private plane. He didn't want to read the words, which were probably an invitation. But instead of getting upset, like he had the first few times, he decided to engage her. *The best defense is an offense.* Besides, *he* was sitting next to Opal, not Donohoe.

"Those pictures you took up on the deck are amazing. The clarity was incredible."

Her eyes shone with the compliment.

"When did you take up photography?" he asked, his voice low as to not disturb the other passengers.

"In high school. Because my mom strictly forbade me to do it."

"Why? What's wrong with photography?"

"I don't know." She replied and brought up her phone, flipping through different pictures that she had taken. He didn't push her, but knew it was important. "I wanted to show you this one." She had stopped on a picture of gutter water, but she zoomed in on the reflection of the water and you could see a tall tree.

"It's really cool. I love the tall tree in the reflection of the puddle. It's like a juxtaposition, almost."

"It was one of first pictures I ever took after my dad died."

She pushed back a loose hair behind her ear. She took a deep breath and started again. "He died when I was thirteen. My mom went nuts. I mean, with me. She watched over every little thing. Made sure I was in the best of everything. In ballet, I was good, if not excellent. And I wanted to be Clara for the Nutcracker."

Link wanted to comfort her, he wanted to put his arms around her, but instead, he let her know that he was listening attentively.

"So she made deals with the patrons and the director, and voila! I'm the lead. So you know what I did after the show? I took my shoes and threw them at her and I walked out."

Link adjusted his seating so that he was leaning a bit towards her. "I'm sorry to hear that."

"I took up photography to piss her off. She couldn't get involved. And I teach lessons to the poor kids now to piss her off too."

"But you love teaching the kids right? You're not doing it out of spite?"

"I do love it, but when I first started, my real reason was to annoy her. I wanted to throw it in her face that she wasn't invited. But then I got to know the kids, I got to dance again, and well, my problems weren't so big anymore."

"I see. I totally understand what you're going through."

"Oh?"

"I'm third generation Navy. My grandfather and my dad were in the Navy. I was legacy, so I was expected to be at the top of my game all the time. It was like having a stage mom in every person I met. Everyone expected me to be better. I guess, in a way, it makes you better."

"That's a way I hadn't thought of before."

"It's not a happier or more pleasant way to better yourself. I'm sure there are healthier ways to improve oneself, but it does have that affect."

"Yeah. I'm still a perfectionist because of my mom."

"Tell her I thank her for that."

"Ha. No, I don't think I will. She's already got an ego the size of the Spruce Goose. I'm not going to give it any more fuel."

"But I want you to know I appreciate you the way you are. It's funny. You know, not a lot of people know this about me, but I used to be in a band. We mostly did covers, but we had a couple of original songs. I sang once in a while, but mostly played guitar."

"You did not. Seriously? That's cool. What kind of music did you like to play?"

"All kinds, but I mostly like what the kids these days are calling classic rock. Queen. Journey. Aerosmith. I was a pretty good singer too. Anyway, in the Navy, playing the guitar was my way to blow off steam."

"So what was this band of yours called?" she asked.

"Oh, now that's a secret. Let's just say it was lame enough I'm not admitting it to anyone."

She gave him a long look before glancing down at the bag between her feet. "Hey. I'm going to listen to some music for a while." She leaned down and pulled ear buds out of her purse and plugged them into her phone. "Thanks for listening."

"Happy to, Opal. I'm going to read," he said, holding up his e-reader. "Non-fiction, political."

"Thrilling," Opal said, popping her ear buds in. He could hear the faint sounds of Tchaikovsky through the speakers and for a moment, he closed his eyes, imagining her in his kitchen again dancing to music.

THEY ARRIVED at midnight DC time. Lincoln wasn't surprised by the rows and rows of slot machines blinking bright lights and annoying sounds in the terminal; he'd seen them before, but he laughed when Opal practically stopped mid-stride off the terminal to stare at them.

"Oh my god. We are in Vegas, aren't we?"

Opal had made the reservations for all three of them, so she checked in and got their room assignments. As they got to their rooms, he realized they had rooms next to each other with a connecting door between them. Carleen was across the hall from them.

As he settled into his room, Link almost knocked on the door between them to invite Opal in for a drink. The fully stocked bar begged to be used, but doing so could lead them down a path he wasn't sure he wanted to go.

He was finally starting to get to know her outside of a work context, but it wasn't enough for him to make a move. Lincoln needed to be absolutely sure Opal knew he'd welcome her interest without being the one to make the first move. And after the plane ride, he was pretty sure.

If she made the initial move, they could shift from coworkers to dating secretly, and when she was ready, move their relationship into the open. They could work through things one step at a time to ensure it was all above board—emotionally and politically. Maybe being so close to Opal had skewed his thoughts and made him see something that wasn't actually there. *Crap.*

His impulse was to scoop Opal into his arms and tell her exactly what he wanted to do with her.

Instead of inviting her over, he had a drink. He'd be meeting Kendra Gilroy soon, and, by all accounts, she was a near perfect match for him—socially and politically. Even Opal said she'd make an awesome running mate. Maybe vying for Opal was too much like running the gauntlet. Maybe he should seriously consider a political marriage. It wasn't like his own dating life had gone anywhere special.

Even so, Opal was worth it. He didn't want to settle. The tiredness of traveling all day suddenly hit him. He needed sleep. He stripped to his boxers, brushed his teeth, and crawled into bed.

LINCOLN WOKE EARLY the next morning to get a jog in. When they'd arrived the night before, the sidewalks outside the hotel had been jam packed with people, making it difficult to get anywhere. The morning, however, was a different story. There was plenty of space for him to jog around the hotel and beyond. The only problem was all the garbage on the street from the night before. Street workers were working hard to sweep up all the empty promises.

There was a fantastical feel to Las Vegas. The buildings were architectural hyperbole, fake and yet over the top fun. There was something refreshing about the tongue in cheek brashness the city offered. He marveled at their odd similarity to the feeling he got in DC. Government buildings were, by and large, theatrical in their presentation. The original architects wanted to incite grandiosity and respect for insti-tutions.

He paused to watch as couples left hand-in-hand to do some sightseeing along with the never-ending row of Cadillac limos waiting. After his run, he had to walk through the casino to get to his room. He ordered room service and took a shower. Just as he was step-ping out of the shower, Opal knocked on their connecting door.

He wrapped the fluffy white robe provided by the hotel around him and opened his door. "What's up?"

"Sorry to interrupt," Opal said, her eyes widening on his bathrobe briefly before looking away from him. "I texted earlier this morning and didn't get a response. I just wanted to make sure you're okay."

Lincoln adjusted the robe; he was pretty sure he hadn't accidentally flashed her. "I took a run. Haven't looked at my phone this morning. I'm getting dressed and then I'm going to eat breakfast." A food tray had already been delivered by room service and was on a nearby desk.

"Andrew texted me this morning. He ran into Yukika and August at the breakfast buffet."

"Crap. You think I should head down there?" He didn't like the idea of the others spending time together without him.

"No. That was an hour ago. I tried to text you a

couple times and decided to join them. Andrew made sure to keep everyone to social niceties and no one talked about anything sensitive. You have about ten minutes to get to the conference room, sir." Opal tapped her watch before turning around to exit. She closed the door between them.

Link scarfed down the breakfast he'd ordered and dressed in a polo shirt and dress slacks. He couldn't even take a jog without something happening in his absence. At least it wasn't a huge deal, and he hadn't missed out on any substantive conversations.

The conference room Opal had secured for the meeting was a spacious suite with a kitchen, two bathrooms, and a conference table that easily sat ten people with laptops and paperwork. What would normally serve as a bedroom had been converted to a miniature office with printers, a separate and secure wi-fi network, and a variety of office supplies.

Link arrived a few minutes after Opal and Carleen so he could greet everyone else as the host of the meeting. Link had intentionally dressed casually so as to appear like he was taking a vacation day. Yukika Mathews showed first. She had dressed down as asked, though there was a style about her that would never say 'casual' to anyone looking at her. Even her jeans and silk button up blouse screamed couture.

Jack and Andrew Donohoe arrived with two

staffers. *Nodding yes men.* Lincoln wondered what Jack and Andrew valued in such grinning sycophants. Was it possible that they were on more of a power trip than Lincoln had thought?

Lincoln and Andrew shook hands firmly, but when Andrew got to Opal, he took her hand and leaned in to kiss her on the cheek. This kind of greeting was normal in DC social circles, and usual with Europeans, but Link rarely saw it during business meetings. Lincoln watched the interplay closely. Opal did not look particularly shocked by the gesture, but simply accepted the light peck on her cheek. She touched her cheek lightly and her skin pinked with a slight blush.

"It's good to see you again, Opal," Andrew said.

Andrew leaned in closer to her ear and said something Lincoln couldn't make out, but her blush deepened.

"Dad, this is Opal," Andrew drew his father away from everyone else to force the introduction. "She's the smart one that I've been working with the last few months."

"Pleasure to meet you. I've heard quite a bit about you."

"Yes, sir. We worked together to make sure this conference would be a success," Opal said with a charming smile, deflecting any insinuations.

Lincoln unclenched his fist to gain control of the rising emotion and forcibly lowered his shoulders. Decking Donohoe would be a pretty bad move on his part. And irrational, to say the least.

It wasn't long before everyone had arrived and settled into seats around the conference table. Lincoln asked Opal to hand out the packets they had prepared for everyone. As she made her way around the room, Lincoln took the time to study all the faces around him.

Jack and Andrew Donohoe sat next to each other. Each had a simple yellow tablet and pen in front of them. Their lackeys were on chairs on either side of them, computers open and ready for whatever the Donohoe's commanded. Yukika Mathews had an aide with her. She sat next to Yukika with a laptop open in front of her. She was so short he couldn't see her face above the computer screen.

August Thorne had brought his wife who acted as his personal assistant. If Lincoln remembered right, this was his second wife. She had started out as his secretary while wife number one was pregnant with their second child. She looked happy enough. Staying close to a man who strayed at work made sense. They both had yellow notepads and pens. August had an expensive-looking new smartphone on the table next to his paper.

Just before Lincoln was about to delve into the project, Yukika stood up and made a half bow toward everyone.

"I'm sorry, Congressman Pierce, but before we begin, you need to address the proverbial elephant in the room."

"Would you like to clarify, Yukika? I'm not sure what concerns you might have."

"Yukika and Company cannot be seen to be part of any scandal. Your office has had a fair number of them recently. I would like to know exactly what is going on with your staff and how you intend to mitigate the various dramas of late."

"What might you be talking about?" he asked, wondering just how much had made it out into the world and how accurate it might be.

"There have been rumors floating. The Chinese gala, a sex tape. Your staff appear to be out of control."

Her sources were good, he had to give her that. He spread his fingers wide and held his palms upward before looking around the room. "I am going to be one hundred percent transparent with all of you here. For SUNFLOWER to go forward, we have to trust one other. As part of that, I am offering to share some intelligence with all of you so that you understand my involvement. However, some information is classified, and I ask that you treat it as such. It should not be repeated outside this room. Clear?"

Not that he would give them anything more than necessary. After giving them a brief description of the gala events that did, indeed, involve a defection of a Chinese official to the United States, the murder of another Chinese national, and the involvement of his staffer in the events, he assured them that she was no longer a staff member and the incident was considered closed by all parties.

"And what about this blackmail threat?" asked Yukika. "Is this pornography threat entirely taken care of?"

Link was prepared for that question as well. Opal had let him know that Andrew was asking and so he was ready for it. Kenny had managed to fix that entire issue without it leaking to anyone. And since he knew that there were no digital copies, that Yukika had no substantiated evidence, he decided a different tact.

"Yukika, I'm not sure I know what you're talking about. Can you elaborate on this...pornography threat?"

Yukika sat with her hands in front of her, fingers laced together. She raised an eyebrow and contemplated him for a moment. "Just a rumor I heard. Obviously, it was erroneous." Her smile barely made it to her lips and stopped there. Her dark brown eyes narrowed ever so slightly. Yukika had some pretty good sources, but there was no way he was going to add credence to something his team had squashed dead in its tracks. Opal smiled at him, as if he'd handled it perfectly.

"Anything else before we get started in on our real business here?" Lincoln scanned the room and was met with shrugs and nods for him to continue.

After welcoming everyone officially, Lincoln led them through the contents of their packets. The basic program was simple, but it required all of their agreement to make it work. As the morning went on, it became clear that Andrew and Jack Donohoe had been receiving a great deal of external pressure from various lobbyists. The talking points they had covered earlier had changed slightly, masking the oil lobby's agenda.

It appeared that Opal was right on about Gordy's interest in Andrew. Ellis and Levin Associates had hit Andrew hard from the oil lobby perspective. Gordy had managed to spook the Donohoe's. Opal looked alarmed at the change in discussions, but not surprised.

Donohoe Industries had its fingers in a number of pies, and it could profit from a number of models and variations on their initial proposal. Lincoln would be happy to see their subsidiaries that had anything to do with oil flounder and die a nasty pecuniary death, but he wouldn't admit that to anyone.

"My biggest concern is all those jobs that would be lost by this particular part of the deal," Andrew said. "If we meet the oil industry halfway, it would go a long way to keeping them off our backs while we are working Research and Development."

"You're being swayed by people who can't see beyond the end of oil, Andrew. They are stuck in a mentality that everyone will be driving gas-powered cars in ten or fifteen years. Oil is running out, and, one day, there will be no choices left. It's better to move things along now. Profit comes from getting in on the ground floor so when the crisis hits, you have a strong and solid foundation."

"Lincoln, I get what you're saying. But my shareholders require I look at the bottom line. A transition like this takes time. There's not going to be profit for at least eighteen months while I retool the assembly lines. I've got thousands of employees firmly in the oil industry, and moving operations to future technologies doesn't happen overnight."

"I agree it's all about the long haul, but without the vision for where you're going, you'll end up staying in the past."

"You have to give on a few things, Congressman, that's all I'm saying." Andrew cast a glance at Opal.

"You can't have everything coming into these negotiations. I'm happy to give up a few of my pets, of course, but you'll have to do the same."

Lincoln got the sense that Andrew was no longer talking about alternative fuel sources. "I won't compromise a good bill, Andrew. We worked these questions a long time ago. What's changed?"

"It's reality, Link. I'm just dealing in the real world here. You don't know what it's like to be slammed up against the wall and pinned to a way of life."

"I do know that feeling, Andrew. I have to deal with it every single day. One day I have folks who want to build a dam to provide cleaner, cheaper, more efficient energy. The same day I have environmentalists saying it's a travesty and that the dam is going to ruin the surrounding land. I can either provide noninvasive electricity or I can ruin a land that I love. I deal with it every day, and your insinuation that I don't is just plain bullshit. How'd Gordy get to you?"

Andrew glared at him. "He didn't get to me. There are certain realities of the business you don't understand."

"We've made concessions for you in the bill with employee retention packages and retraining. I suppose we will be renegotiating those as well. Along with the tax relief package I also promised. I can have Opal call our lawyers to rewrite that aspect of the bill."

"We will need our lawyers to review any changes as well," Andrew stated. He straightened up his shirt and looked like he was ready to leave.

"Sit down, son. And be quiet. I'm trying to think." Jack Donohoe had sat quietly throughout, seemingly absorbing the meeting. He rubbed his hands together. "You know, boys, as long as these changes make me money and they get you in line with the next generation, I don't really give a shit about anything else. We aren't going to turn out like Blockbuster, for god's sake. I didn't work my whole life to build a business that I wanted to pass on just to lose everything. I'm not that old, but I'm looking to hang up my spurs in another ten years and hand the whole kit-and-caboodle over to Andrew. But first, I got a bee in my bonnet to get us moving out of the dark ages before it's foisted upon us. And I reckon we're on a good path here. Truth is, I've got friends who aren't going to like this, not one whit. I'll be taking plenty o' heat for this, and it better be worth my while."

"There are no guarantees in life, Jack," Lincoln said. "But the one that we know of is limited resources run out. The sun? It's always going to be there; the more we use it, the better."

"Get to work convincing people of that," Jack said. "Some people are so stupid, they think the damn sun turns off at night."

"It's in the plan. Part of the national marketing is an extensive media campaign," Link said. "Yukika Mathews' company is at the forefront of messaging here. Yukika can you go over the tiered marketing plan?"

Yukika stood and pointed at the smart board on the wall behind her. Everyone turned to watch as she brought up her presentation. While she spoke, Lincoln watched the reactions of everyone else in the room. Jack Donohoe clearly wanted to lead Donohoe Industries into the new age, but had his concerns. Andrew actually seemed skeptical, but he didn't really care what they did as long as it looked good and they made money. He was the sketchy horse in this race, and Lincoln would have to spend some extra time schmoozing him over.

Opal met his eyes; she'd caught him with his eyes off the presentation. Her warm, encouraging smile was all he needed right then.

The meeting continued with Lincoln countering each contentious point with facts and figures, with Opal's help, one at a time, chipping away at all the skepticism and worry in the room.

As the day's agenda came to a close, Opal ordered up a round of appetizers and drinks to be delivered to the room to end the day with a bit of relaxation. The mood shifted into one of camaraderie and common purpose as they toasted a day of excellent work.

As everyone was leaving, and just as Link was about to ask Opal if she'd like to join him and Carleen for a private dinner, Andrew asked Opal if he could speak to her privately for a minute. She excused herself from Carleen and Link and followed him out the door of the suite. She paused at the door and gave Lincoln a questioning look. He held up his hands in a 'do what you feel is best' gesture. She turned away and left with Andrew.

Chapter 11

Opal was in her room, alone, getting dressed for another dinner with Andrew. After the big meeting today, Andrew walked her back to the elevator and told her to be ready in an hour. He was taking her out for a surprise dinner that evening and had already set it up. Of course, she said yes. There was a minor irritation of actually having him tell her that she was going rather than him asking. She felt guilty about skipping dinner with Link and Carleen. She should be there to review the events of the meeting and be on the same page for tomorrow. To top it all off, she was tired from the traveling and exhausted from the strong-arm negotiations amongst the powerful groups of people trying to work together.

There was a knock on her door. At first, Opal thought it was coming from the door she shared with

Link, but when she realized it was her main door, her heart sunk a little.

She peered through the peephole and saw Carleen. What was she doing there? She opened the door. "Would you like to sit down?" she asked, pointing to a small table in the corner, awkwardly offering what little space there was to the other woman.

Carleen came into the room, forcing a closeness between them Opal didn't want.

"So far, I have to say this event has taken on the attributes of a god damn circus."

Opal was shocked, but not surprised. For the last two months, Carleen had been playing hard defense for so long that any offense plays were minuscule at best. There were no new agendas or great ideas that usually signified her stamp on the job, so understandably she was upset.

Opal hadn't expected her to unload like this. She assumed that Carleen was referring to Monument Bingo and needed to respond in a way that didn't blame everything on her officemates. Otherwise it would appear as if she couldn't do her job. Taking responsibility for her part would suck, but it was the right thing to do. "But I...we...the game was shut down. I heard Eleanor removed any and all social media pictures. I'm assuming you are going speak to each of the women about personal responsibility?"

"I'm not talking about the game."

Opal's eyebrows furrowed. "I'm not sure what you're referring to?"

"It's obvious to anyone with a pulse in that room today," Carleen said, standing tall, her glasses perched on the end of her nose.

Opal still wasn't sure what Carleen meant. She hadn't behaved in an unprofessional manner in any way during the day.

"The way you and Andrew were with each other today. I heard from Lincoln that you went out with him to the Mélange ballet on Saturday. Are you having sex with him?"

"Excuse me?"

"I need to know. If you're screwing him, we may need to make sure this project—once it goes live—isn't impacted by negative press like, let's say, collusion or coercion."

"How dare you, Carleen. How dare you say something like that to *me*. How long have we worked together?"

"A long time. That's why I'm here talking to you, instead of you being out on your ass without a job or reference."

"Is that a threat?"

Carleen shrugged, but didn't lose eye contact with her.

"As a *thank you* for all the work I've done putting this meeting together, Andrew wanted to take me to the ballet."

"That's not what it sounded like. Handsome, rich man like that? You could see the stars in your eyes today."

"No way. I looked professional. I wasn't making eyes with him. That's ridiculous."

"You're missing the point, Opal. We finally had all of our PR nightmares locked down. Liz and the Embassy events, Monument Bingo, even a fucking blackmail scandal. Everything was in the clear. Until you went out on that date with Andrew."

"Are you saying I am going to blow this deal? It's *me,* Carleen. It wasn't a date. I have done nothing wrong and this is completely above board."

"Are you seeing him again tonight?"

"Yes."

"And you invited Gretchen here? Is she going to cover the date?"

"She's here to cover the fundraiser. The press of Lincoln meeting the governor will be perfect. She doesn't fly in until Saturday morning."

"You don't see a problem with this?"

"I had to. She had pictures of Gordy and

Harrison about to get into a fight, Chloe in the middle." Opal crossed her arms and held her head up high. "And she had pictures of Link at the Chinese Gala."

"Why didn't...? Oh, never mind. I don't want to know. My feeling? She's screwed us before with that exposé, she'll screw us again. This is unbelievable. You, of all people, can't see how stupid this is. All I can say is, don't go out on a date with Andrew. Besides, he's known as a player. Not only will you ruin the congressman's chance of decent legislation, you're going to get hurt."

Opal stepped back, running into the dresser behind her. Carleen took up too much space. Opal had withstood abrasive verbal attacks before. She had seen Carleen's tell-it-like-it-is conversations with others before, but always from a professional perspective and a distance. Carleen was telling her how to manage her private life.

"Dinner with Andrew is not going to ruin SUNFLOWER. It's dinner. I'm not some naïve little girl, Carleen. I know how this game works. I know how to handle this."

"We've worked too long and too hard to lose this deal, between our partners or in the public arena. We need all-hands-on deck to win."

Opal crossed her arms and willed herself to keep

her gaze steady on Carleen. She'd do what she had to do. "Thanks, Carleen. I've got it handled."

"You're going out with him anyway, aren't you?"

Opal considered lying to her, to shrug it off, but if they were going to move up together into higher offices, she had to tell her the truth. "Yes. I'm going."

Carleen tightened her arm against her purse. "Keep it on the up and up." Carleen put her hand on the doorknob, fingers whitening around the lever. "If you sleep with him, you need to tell me."

Opal didn't budge. She didn't smile, she didn't nod, and she sure as hell didn't say anything in response.

"You manage Link's dating life all the time, you *know* the impact something like this has. Be ready, dear. You may have to choose between Andrew and Lincoln." Carleen walked out the door and it solidly closed behind her.

Chapter 12

The door shut. Opal took a deep breath, not realizing she'd been holding it, and felt her lungs taking in the extra air, but she had to breathe in hard. Her ribs vibrated with the inhalation and she let it out all at once. Carleen had no right to come in here and treat her like she was a teenager who had broken curfew. *Fuck that.* After all the hard work that she had done for her over the years, after all the hours she had put in overtime without so much as a dime or sometimes even a thank you, who the hell did Carleen think she was?

Opal yanked the clothes hanging in her closet over to one side. A dress fell off one of the hangers and crumpled to the floor. She looked down at the dress, mad at it. How dare it fall off the hanger? She did all the right things and then gets treated like an errand girl, treated like an idiot. If she wanted to eat dinner with Andrew, she was going to. If she wanted to date Andrew, she was going to do that too.

Opal picked up the dress that had fallen to the ground. She had planned to wear it for the fundraiser, but screw it. Now was the time. It was a gorgeous dress: a vintage Italian summer-evening dress with a gray background and a smattering of cornflower blue flowers. She slipped it over her head and it slid over the curves of her body. She looked in the mirror to see if it was the right choice. *Oh yes.* It was definitely the right choice.

She applied fresh makeup to highlight the blue in her dress and in her eyes. She ran her fingers through her wide curls, giving her hair a bit more volume before turning around in front of the mirror so she could see her backside, checking out all angles. *Nice.* She admired the swirl of the dress, the way the bottom edge of the fabric wrapped around her knees. It would be perfect for a night of dancing. She stopped and looked at herself in the mirror, her hands on her hips. She couldn't go dancing. Not with Andrew.

The alarm on her phone chimed. It was time for her to go downstairs and meet him at five thirty pm on the dot. She still had a chance to call it off, but she dismissed the idea. With a longing glance, her eyes swept across the door that separated her and Lincoln.

That whole idea needed to be nipped in the bud. Even though she felt closer to Link, there was no way she'd ever do anything romantic with Lincoln, ever. Not that she couldn't imagine being with him, that wasn't it. There was too much at stake: her present and future career. Andrew may not be perfect, but he was perfect for right now. She grabbed a shawl and purse, left the room and didn't look back.

In the lobby, Andrew was waiting for her. He wore a pair of khakis and a button-down shirt, and, *of all things*, sneakers. The shoes were upscale, made with leather and suede, but still, they were *sneakers*. She had expected him to dress up a bit more.

"You look wonderful, as always." He kissed her on the cheek.

Opal almost wanted to pull back. Carleen's words rang in her ears: *PR nightmare*. What if Gretchen had gotten a shot of that; what would the headlines say? How would she explain that to Lincoln? She exhaled slowly to calm her body down.

"Let's go," she said.

"Is something wrong? You seem a little tense."

"Nothing a glass of Champagne won't fix," she said, but then she saw his expression. He had pulled back, hesitant about being with her. The stress of the job, Carleen, everything was getting to her. She forced herself to relax, dropped her shoulders, and took a deep breath. "Andrew, I have been very excited for the last hour to go with you. But I've also had a stressful week. I would very much like to go on this date with you."

"You would like a glass of Champagne? Would that help?"

"Very much so. Thank you for offering. I'd love one." He motioned to someone in the bar area and a young woman appeared with a bottle of Champagne and two glasses.

Andrew led her to the elevator, swiped his room card, and pressed the top floor button. She took another sip of her drink, excited about the prospect of a dinner with Andrew. What restaurant would he take her to? Paris? She was sure it would be an exclusive spot. When she got out of the elevator, she heard...*heli-copter blades?*

"Are we going on a tour of the city first?"

"Yes, and there's more," he said. "The destination is a surprise. I want to see the look on your face when we land."

He's taking me to the fucking Grand Canyon.

She should be excited. She'd always wanted to go there. It was on her bucket list, for crying out loud. But not in a vintage Italian dress with sling back heels.

They exited a set of double doors to the rooftop. Chopper blades were in full force and she grabbed her hair back just as the strands swirled around her face, hitting at her like tiny little whips. Andrew brought the Champagne bottle and two glasses. He wrapped one arm around her shoulders and they walk-jogged to the chopper.

She got in first, and once she settled, the pilot handed her giant, black over-the-ear headphones. She looked at them as if they were something from Area 51. The pilot mimicked putting them on his head. She knew exactly where they were meant to go. But she would have preferred to be prepared had he actually told her that they were going to the Grand Canyon. She would have worn something less out-on-the-town with appropriately comfortable shoes, like his tennis shoes, and pulled her hair back into a tight bun.

But she didn't want to seem ungrateful. She didn't want to appear like she couldn't be flexible. After all, she should have expected that Andrew, of all people, Mr. Speed Demon Adventure Type would take her on a date to the Grand Canyon. But she hadn't expected it at all, until he told her, of course. She put the headphones on and sat back in her seat. *Buck up, sourpuss. It's the GRAND CANYON! At least, it better be the Grand Canyon with all this fuss.*

She was going to one of the most awe-inspiring places in the country with the most eligible bachelor in the entire US. So what if her hair got a little messy? So what if her shoes weren't right? She was going to get to mark off a bucket list item. A BUCKET LIST. For free. In a chopper. And not just any chopper, but a luxury one complete with new-car smelling leather seats, shiny chrome knobs, and digitized console. This was no Vietnam reboot like the one she had flown in for a photo op with Congressman Pierce to promote his military experience. This chopper was top of the line.

"It's loud in here!" Andrew said. He had just put on his headphones and his voice came in clear as day.

"I can hear you," she said.

"Good. This setting allows you and I to talk privately, but the pilot can patch in to speak with me when necessary."

"Okay." Opal put the seatbelt on and tried not to think about all the wrinkles it would cause. Focus on the positive. *Grand Canyon!*

The pilot spoke through the headphones to which only Andrew could hear. He responded with a short quick nod. They lifted, and they spun off over the city. The pilot was a fantastic tour guide full of historical trivia. Las Vegas, at the height of the day, wasn't all flash. With a bird's eye view, the city was literally an oasis in the desert. The chopper was air conditioned, and she was going to mark off her bucket list in style. Andrew poured her another glass of Champagne.

The edge was starting to wear off. The pilot hovered over Old Las Vegas, the historic city center where the gambling first started, where some of the famous mafia fights took place, and then they moved over the strip where he explained the new build, the Wynn Hotel and the Bellagio.

"I've always wanted to see Wayne Newton then have a gin and tonic where Frank Sinatra and Dean Martin used to drink."

"That nostalgic, romantic side of the city is gone. Better to just make way for the new."

Opal looked at him, surprised. She didn't think that was something he would say.

"Excuse me, Mr. Donohoe. We're headed out to the location."

"Thanks, Jr."

"Sit tight, my dear. This is the best part!" Andrew said as they clinked glasses.

Opal cringed when he said 'my dear.' It didn't sound inviting, it sounded like ownership. The chopper headed towards the desert, and within minutes the city was well behind them. She tried to relax and be excited for the moment, but she would rather be comfortable clothes watching Casablanca.

AFTER AN HOUR of flying and chatting, they fell silent. Both of them were skilled conversationalists, and they talked about everything under the sun, from podcasts to pickled tomatoes, before running out of easy things to say. Even though Opal normally had an iron stomach, the Champagne had made her feel slightly queasy. Nothing she couldn't suppress, but the ride was making her uncomfortable. The chopper seemed to be going abnormally fast. She tried to relax, but didn't feel like she could be herself around Andrew. The feeling was so slight, that she brushed it off. Maybe she was expecting too much too soon.

"We're approaching the site, sir," said the pilot.

Opal wished he would just tell her that they were at the Grand Canyon. She checked her watch. It was six pm. Thankfully, the temperature should be cooling down, but the sun wouldn't set for at least another hour and a half.

"Opal, close your eyes for a minute."

She did as he asked. She already knew where they were, but his boyish charm and excitement was contagious. Even though she thought it all a little dramatic, she did as he wished. The pilot did a quick up and then they seemed to fall down. The vertigo scared her, and she reached out for his hands. He caught them, and soothed her.

"Okay, now open them."

The chopper was over the edge of the canyon and before her was awesome nature. Not awesome in the watered-down way everyone and their dog used the word, but awesome according to the dictionary: extraordinary. Layer upon layer, the sediment a record of epochs.

"We're on the move, Mr. Donohoe. Landing site coming up next."

Andrew nodded to the pilot. He lifted off and they sort of did a curve dive. Opal felt the change in her stomach and clasped it with her hands. Usually she was pretty good in these situations; her mom had always teased her that she had an iron stomach, but her stomach was a bit queasy.

The pilot landed softly, for which Opal was thankful. Or at least, her stomach was thankful. They stepped out of the chopper. The view was magnificent. Straight ahead of them was the Colorado River, and in the distance, it seemingly ended between two bluffs.

"Oh Andrew! This is lovely. It's incredible. Thank you!"

"I aim to please."

The pilot turned off the engine and exited the machine. Opal and Andrew walked towards a picnic table that had been set up for them with a crisp white tablecloth and expensive linens. A waiter was getting a tray ready with drinks. He wore black trousers and shirt and a white apron from waist to ankles. To the side of the table was a barbecue, and the smell of chicken and roasted potatoes wafted through the air. A chef tended the flames with experienced movements as they approached. As soon as they sat down, the waiter placed the drinks down on the table and then walked behind a white screen where the chef, pilot, and waiter discretely had their own fare.

"This is incredible, really, Andrew. It's too much."

"Not for you. I'll let you in on a little secret," he said. "I've wanted to do this for some time too, so it's for both of us."

That's so not romantic.

It was supposed to be just a friendly get together, the way she had framed it to Carleen, but here she was thinking of him as a possible romantic partner. The juxtaposition had her flummoxed and she took a sip of water. Didn't flying your date via helicopter to the Grand Canyon count as some sort of romantic gesture?

"Very smart of you, Mr. Donohoe," replied Opal, unwilling to let Carleen's earlier interference ruin her evening. No one else in the office had to date like this. She wanted to turn off the pragmatic side of herself and enjoy the moment.

"The chardonnay is from the Montrachet vineyards. They plant only chardonnay grapes and have for centuries."

Opal didn't know much about the pedigree of vineyards, but she knew Andrew and was sure the bottle was expensive.

He lifted his glass. "To us, Opal. And to a fantastic new deal." They clinked glasses.

Of course, it wasn't just a work event. And of course, it wasn't just a romantic gesture. Was it possible to separate the two with a man like Andrew Donohoe?

"I love spending time with you. It's really refreshing from the...other kinds of women I usually date."

He usually dated models. *Am I too fat? Am I too short?* The Victoria Secret model he had dated six months ago recently checked herself into rehab for exhaustion. *Am I not crazy enough?* Not that she usually read up on society mags, but Madeline had started forwarding every article she found about Andrew when SUNFLOWER was first beginning to take shape. She'd also linked Opal to articles on everyone else that had been at the meeting. Research.

"So how is your Dad reacting to the shape of the deal?"

"Too early to tell," he said. "I think that chicken is going to be good. It sure smells good."

"My mom was really jealous over the Mélange tickets. Thank you, again, for that. It was lovely."

"You're welcome. Lucky we didn't hit major paparazzi."

"No kidding."

"We look good together, you and I. That phone picture turned out excellent."

"I thought it was nice too."

"Yeah. I could see the two of us making babies together."

"You could?"

"I'd like you to think long term with me. Maybe we can try a couple more dates and see how it goes?"

"Oh. I. Well." *What was this? A job interview to be his wife? So not romantic.*

"Don't worry about an answer right now. I can see it's a little overwhelming for you."

"Andrew. We're here to eat dinner and enjoy ourselves. This isn't financial planning or a corporate strategy meeting." *Or find a wife meeting.*

"I know, I just...you're the perfect girl for me."

The waiter brought two exquisitely plated dishes to the table. The chicken was grilled to a nice crispiness, the skin left on to add flavor. Rosemary and olive oil roasted baby potatoes and grilled asparagus completed the meal. She was so glad it was fresh cooked and not brought in and reheated like bad buffet food.

The waiter filled up the wine glasses and Andrew

took a long drink without cheering, and started right in on dinner. Maybe he was nervous. She had one sip and commented on its flavor, but then she didn't touch another drop.

AFTER DINNER AND DESSERT, they walked back to the chopper. She'd always wanted to hike down into the canyon, or maybe ride donkeys, and though the date was incredible, the whole event had an aftertaste of disappointment. The pilot appeared at the table and let them know that they had thirty minutes left since the sun was setting. They had to get out of the canyon before nightfall.

Opal got up and started for the helicopter. She had assumed that the pilot would need to take off right away.

"Wait, Opal, before you get in, come stand next to me." Andrew held his hand out for her. Opal took it and stood next to him. Flanked on both sides was the canyon, in its layered striations. The sun was starting to set, shading everything a dusky rose. He put his arms around her waist and pulled her in gently. She put her arms around him, willing herself forward.

"I wanted this night to be special. And it is, because of you."

Opal nodded her head, to agree with him, and just before she was about to say something, he kissed her. Her slightly open mouth appeared as an invitation and he tried to take the kiss deeper. She pulled back slightly and kissed him on the lips.

"It was incredible, Andrew." Then she tried to kiss him again, but the momentum was lost. He seemed to look at her as if she were strange to him.

"Definitely different. But it's good for me." He took her hand and they walked back to the helicopter. He nodded to the pilot, and the blades started. They rose up to ground level and hovered, granting the passengers one final view. Shadows fell across the two hundred and seventy-seven miles of the canyon, continuing beyond what her eyes could see. Andrew fell asleep on the helicopter ride back. Perhaps he'd had too much to drink, perhaps he had partied too hard the night before, Opal wasn't sure. She leaned her head against the tinted glass of the chopper. Could she see herself realistically with Andrew? Carleen's words crept back. *You may have to choose between Andrew or Lincoln.*

Chapter 13

*L*ink went to dinner with Carleen at the restaurant in the hotel. The fact it was owned by a television celebrity chef drew in hordes of fans of the show while delivering on the food. Even with Lincoln's creds, they had to wait an hour to get in. Spending time with Carleen was like spending time with an older sister. They had an ease about them and a short-hand way of talking.

As they left the restaurant, Link saw Opal and Andrew Donohoe step onto the elevator together. Andrew had his hand on the small of her back, his fingers spread wide against her with an air of owner-ship. As if he were claiming her openly. The doors swished shut behind them before he could get to them. He pushed the *up* button with impatience, smashing it three times in a row and swearing under his breath. Was Opal taking Andrew up to her room?

Carleen put a restraining hand on his arm. "You know, Lincoln, she's a big girl."

"What are you talking about?" He tried playing it cool, as if he hadn't seen Opal with another man.

"Oh, come on. I saw them too. We'll need to watch things as they develop, but I've been thinking about this all evening. If Opal and Andrew do end up an item, I think we can spin it the right way. It's maybe not ideal, but if we stay on top of it, I think we'll be okay."

The hell you say.

Lincoln leaned in close to Carleen. "I hope you're right. Of course, I'll be happy for Opal if she is happy, but I don't trust Donohoe."

"He's got a lot to offer, but this doesn't bode well for negotiations, does it, Link?"

"I don't see how it matters? Maybe after we present the bill, but they aren't going to use her as a bargaining chip. That wouldn't make any sense." A different elevator than the one Opal and Andrew had disappeared into opened for them. No one else got on with them so they had the space to themselves.

"Honestly? I think he's talking out of both sides of his mouth. He's definitely got some oil and coal rhetoric going on from somewhere. Opal said that

Gordy was calling him. Everything he brings up as a possible issue stems from oil and gas."

"Gordy is the only one who could have told Yukika about the blackmail threat. I'm certain the only other people who knew about it wouldn't dare go there. Kenny? Dallas? Cheyenne? Opal?"

"You're right. Gordy makes sense. Yukika wouldn't want to admit to talking to Gordy either. I think that's why she dropped it so fast."

Lincoln tried to play it cool when the elevator opened onto their floor. He walked Carleen calmly to her room, trying to not make it obvious he was looking to see if Opal's door was open or if Donohoe had already left.

He closed his door behind him and put his ear against the door between his and Opal's room. He heard the soft sound of a woman speaking, but nothing else. She was either on the phone or had the TV on. He backed away, semi-appalled at his own behavior. Had he really just done that? And what if she were in there right now with Donohoe? Link raised his hand to knock, pretending that he just wanted to say good night, thought better of it and backed away.

THE NEXT DAY was a painful game of cat and mouse

played at a snail's pace. Jack Donohoe had insisted they read through the proposed agreement line-by-line. All eighty-seven pages, with each possible point of contention being discussed yet again. Spelled out, questioned, discussed, and initialed. Every single line had a red mark on it. By the time they were done, though, all parties were in alignment and their long-term goals fixed.

Profit was the only thing that spoke to Jack Donohoe, so that was the language Lincoln used. He wanted to make sure his company didn't get bottom-barreled when new technology came out. Tax-breaks for new and inventive technology and a slow shift to punitive measures for oil and coal. Phase out the old and in with the new. The better. The brighter. More money.

By the end of a long day, Lincoln could see the shift of new ways overcoming the old in his lifetime. The planet might still be inhabitable for his grandchildren someday. And, as far as he knew, no one had seen the small group of people meeting together in a private conference room. They'd done the first step of setting SUNFLOWER into motion. It was more than just a seed of an idea, it was a fucking stalk with a flower bud ready to burst into full bloom.

After the meeting was over, Lincoln, Carleen, and Opal returned to Lincoln's room. He had a larger room than hers, with a spacious area for a desk and small table. The general air was tired, but relaxed. They were on constant watch for signs of interference and willingness, but the nice thing about brokering a win-win deal was that people were usually happy.

The only points of contention were the Dono-hoes' demand for certain exceptions that would eventually work in their favor. Oil and gas would have space to respond, and the deal made him look fair and balanced. Plenty of hurdles would be thrown in their way moving forward, but, for now, Lincoln wanted to celebrate. Unfortunately, a public display of celebration would draw unwanted attention. "I'm still wired from the day. You ladies up for some dinner?"

"Lincoln, I'd love to go out, but I have some personal business I need to tend to," Carleen said. "Why don't you and Opal go have dinner. Discuss some of the finer points of the deal? Celebrate quietly."

Opal jumped up from the ottoman she was sitting on. "No. Quiet won't work. I'm all keyed up, aren't you?"

Carleen sighed heavily. "No. Not me. I'm not up for anything. Sorry."

"You've been down in the mouth since this after-noon. I saw you texting under the table. Is there something I should know about, Carleen?" She had been known to protect him from drama in the office. He hoped that nothing new had popped up back in DC.

"Oh, Lincoln, no. It's personal, like I said," she pursed her lips. "There's a chance I may need to go to Scotland to be with my ex. It's complicated, and I don't want to get into it right now. You two are practically bouncing off the walls. Lincoln, stop pacing. Opal, help him find something to eat, will you?"

"Hey," Lincoln said, "I appreciate and love you, Carleen, but this guy can take care of himself. Opal, I would love to have dinner with you, but not under duress."

After Carleen left, Opal tapped her lips with her finger, then pointed to him. "You do want to do something other than hang out in your room all night, right?"

"I might go stir crazy if I stay here." There was something mischievous and impish about Opal's grin.

Opal stood up from the ottoman. "I have an idea. I think you'll love it, Link. But, for it to work, I need to figure something out. Can you relax for a few minutes?"

Lincoln shrugged and put his palms up. "I'll take a quick shower and change. Does that work for you?"

"Sure."

He unlocked the connecting door between their

rooms. "I'll just leave this open. Just knock and come in when you're back."

"Okay then. Half an hour, tops."

As soon as Opal was gone, Lincoln undressed and turned on the hot water. The bright light in Opal's eyes when she asked if he wanted to do something other than hang out in his room told him she had something fun up her sleeve. The way her lips quirked upward when she had a secret were ever so kissable. He shifted the water to cold to staunch the sudden arousal flooding his body.

He had wrapped himself in the thick terry robe and poured himself a drink when there was a light tap at the connecting door and it swung open.

"Sorry. I didn't want to get dressed and have to change depending on what it is you have in mind here." He tightened his robe.

Opal was flush with excitement. Her usually beautiful complexion was made even more compelling by the twinkle in her eye.

It took him a moment to realize that she held something behind her back, concealing a surprise of some sort. "What do you have there?"

Opal thrust a plastic hanger bag into his hand. "Your disguise." She said it with a chortle, bopping up onto her toes.

What he wouldn't give to hear that kind of happiness every day. She made him feel young and carefree. He unzipped the bag. Inside was a pair of chaps, a pair of jeans, an ornamental western shirt, cowboy boots, a hat and a set of whiskers that didn't quite match his hair.

"What in the world?" he pulled the chaps out and looked at them dubiously.

"And I'm going as a saloon girl," Opal said, holding up a second bag. "Let's get changed, and then I'll tell you the rest of it."

Opal stood there for a moment. "I mean, I'll get changed in my own room and you...uh...okay. You know what to do." Red faced, she turned away and shut the door between them. Lincoln put on his outfit, adhering the whiskers to his face with a little bottle of glue provided. The costumes were high quality, and when he was done, he felt like a cowboy dressed up for the rodeo awards. With the hat on, he didn't even recognize himself.

Opal knocked on the door a minute later. She clutched her dress between her arms and her sides. "I'm so embarrassed," she said. "I cannot get the zipper up the back. I think it's stuck. Would you mind?"

She turned slowly, with the grace of a swan. The back of her dress gaped open, revealing her even, smooth skin from neck to the little dimple above her buttocks. Lincoln shouldn't be seeing Opal like this.

Almost naked, but fully clothed. No bra, just her bare skin under the dress. Lincoln pulled the top of the dress together and tried the zipper, but it was stuck. "Needs a little WD-40," he said and yanked on the zipper. It moved upward in fits and starts until the soft, kissable skin was hidden beneath clothing.

"Okay then." Opal turned, smoothing the front of her dress. It was low cut, a fake corset with a flared skirt. Underneath, she wore fishnet stockings. "I'll grab my wig and we can get out of here."

"And, where would be heading dressed up like this? I feel ridiculous."

"We, my dear sir, are going to be in a karaoke contest."

Lincoln followed her into her room. "Are you serious?"

"One hundred percent serious. I was thinking about what you told me on the plane, about singing and playing the guitar. Thought it might help you blow off some steam. No one will recognize us in these get-ups." Opal adjusted the wig on her head, tucking her hair in expertly underneath. The old fashioned updo with lots of ringlets hanging off the back was a good look on her. So were the stockings. *Fishnet.* She slipped on the shoes that came with her costume and held out her arms for inspection. "What do you think?"

"You look perfect," Lincoln said, meaning it in every way possible. *Damn. Damn. Damn.* He didn't want to go anywhere. He wanted to take Opal by the hand and kiss every inch of her, taste her. Make love to her in every way possible.

"Are you okay, Link? You look like you've seen a ghost or something."

"I'm fine. The jeans are a size to small, maybe." They had been fine when he put them on, but the growing erection was proving painful. He turned away and adjusted himself.

THE KARAOKE BAR was in another hotel only a block away, so they decided to face the masses of people on the weirdness that was Las Vegas sidewalks. Promenades, more like. The sheer throng of numbers threatened to separate them unless they held hands. Even that proved to be not enough, so at one point, Lincoln grasped Opal by the waist and held her close to his side so that no one could get between them. It felt so natural and right to be walking like that with her side-by-side.

Their concierge had reserved a spot for Cowboy Bob and Dolly and that included a slot in the karaoke competition. Lincoln's original energy was flagging, so he ordered two Red Bulls with shots of vodka. Opal's eyes widened, and Link realized that he'd made some sort of faux pas.

"I'm sorry, let's order you something. I really need the caffeine right now. I should have asked what you wanted."

Opal waved it away. "I'll be fine." She looked at the drink, then down at her hands. "Let's make sure to order some food to go with that."

He put randomly pointed to a few appetizers on the menu and the waiter disappeared again. Link took three big gulps of his drink, letting the caffeine into his body. The combo would loosen him up to sing in front of a crowd. Though, with this disguise on, he was pretty sure he could do almost anything in front of a crowd and get away with it. He felt twenty years younger, just like he did in college, right before getting up on stage. He loved the adrenaline flow, the energy from the crowd, he couldn't wait to sing again.

The emcee for the evening was getting everyone's attention. "Now, tonight is all about FUN. Contestants will be singing together for a contest called *Duet Roulette*." He spoke the words as if they were at a boxing match.

Couples took their turns singing after they spun the roulette wheel. Link sat back and relaxed. He wondered what Opal's voice sounded like. He'd been good enough at singing that he could help cover a bad voice, but whatever her skill level, the night was about having a good time. Letting loose. The wheel had the names of songs on the spokes, and wherever the pointer landed, you had to sing the song.

"This sounds cool."

Opal grinned at him, sipping at her drink. "I should warn you, I'm not the best singer on the planet, but I'm not entirely tone deaf."

"Looks like you're not in love with that drink? How about some wine instead?"

Opal shrugged. "I'm okay with this. It's just...I'll be wired for hours."

Lincoln realized he had no idea what was in Red Bull other than caffeine and more caffeine and that a shot of vodka added to it usually took care of any lingering headaches or nerves he might have. "Are you sure?"

She held up her glass as if she could see all the chemicals inside it. "You do have to wonder what all is in here."

"If you're sure..."

"Hey, the first act is up." Opal pointed to the stage.

Two young men dressed in leather bondage gear took to the microphones. One of them spun the wheel and it landed on, "The Boy is Mine." The crowd roared and the men high-fived and dove into singing.

Lincoln slid over in the booth to get a better view, not quite realizing how much closer he was getting to Opal. The appetizers he'd ordered came, and they picked at them as they listened to the music and joined in on choruses where appropriate.

"So," he said, slowly feeling like a gawky teenager. "You went out with Andrew Donohoe last night. What's up with that?"

Opal put one of the deep-fried stuffed olives in her mouth and chewed, her eyes narrowing thoughtfully. "Honestly? He said he'd marry me. Apparently, I am the perfect woman for him."

"That's fast, don't you think?" Lincoln wondered briefly why she was sitting next to him then. Their legs pressed against each other in the booth, and neither of them moved.

She shrugged one shoulder. "He's nice enough. Took me on a helicopter ride to the Grand Canyon for dinner."

"Wow. I don't think that would have entered my mind," Link said. How could a guy compete against endless pockets and grand gestures like that?

"But he didn't tell me where we were going. So, I had this super nice dress on, heels, my hair was down."

"Ouch. In a helicopter?"

"Exactly."

"Are you thinking of marrying him?" Link asked.

"I'd be stupid not to consider it, wouldn't I?" she asked. Her eyes met his, open and questioning—almost daring him to counter her.

Their number came up before he could answer. "Cowboy Bob and Dolly! Come on up!" The two of them got up from their seats and headed through the crowd. They passed the roulette wheel, which only had six songs left on it, and Lincoln didn't recognize any of them. He hoped that whatever they landed on sounded familiar once the music came on. If they were lucky, this karaoke machine would have the music notes for him to follow, in addition to the words. Both of them onstage, he held out his hand, inviting Opal to spin the roulette wheel. The colors whizzed by for a moment and shuddered to a stop. The song was *"Marry You."*

Lincoln's heart skipped a beat. He didn't believe in coincidences, nor did he believe in fate, but there was something about this moment that slowed the world for him.

The stage hand helped them adjust the fancy headsets and guided them to their places on stage. The spotlight landed on the two of them, and the audience was blinded out. Though he could sense their presence—but muted and in the background. It was as if he and Opal were the only two people on the planet. For sure, she was the only other person that mattered to him. She was on the center of the stage and the center of his universe.

After the first few bars, he recognized the song as soon as it started. It had been popular a few years back, though he couldn't remember paying attention to it. The words were simple and they got into a good groove. And they couldn't be more appropriate. He put his heart and soul into the singing of it, making the words his own reality. He had no idea if Opal understood he wasn't just singing along to some old karaoke music, but that he singing what was truly living in his heart.

Near the end, Lincoln reached out to Opal and all those ballroom dance lessons his mother had pushed on him kicked in. He led Opal in several spins around him, ending the song with her in a low dip, her back arching comfortably around his arm, one foot up in the air a perfect ballerina's point.

The crowd cheered and hooted their approval. Lincoln brought Opal to an upright position and held her close. He could feel her laughing but the cheers were too loud to hear her and had shifted to a chant. "Kiss, kiss, kiss, kiss, kiss, kiss..." People clapped and chanted, waited for them to comply.

Lincoln swept a stray curl from Opal's wig away from her cheek, his thumb stroking the smooth line of her jaw as he slid his hand behind her neck. He brought his face in close to hers, questioning, making sure she was okay with it. Opal nodded ever so slightly and parted her lips, inviting him to her.

It was as though the world went silent. He could vaguely tell the crowd still chanted, clapped, and hooted, but the only thing that mattered was Opal. A tunnel vision brought all his focus to her face. Her welcoming and bright eyes. Her sweet, red lips.

His arms slid around her back, bringing her in tight against him. When their lips touched, Lincoln knew, in that moment, that Opal was The One. The One with a capital O. As if there had been any doubt before, but the electric heat of it was unlike any kiss he'd ever experienced. Unlike other, awkward, first kisses, this felt as though he knew her better than anyone else. Knew where and how to move his lips, his tongue gently dipping in.

Gradually, the clapping and chanting made it back into his senses and he slowly pulled away from Opal. Breathless. Heart beating a thousand times a second. Hope bursting bright. Their eyes met and the same wondrous sensations he was feeling were mirrored in hers.

After the song, they started back to their table, hand in hand, and instead of sitting back down, he tossed enough money to cover their tab down and led her out of the bar. By leaving, they forfeited any chance at winning. He didn't care. Being with Opal was far more important than a little karaoke competition.

They half-ran, half-stumbled back to their hotel, pausing every twenty feet to kiss. When they entered the hotel, some sensibility came back to him, and he suggested they be more discreet. As soon as the elevator door was shut, however, and they found themselves alone, Lincoln wrapped his arms around Opal.

But then, a moment of niggling reality intruding upon him that made him pause and cup her cheeks in his hands. "I just need to know one thing," he said.

She blinked rapidly, a look of wary confusion flickered over her face. "Okay?"

"Did you play that Bingo game? The kissing game to win this trip with me?" It would be impossible for them to move forward if she had.

She obviously wasn't expecting that particular question. Her lips parted in a silent oh. Then she shook her head, eyes crinkling and warm. "No, oh, good lord, no. I didn't play, not for a single, solitary, kiss. What made you think I'd played?"

"Oh, never mind. It's just...I heard about it and wanted to know. I didn't think you were part of it, but then you were going to Vegas. I'm sorry, I had to make sure."

She became serious. "Not even for a minute. I

can't believe I even agreed to it. The whole thing was stupid. Why do you ask? Liquid courage? You have too much to drink?"

"No. I haven't been this clear-headed in ages. Opal...come to my room. Spend the night with me." His lips pressed against her neck as he whispered. "I hope I'm gonna marry you..."

Chapter 14

Opal took Link by the hand and they walked together down the hallway. As they approached his room though, a moment of clarity struck.

"Just in case anyone happens to see us. You go into your room. I'll go into mine," she said.

"Smart. Another reason..."

Opal put her finger on his lips, cutting him off, and slipped past him into her room. After the door shut, she wasn't sure what to do. Should she slip into something more comfortable, or just open the door between them? He knocked on it before she had a chance to decide. She opened it, and Lincoln was there in full gear, tipping his cowboy hat at her, a rakish smile on his lips.

He tossed the hat on the floor and rubbed the

whiskers off his face. She stepped over the threshold and into his arms.

He closed his arms around her and brought her in close, holding her against his warm, strong body. After a few moments, he leaned away, placing a hand against her cheek and lifting her chin gently, "I want to make sure you're okay with this."

"I am."

"This isn't some drunk thing."

"Do I look drunk to you?"

"I want to be sure. What about work?"

"We'll figure it out. Do you want this?"

"More than anything."

"Were you serious about what you said?" she asked. "I get it's the heat of the moment."

"I didn't say it to get into your pants." He ran his hand down her back. "Not that you're actually wearing pants."

"Why don't you come here, cowboy? I think this damsel needs a kiss," she said, affecting an accent.

"Righty-O," he said, shifting his hands to circle around her waist. He started with a sweet, simple kiss on her lips.

The heat from the touch traveled down her body, through her heart, and straight down to her clitoris. She opened her mouth to him, and he kissed her deeply. He gently bit her lip before slipping his tongue into her mouth. His hands pulled her into a deeper embrace. She leaned her head back and his hands moved up her back and behind her neck.

"Lincoln," she said.

"Opal."

"You know what this means."

"Yeah. I do." He unbuttoned his shirt.

He was mere inches away, but she wanted to feel his skin against hers, his hands in her hair, his lips on her body. "Will you unzip me?" she asked.

"My pleasure."

His grasp around her waist tightened slightly and he turned her around, slowly but firmly. She felt him grasp the zipper and take it down. He lightly pushed the fabric forward. The back of his fingers lightly caressed her neck and then skimmed, butterfly soft, over her skin, causing her forearms to ripple with goosebumps. Light kisses rained down the back of her neck. He swept his hands underneath the corset, just under her breasts, and pulled her closer against his body. Her nipples swelled in anticipation.

His hot breath, the lightness of the kisses, the firmness of his hold, and the hardness of his body were everything she'd imagined they'd be. She was drowning in bliss and acutely aware of every single hair on her body. She faced him and stepped away to turn off the overhead lights. No lights were on in the room, but the curtain was open. Shades of neon red and white lights filtered into the room. Watching him watch her, she pushed down the corset, wiggled it over her hips and let it fall.

He took a step forward, pushed her hair back off her shoulders. He traced his hand along her shoulder, fingers light as a feather. The gentler the touch, the more she craved something firmer. He paused and his fingers traced her areolas. "Beautiful."

He rolled a nipple between two fingers. It felt like fire on ice. She moaned and that seemed to excite him even more. He leaned over and kissed her breast before taking her nipple into his mouth. He caressed the fullness of her other breast with an open palm; squeezing, he nipped at her bud, causing her to cry out. He released her, grinning in challenge.

She lifted his chin to her and kissed him, pushing the shirt off his shoulders. Finally, she was able to touch him, to feel his strong muscles on her fingertips. The movements, the actions all felt erotic and yet natural, as if they had been lovers for years.

His hands curved around her bottom, caressing her through the coarse fishnet. It was rough against her skin, but not painful.

"May I?" he asked, his fingers tugging at the band of the stockings.

Whatever he was about to do, she wanted. "Yes," she said. "A hundred times, yes."

He led her over to the bed, guiding her onto her back. She obliged with the same dancer's grace she'd shown on the stage less than an hour before. She fell onto her back, ready and willing to take his lead in all ways. With a knee between hers, he rubbed his hands back and forth over her thighs. The roughness of the tights against her skin sent an exquisite charge of desire through her. She arched her back and her knees popped up. He hooked his fingers around the top of the fishnet stockings. She lifted her hips so he could remove them easily.

"...marry you..." he sang as he pulled them off.

He fell onto her, his body hot, his eyes closed, his lips seeking her. She met his mouth with teasing, testing, and a nip on his lip. His hips rocked into hers. His hardness against her softness. Seeking more, he lowered himself so that his mouth could take in a nipple, first one and then the other, rubbing, pinching, pleasure building. He kissed a trail to her navel, circling his hand around it. He looked up at her, and their eyes met. Unsaid words passed between them in a language only lovers understand.

His hand moved between her, and he slipped a finger inside her. She had no more words, but her body knew what to say. Her knees fell to the sides and he put two fingers inside her. "It's a beautiful sight..." he said.

She groaned and lifted her hips to him. Instead of words, he started to hum and his fingers moved to the music, swirling around her, he stroked his thumb against her clitoris.

"More. I want you."

"Not yet, love." He lowered himself to her. "I have to taste you first." His fingers splayed her apart. She was totally open to him and his fingers swirled around her opening once more, then two came inside her. She squirmed, her body wanting more, wanting release. Then his mouth was on her, firm and fast, with two fingers still inside her. He pulsed his fingers while he sucked and nipped at her clitoris. Her head lolled back against the bed, pure pleasure coursing through her body. She relaxed and tensed at the same time at the pulsing of his fingers, the pull of his mouth.

"Oh my god," she said.

He withdrew his mouth and removed his fingers. Opal's eyes flew open in surprise.

"Do you take me?"

Opal swallowed hard. Her body screamed at her to say the words, but she knew it was more than that. He was *The One.*

With a deft hand, she opened herself for him. "I do."

She wanted him, she wanted all of him. His penis was thick and hard, a manly thing of beauty. Without a word, he slipped on a condom. He put his hands down beside her, he was on top of her. He angled his hips so that the tip of his dick touched just the vaginal lips. "You're ready for me. Wet and ready."

"Yes," she said.

He slid his throbbing hardness into her, splitting her, separating her, coming into her until they were one. He moved his body down upon her so that all of him was touching all of her.

"And a man and woman shall become one," he said, rubbing the roughness of his cheek against the smoothness of hers.

"I'm yours."

Staring into her eyes, breathing her breaths, he pulled back slightly and came harder into her. Opal groaned and squeezed herself onto him, not wanting to let go, wanting him forever. He pulled back ever so slightly and plunged again, the motion slow but deep, uniting them. Her body floated, she fluttered like a leaf, but he drove into her the roots, grounding her until she felt a rhythm take over that was no longer either of them. His heart beating wildly, her body taking him fully until he shuddered and she was free, the release rocking through her body like lightning, eternally changing her.

He collapsed on her. They were still one. Both breathing heavily, trying to keep up with themselves, be present. She knew. He knew. They took care of each other. She brought him a towel. He brought her a glass of water. Nakedness now was tenderness. They fell asleep against each other. Opal dreamed of sugar plums and mistletoes in the middle of the bone-dry desert.

Chapter 15

Lincoln woke while Opal still slept, the dawn light peeking in through the curtains and lighting up her hair. Her eyes moved behind closed lids, and her lips twitched upward at the corners in a smile that told him her dream was a happy one. Moving would mean waking her, so he remained still until she rolled onto her back and stretched. Her arms lifted over her head and the sheet slipped to below her breasts with the movement.

Lincoln took the closest nipple between his lips, and swirled his tongue around the areola, coaxing her nipple into hardness. He watched Opal's face for any hint as to whether she was waking up. He cupped her other breast with the palm of a hand, drawing the nipple upward between thumb and forefinger.

Opal groaned softly.

Lincoln continued tonguing one nipple while pulling gently at the other until Opal arched her back slightly, her breath hitched. She opened her eyes.

"That feels just right," she said, pushing his hand from her breast down to her dripping pussy.

She curled her fingers around his, shaping three of his fingers together, and directed them inside her. Sliding her hand up his wrist, she grasped him firmly and moved him in and out. Link turned his hand so that two of his fingers slid alongside her clit with each movement. "Yes, just like that."

Her legs parted. When he would have lightened up, she pressed him all that much harder against herself.

Lincoln propped himself on an elbow to watch her, taking note of exactly where and how she liked to be touched. There was something so free-form and hungry about her need. It was also refreshing to be with a woman who was so clear with her desires—telling him and showing him exactly what she wanted. Her whole body started trembling, and he sensed she was on the brink of an orgasm.

She wriggled under him as he hooked two fingers inside her, stilling her movements and pressing his palm against her clit.

She turned toward him, her eyes wide. "I was so close. Why are you stopping?"

He brushed his nose against hers. "Third time's the charm."

Exasperated, she pressed her head back into the pillow, exposing her long, graceful neck. "What?"

Lincoln circled his fingers slowly around her clit, changing the motion completely from what it had been while lowering his lips to that delicate expanse of skin just below her ear. He kissed her gently, sucking in a tiny bit of flesh and dragging his morning beard across the nape of her neck. Her body trembled.

Link rolled onto his knees without breaking contact, dragging his chin along Opal's neck and collarbone. He caressed her with his fingers, but never hard enough or fast enough for her to reach a peak, bringing her close and backing off before she ever quite got there.

His cock ached for her with every moment. He wanted everything about her—her smooth skin, her lean dancer's muscles, her intelligence, her quick wit. She opened up for him, like a blank canvas to a painter, full of trust and desire.

He continued his slow, teasing descent, alternating smooth soft kisses with the caress of his morning beard. He traced the outline of her breast with his chin, the short growth leaving the briefest of pink marks. He laid his cheek against her belly and drew an imaginary line down to her thighs.

She groaned in frustration, pushing her hips upward. "More, please, Link. I need more."

Lincoln settled in between her spread legs, poised over her, fingers still rocking slowly in and out of her, drawing out the pleasure for as long as possible.

"All right, my love," he said. "I'll ramp things up until you tell me to stop."

"Yes. Yes. Faster. Harder. Now."

Link's fingers were coated with her slick juices. He picked up his pace, fingers sliding in and out, focusing on her pleasure. She met him thrust for thrust, her hips lifting off the bed with surprising force. Link could not take his eyes off her. The wanton desire she displayed was so real, so unabashedly open and unforced. She could not be denied now.

The real deal. The One. Her breath grew shallow; he marveled at her exquisite lips, parted just so; her perfectly shaped breasts, nipples hard and erect; her lean dancer's legs on either side of him, warm and strong.

"Come, my darling," he said, his eyes riveted on her face, waiting for that moment.

Opal looked at him briefly through clouded eyes, mouth working for a moment before she threw her head back against the pillow, her eyes rolling upward. Her pussy clenched hard against his fingers, almost holding him inside as she jerked nearly upright toward him, her entire body shaking and trembling.

Her eyes met his, wide and round. "Yes. Oh. God. Keep... Yes." Opal was nearly incoherent as her body jerked and twisted beneath him. She grabbed a pillow and yelled into it. "Yes. More. Yes. Yes. Yes."

Lincoln responded to her body as she slowed and caught her breath, eventually cupping her with the palm of his hand, smoothing over her inflamed pussy.

"Your turn, mister," she said, looking up at him with a glint in her eye. "On your back."

Lincoln held up his hands in mock surrender and rolled onto his back. "Whatever the lady wants."

Opal rolled onto her knees, straddling him over his thighs. She slid her arms along his chest and up his body and along his arms. She grasped his wrists and pinned them down to the mattress over his head. Her lips quirked upward into her mischievous grin and turned her head so that her long hair cascaded across her face and against his chest.

"Hey, that tickles," he laughed and squirmed playfully.

"I know," she said. She draped her hair along his sides, then along his chest.

"Tit for tat?" he asked, breathing heavily.

"You got it, buster."

With her whole weight on him, he couldn't escape

without a great deal of effort. Not that he wanted to. He'd never had a woman so easily take control of him before. And he liked it. He'd teased her, almost mercilessly, and now she was giving it as good as she'd got.

She alternated kissing him with tickling him with her hair. When she leaned over him, her taut belly pressed against his cock. Knowing how close he was to her made him harder. He wanted to sink into her softness. He wanted to flip her on her back and take her, but instead Lincoln relaxed into the pleasure, relishing every slight movement of her lips, her hands, her hips.

"Opal, I want you. I need more." He thought he might lose his mind. He shifted under her, trying to position her in his favor.

"More what?" she asked, her voice low and teasing.

"God. You imp. Fuck me, or let me fuck you," he growled.

She hovered over him, her eyes shining. "Say please."

She had him pinned to the bed and had worked him into a frenzy of desire for her. He wanted to explode into her, to feel that final release. "Please. Opal. Fuck me. Please." He tried to free his hands, to reach for another condom from the bedside table, but she held on tight. "Condom, darling..."

Opal moved up from his thighs, still not releasing his wrists. "No, I want to feel you. Just you."

She slid her pussy along the length of his cock. She remained there, her warm soft folds wrapping around him. After a moment, she shifted and took him inside her in one smooth movement. She squeezed him as she rocked against him. Finally, she let loose his hands. He grasped her at her waist to give her balance as she rode him hard and wild, taking her own pleasure from him again.

Watching her come for a second time sent him over the edge. He arched his back, plunging deeply inside her. He sat up, his arms wrapping around her pulling her to him. He sought out her lips and kissed her hungrily as he released himself inside her. She ground down against him, her arms wrapping around his back and nails biting into his skin. They didn't move for a long while. Not until their bodies had both stopped trembling. Not until they both caught their breath.

"Wow," he said. Lincoln met her eyes and held them, looking for confirmation of what he was feeling. "Wow. Wow. Wow."

She pressed her forehead against his, her eyes closed. "Perfection," she said, her whispered words soft against his lips.

At length he gathered her into his arms and held her close, spooning along the length of her body. He gathered her long hair into a thick ponytail at the nape of her neck, breathing in her sweet scent, kissing her gently. She wiggled against him until there was no air between them, until they were, once again, one.

"I could stay like this forever," he said dreamily.

"We have a banquet to get to," she said.

"Ugh. I don't want to let you go. Let's cancel everything."

"Yeah, right. I can see that happening. I'll make this easy for you. I'm going to go shower, and you are not allowed in my bathroom." She backed away from him toward the door.

"You know, I am pretty good at shower sex," Lincoln said.

She rolled her eyes, her back against the bathroom door. "You know, there are more injuries in bathrooms?"

"Fine. I'll go to my room and shower all by myself," he said as she closed the door on him. He flopped back onto the bed, grabbed her pillow and pressed it against his face and inhaled.

LINK LEFT the door between their rooms open as he shaved, showered, and dressed, but he gave Opal her space to get dressed and do whatever she needed to do to get ready. He loved that she had long, thick hair, but the blow dryer was going for what seemed like an hour. They still had some time before the benefit, so he decided to get some work done. He opened one of the many documents he needed to review and lost himself in the words.

Opal's voice, loud and angry startled him. "Fuck. Oh holy, fucking hell."

Lincoln tossed his computer aside and raced to Opal's room. Opal stood in the center of her room, dressed in a cream slip, staring at her phone. She had obviously been checking messages while getting dressed. Her lips were drawn into a thin white line, and she shook her head as she scrolled through her screen.

"Opal? What's going on?"

He approached cautiously. He'd never seen Opal quite so angry before. Or white in the face. She held out her phone toward him, too close so that he had to lean back to see it.

On the screen was a photo of the two of them kissing on stage at the karaoke bar. Lincoln took the phone and guided her to the bed, sitting next to her so he could read the message.

Gretchen: So, Congressman Lincoln Pierce gets down and dirty with staff? You've been holding out on me, Opal. Boinking Andrew Donohoe and the congressman? Some nerve. Meet me half an hour before the luncheon or this shit goes viral. May reconsider posting Harrison and Gordy too.

"What does she mean, holding off on Harrison and Gordy?" he asked.

Opal's lips parted for a second and then she swallowed. "Harrison Rousseau and Gordy Carpenter got into a bar fight a couple weeks ago, with Chloe in the middle. I asked Gretchen to put the kibosh on it. Offered her a chance to cover the fundraiser."

"Chloe the intern? Wasn't Rousseau at the BBQ?" Lincoln asked. "And Gordy, is he the asshole who..."

"Yes. Yes. And the same asshole lobbyist."

"Did you promise her anything else?"

"I promised her time with you in Vegas. I promised her SUNFLOWER. She doesn't know it, but I told her I would give her something real. Something big, if she held out."

"Without talking to me about it?" Lincoln clenched his jaw tight to keep himself from saying something he couldn't take back. Opal was no longer 'just an employee,' and he had to tread carefully here. She was still an employee, one he had become extremely intimate with. Yes, he could justify it with being in love, but...he'd crossed a line before figuring out the rules.

"Yes."

"What are you going to tell Gretchen?"

"I don't know. I'll call Kenny and see what he thinks. The best way to spin this."

"Spin? You want to figure out how to spin what's going on between us?" Link stood up, horrified. "What exactly do you think is happening here, Opal?"

She had been angry at the text, but now he saw no emotion in her. She was being businesslike, thinking through what needed to be done.

"What kind of spin do we need other than to declare our love for each other? Let's just be open and tell the world," he said. "I love you, Opal. I have loved you for..." he ran his hands through his hair. "Forever. Since you entered my life, but I've ignored all those feelings. I can't ignore them any longer. Not after last night."

She looked down at her feet. Her silence was damning.

"Wait," he asked, as it dawned on him. "'Boinking Donohoe and the congressman?' What is that about?"

Opal's head jerked up. "She's connecting two dots that aren't connected, Lincoln."

Lincoln could see how it all had happened, and he jumped up and away from Opal. Her sudden interest in him, last night, everything she'd done was designed to make Donohoe jealous. To get Andrew to hasten his proposal. The flagrant karaoke disguises hadn't fooled anyone.

"I see what's going on here. First, you go out with Andrew Donohoe and be a little rich man's girl. Then, he whisks you away on a fucking helicopter to the Grand Canyon. Am I some pawn in a game? Is this all related to that game you were playing?"

Her face drained of color. "I'm not into playing games, Lincoln. You're way off base here."

"Were you with Andrew Donohoe, kissing him for that stupid game of yours?" he asked.

Her eyes narrowed on him and she straightened up to her full height. "How dare you. I...We...You are a son of a bitch to say that to me. And you know what? Andrew and I? None of your fucking business."

"Exactly how do I figure into this, Opal? Am I just another pawn?"

"Get out of my room. Now." She pointed through the doorway back into his room.

He stomped through it and she slammed it closed. The deadbolt clunked loudly behind him.

Chapter 16

Opal locked the door between them and sat on the bed. The bed that still smelled of them. The whole room smelled of him. The last thing she needed was emotions to cloud her thoughts. Good decisions were made with clear, logical heads. She didn't have time to think about Lincoln and his accusations. She didn't even have time to even enjoy how incredible the sex was last night and this morning. The bottom line: she worked for him. The bottom line: he accused her of playing games. And that stupid idea to let everyone know they were in love? The ludicrous notion that he could use "love" to counter Gretchen's story? Even if it were true, no one would believe it now.

Did he really mean what he said, though?

Did it matter after his accusations?

The incredible swing of events—the declarations of love to the spewing of jealousy—was overwhelming. She pounded a fist on the bed. The truth didn't matter right now. The most important thing at the moment was to get Gretchen to drop the photo and focus her attention on a shiny new object. But first, Opal needed to get her game back. There was no way she could go down to meet Gretchen in this state of mind. With a deep sigh, she forced the rollercoaster of events and emotions from her mind.

Even if she and Link hated each other, she still had to fix the issue at hand. Opal picked up her phone and texted Gretchen to meet her in fifteen minutes.

Gretchen responded that she had to attend the luncheon first. Then they could talk.

Opal was furious. First she wanted a quick turn around, and now Gretchen wanted to attend the luncheon. Probably to get more photo ops between her and Lincoln. *Well, good fucking luck getting one where we are gazing upon each other with love.* The words he said to her this morning, those horrible awful words, threatened to overcome her, but she shoved them aside, refused to let them get to her. They would take her right down the rabbit hole, and she couldn't go there. Even if avoidance wasn't a mature or responsible action to take, at the moment she didn't have the emotional stability to consider other avenues, other possibilities, and she needed to have her game face on.

She put on a pair of dress pants that made her feel like she could conquer the world. They were expensive, they fit perfectly, and they screamed a message: get shit done. She paired it with a severely cut silk blouse and a knotted small scarf around her neck. She pulled her hair up into a tight bun she used to wear when she performed on stage.

Opal meant business and if she had to jeté all over Gretchen and even Lincoln, that was exactly what she would do to turn this circus into a dignified performance. It took strength of will and making sure the players all knew their parts. Opal's performance instincts kicked in, and her body relaxed in the midst of stress. With that, she walked confidently down the hall, ignoring Lincoln's door. On the elevator, she pressed the button for the third floor, where the ballroom was located.

The luncheon would start in about thirty minutes. People had come down early to meet and greet, to buy a drink before having to sit down. Her first order of business was to scan the room and find Gretchen. Jack Donohoe and Carleen Bigalow were talking to each other. Link was in the corner, talking with—oh my god —Gretchen? He looked relaxed and happy, in his element.

Is he flirting with her? Oh hell no.

Opal started towards them, but before she got going, she noticed a man with red hair. *Oh no.* Opal stopped midstride to look. Gordy Carpenter was here too. *What the fuck was Gordy doing HERE?* And he was at the bar speaking to Yukika? Opal swiveled her gaze between Link and Gordy. She wasn't sure who to go to first. Which fire was bigger?

Link patted Gretchen's arm and then turned towards the bar. She watched his expression change as he saw Gordy and Yukika talking. He stopped in his tracks, like Opal had done, and as he turned to check on Gretchen, he saw Opal. Across the crowded room, their eyes connected. A wave of intense joy lit up her body, followed by sharp anger. The mix was a dangerous combination. She couldn't run across the room into his arms. She didn't want to admonish him either, but his recent words burned in her heart. There was nothing she could do other than turn away from him.

Tears threatened to bubble up, but when she saw Gretchen coming towards her, she swallowed hard and pushed back every single feeling she had, leaving only a mask.

"Hi, Gretchen," Opal said, hoping she didn't sound angry or sad, but rather in control.

"I was just having a chat with our favorite person,

the Honorable Congressman. He's so handsome, don't you think? I mean, he might be a little old for you. Daddy issues, much?"

"Why are you doing this to me?" Opal whispered. She hadn't meant to say it out loud, but she had and Gretchen had heard her.

Gretchen looked away. Embarrassed, maybe? Her lips twitched, possibly thinking of her options. Now was the time to say something before she decided one way or the other.

"We can help each other. You and I," Opal said, knowing that threats would not work with Gretchen. She might not always see the obvious story, but she wasn't a pushover.

Gretchen swiveled back, fast and hard. "You keep selling me short. Letting me think Gordy and Harrison was the big story." She glanced over towards the bar where Andrew and Jack Donohoe were talking, "Not commenting on your exclusive with Andrew."

"Gordy and Harrison was out of my control. I didn't know about that until..."

"Really? You're gonna lie to me now? When we're having a moment of truth?" Gretchen said, standing her ground.

Opal met her glare. "It's true. I didn't fucking know. All of those stories will hurt the congressman."

"People should know that his office is being uh, shall we say, *mishandled*."

"Let's skip the bullshit. You don't care about bringing the truth to the people. You want numbers. What do you really want?"

"Why is everyone here? The real reason everyone is here." Gretchen tilted her head toward the bar. "Yukika Mathews? August Thorne? Andrew and Jack Donohoe? None of them give a flying fig about service dogs."

Just then, the room erupted in applause. The governor of Nevada, Kendra Gilroy, had arrived with her entourage. She shook hands with people as she made her way to the front of the ballroom, where the president of Service Dogs of America stood. Before posing for pictures, they called out for Link to join them.

Gretchen turned to Opal. "Ohhh. There's a fancy angle. Is our favorite congressman wanting to hook up with the governor? VP, maybe? Or is she a First Lady type? I've got a nice photo op. I've got to go." She pulled a camera from her messenger bag, and held it between them. "But we're not done yet. I still have the pictures on my phone. I think last night's photos next to today's might be my juiciest story in a while. 'Lincoln Pierce, who will he pick? Nevada Governor or hot young employee?'"

"You wouldn't."

"I would. I have everything I need. The big question is, what headline will I use? I'll see you after the luncheon, sweetheart."

Opal watched her cross the room to join the other members of the press. Lincoln did not even look at her. Which, with Gretchen present, was a good thing. Opal headed to the bar. As soon as Gordy caught sight of her, he gave a snarky grin.

"Can I get you a drink?" asked Andrew, who appeared behind her. "Coffee, tea, whiskey?"

"Oh, hi." She turned to him. "Tea would be nice."

"Sure," he said. "I had them bring in specialty teas. Much higher end than the usual brands I see at these things. Come with me?"

"I can't. I've got to be over..." she watched Lincoln, the man who was her everything and now her nothing. He seemed to be fine without her. He seemed happy enough. She didn't want to watch him smile for the cameras.

"Is everything okay?"

She straightened up. Andrew didn't need to know anything, either. "I guess he's fine. Let's go."

They walked together to the tea station, and she was quiet, unsure of what she wanted to say. He asked, again, if there was anything wrong and she said nothing. He proceeded to make her a cup of tea and handed her the cup with a smile.

A bell tone rang through the halls, signaling that the luncheon was to begin in ten minutes. Andrew had excused himself to go speak with his dad and some other people he knew. As she walked back to the ball-room, Gordy and Yukika were standing next to each other, smiling and posing for a picture. The person taking the picture was Gretchen.

Shit.

If Gretchen were able to put two and two together, she might figure out that there was more tot his event than a simple fundraiser.

Lincoln's name was printed on the placard for the seat next to Kendra Gilroy's. Opal had seated him next to her to start a conversation about running mates. At the time she'd made the chart, Opal had been looking forward to being part of it—the beginning of something fresh and exciting. A new political empire.

Now? Opal clenched her jaw. She wasn't sure how she'd manage it. Today, she'd have to be the consummate professional. Keep her poker face for the entirety of the meal. A whole two hours, at least, of having the man she loved, The One, so close to her. The knowledge of his jealousy, his horrible words, soured her. That he believed the worst of her, that she would use him like that, made her stomach churn.

Kendra Gilroy was seated already, and there was no one else at the table. Opal sat next to her.

"I'm hearing rumors that Lincoln Pierce wants to make a bid for presidency."

"You heard right."

"Maybe I'm a possible mate, that right, too? It's not like he has a reputation for being, shall we say, indirect."

Opal was surprised, but she shouldn't be. Often times, conversations between two political people was often comprised of verbal shorthand. "It is." Opal didn't want to say too much, and hopefully she wasn't saying too little. Her dad used to always tell her, 'don't sell it if it's already sold.' She hadn't thought of him like that in years.

"The longer I'm in politics, the more I realize that all of this is like an arranged marriage."

"Aren't all political relationships that way?" Opal said, wondering about her and Lincoln. Were they a good match politically? The gold standard for a political relationship was to marry someone who had a connection to money or power. She had neither. Anyway, who was she kidding? They couldn't even make it thirty minutes beyond the bed.

"I'd like to think there is some spontaneity. That there's some serendipity. Makes me feel like life isn't this preordained plan. I think we would work well together. I think our politics meld well, but the press is going to have a field day with a single man and a single woman running together."

"We live in the modern age. No one is going to care," Opal said flippantly.

"Oh please," the governor said. "*They* will care very much. Anything to sell the papers, and sex sells the best."

"We can discuss it further, but as of now, the Honorable Congressman is single." It was bullshit. Opal should be up there standing next to him. She'd make an amazing partner. Instead, Lincoln chose to believe that she was using him. How could he think that? She'd have to quit. There was no way around it. Not after what had transpired this morning. Her knee started to involuntarily shake.

"Or is it just a ploy to keep me from running my own ticket?"

"Hi, Ms. Gilroy. I'm Andrew Donohoe."

Kendra stood up to shake his hand. "Pleasure to meet you."

"I'm not seated here, but I wanted to come over and introduce myself." Andrew sat next to Opal.

Opal put her hand on her knee to steady it. She would make it through this day. She had to make it through.

Andrew put his arm around her shoulders. "And

the real reason is I wanted to check on my friend Opal. Sure you're okay? You seem off."

Opal shrugged his arm off her with a vacant smile. "Gretchen is here," she whispered, not wanting Kendra to hear her. *Good god, did Lincoln see her? This would only add fuel to his fire.*

"Oh? Oh. OH," he said, straightening his posture. "How did she know about this?"

Opal didn't want to tell him that she had to invite her, so she didn't—she pretended as if she didn't hear him. The banquet workers started to move in, placing salads in front of everyone.

"Just relax, Opal," Andrew leaned in to whisper in her ear. "You're gonna fuck this up if you're too tense." He stood up and straightened his jacket.

"Andrew," said Lincoln, seeming to square off with him. "What are you doing here?"

"I came over to see how Opal's doing. She's handling herself, I see."

"We'll be sure to meet back in DC to finalize our PR strategy."

"Yes, we will," Andrew replied. "I have to meet with Yukika. I'll see you all later?"

Lincoln nodded goodbye as he pulled out the chair next to Kendra Gilroy. He sat down slowly, easily, as if he didn't have a care in the world.

"Kendra, I'm so glad we'll have a chance to chat,"

he said. He patted opal on the back, as if there was nothing wrong. As if they were just two coworkers.

Her face felt white, as if all the blood had left.

"You two okay?" Kendra asked.

"Never better. You'll have to excuse me," Opal said, making eye contact with Link, wanting to tell him how she felt, but she couldn't, not in the middle of a luncheon, not in front of Kendra. "I got a call from the office. Katherine says she needs me for something urgent."

Link nodded and turned his attention to Kendra Gilroy, his signature dimples on full-blast. Opal pushed back from the table and escaped the room. She didn't even know where she was going; she just needed distance and privacy.

Except Opal didn't get any privacy, she got lost in the sprawling conference center with its never-ending halls and similar sounding room names. Instead of proceeding with caution, she walked as if she knew exactly where she was going. By the time she returned, the luncheon had wrapped up. Banquet workers wearing stiff starched white button-down shirts with polyester black pants took away the main entrée plates and replaced them with a decadent chocolate cake and quiet offers of coffee or decaf. The Service Dogs of America president got up from his table and walked to the main podium, where he would presumably talk about the good the association has done for the military, the good that the Honorable Congressman Lincoln Pierce had done for our country and the military, and finalize his speech by honoring the governor for supporting and uniting the various groups involved. He did exactly that.

Maybe I've been to too many of these things.

After the speech, everyone was invited over to a demonstration. The SDA members brought in several puppies and young dogs to display the training tactics used to help calm individuals with severe PTSD. Everyone else had already left the table, but Opal wanted to check the fundraiser schedule first before heading over. Gretchen sat down next to her.

Opal set down her phone and tried to keep the anger off her face and stay composed. She wasn't about to say the first word; anything that came out of her mouth now wouldn't be good.

"You know, honestly, I think I would hate to be the First Lady. I mean, really. You're sort of stuck between this traditional role of making cookies, but then expected to make appearances at rather silly functions that only pertain to children or education. That seems rather a dull life, don't you think?"

"Are you recording this, Gretchen?" asked Opal.

"Me?" she asked somewhat seriously, but a lilt in her tone gave her away.

"Yes, you."

"What is the deal with you and Lincoln? The picture." Gretchen pursed her lips and kissed the air as a crude reminder. She held her phone in her hand.

"I can't speak to that, maybe later. But what I can tell you is the bigger picture of what's going on. But you'll have to delete the photo of Link and me from your device and the cloud."

"I don't think so. See I also have a picture of you and Andrew going off. I heard a helicopter was involved. And another sweet little picture of him here with his arms around you."

Gretchen swiped the photo frame over to show Opal a photo taken of her and Andrew taken just thirty minutes ago at the luncheon table.

Opal's mouth dropped, but she closed it—fast. No way in hell was she going to let Gretchen get the better of her. Everything was happening too fast, when even she didn't know how she felt or what she wanted. But she knew this. Gretchen wasn't going to drive the story. She was.

"Is he consoling you, dear? Perhaps you told him about the kiss with Lincoln?" Gretchen shrugged her shoulders looking coy, as if she were a girl overwhelmed by love.

"Look, Gretchen," Opal said, trying to make sure she sounded in control, like she was just fine, like nothing was bothering her, like her heart wasn't in the middle of tearing apart. "There is a reason everyone is here, and it means major legislation in DC. Now you can go with your little story, which really doesn't mean anything. Sure it's a bunch of pictures, it's inflammatory, you'll sell fast and hot, but is that what you *really* want?"

"What do you mean?"

"Do you want to be known for having the first scoop on a major DC event happening outside of DC, or do you want to be a society blogger? You can't be both."

"Sure I can." Gretchen crossed her legs and cocked her head.

"You publish those photos, no one in politics will ever take you under their wing. They will never trust you. They will always think you have an agenda."

"And if I don't publish the photos?"

"I'll give you your first *real* story. A huge political story. A big-time, headline busting, 'Inside the Beltway' story." Opal placed her hands in her lap and tried not to move.

"You've promised me that before."

"You're here. Right in the middle of it all, because I invited you. Because I told you about this event. But you publish this paparazzi bullshit? This gossip-rag speculative nonsense? I won't be able to trust you anymore. You can kiss your spot on the press junket goodbye."

"Maybe. Maybe not. But I'm the one in control here, Opal, not you." Gretchen pushed back from the table, grabbed her bag, and was gone.

Chapter 17

*L*incoln had sat through the luncheon and all the tedious speeches with a determinedly calm poker face being nothing but a mask hiding the roiling anger within. Anger at himself, anger at Opal. Anger at the whole situation. He took responsibility for where he found himself—single, aging career politician—but he didn't have to be happy about it.

Why had he lashed out at Opal after such a perfect evening and morning? She was everything to him, and yet, he had accused her of playing games and machinations. What was he afraid of? He loved her. Wanted her by his side. If they were married, she could still do a lot of the work she would have done as a staffer, but maybe even at a deeper level. She hadn't told him she loved him. Even though he had accused her of it, he couldn't believe that she was sleeping with him as a part of a political move. But was she? Did he really know her as well as he thought, or was she another one of DC players?

The whole luncheon was a painful exercise in trying to ignore what was really filling his heart and mind, and as soon as the formal presentation was over and everyone went gaga over the puppies, Lincoln made a beeline to the bar. It was early afternoon, he was in Las Vegas, and, damn it, he wanted a drink. He had to apologize to Opal, and he wasn't sure how.

Link ordered a whiskey and hunched over the bar, sending a 'do not disturb' body signal flashing for anyone to notice. Leave it to Andrew Fucking Donohoe to ignore it.

Donohoe pressed in next to him, elbow to elbow. "I'll take what he's having."

Link's fingers tightened around his glass as he tried to ignore Donohoe. The last thing he wanted was a discussion of any kind with Donohoe.

"Jesus, Lincoln. You're acting like a spoiled brat today. What's up with you? You're like a different man. You're all stiff and fake smiley. Even with when you were sandwiched between the two most beautiful women in the room. The gov'nur is spanking hot. And Opal? Hold on, I gotta close my eyes for a sec."

Lincoln barely turned his head to acknowledge the other man.

Andrew patted Link's wrist in an awkward comforting gesture. "Oh man. That was hot. Now, let me give you a little advice, okay?"

"That's disgusting," Link said as he stared into his drink, seeking control. Advice from this monkey? Like he needed it.

"We all know you are aiming for the White House. The thing is? You can't possibly think that will fly when you can't even control your own staff, you know?"

Lincoln turned now, standing up straight and on high alert. "No? Why don't you illuminate things for me."

Donohoe took a sip of the whiskey and let out a gasp as if it had burned the back of his throat. "Whew. Damn. That's some good stuff. Look, here's the thing. A little bird told me about that deal with Cheyenne last week. That was a fucking close call. And the Chinese Gala? Wasn't that one of your other girls getting into trouble? You gotta be doing something when someone like Gordy Fucking Carpenter comes up to me to ask me about shit going down. You see what I'm saying?"

The man was talking too loudly and Lincoln scanned the room quickly to make sure no one could hear him "How much have you already had to drink, Andrew?" Lincoln asked. "Let's go where we can have a little privacy."

Andrew downed the last of his drink as Lincoln took him by the elbow toward a corner away from the bar. Most of the party guests were still inside the main ballroom. He took Andrew around the corner where they would be mostly hidden from view.

"What did Gordy tell you?"

Andrew brushed a fake crumb off Link's jacket. "If someone like Gordy has inside information, you know you have got to be doing something wrong. And you gotta tighten up that ship if you want to sail it to the White House."

Andrew was repeating himself and slurring his words. "You're talking in circles, Andrew."

"I mean. I get it. Look, I know it's fun having all these hot babes working for you, but it really isn't befitting a man who is running for the highest office in the land."

"I hire people based on merit. If they happen to be women, it is coincidental."

"Yeah, keep telling yourself that," Andrew said. "Opal is definitely a winner in every respect. That's for sure. You know what? She's the first woman I've dated in years that hasn't tried to seduce me."

Lincoln found that easy to believe. Opal wouldn't

reduce herself to seducing anyone. *Oh, God. What a fool I've been. There's no way Opal was playing that game. Or any game.*

"I took her to the ballet the other night, you know? And I thought I'd totally score with that. I did my research on her, you see? I found out she was this hot-shot dancer when she was younger. So, I knew she'd like the ballet. Nada. Five hundred bucks on dinner and another two grand on the ballet, and not so much as a titty grab."

Lincoln wasn't sure what was more disturbing, the fact that Donohoe was going on about a woman like this—the woman he loved—or that Lincoln was sitting there quietly and listening to it.

"I suggest you change the subject," Lincoln growled through clenched teeth.

Donohoe plowed on, ignoring the warning. "And then? You know she had this blog back in high school? And she made a bucket list that was about a thousand lines long. So, I figure, what better than to impress her with something she wants? So, I do this huge thing with a helicopter and private catering out at the Grand Canyon. Bucket list? Bam. Man, she acted like she was doing me a favor by kissing me. You know that two hours was like five grand?"

Donohoe paused and downed the last of his whiskey. "Jesus. Almost ten grand on her, and nothing but a boring kiss. I even asked her to marry me, and she still won't put out. You know what, though? She'd make the perfect little wife, don't you think, complacent, keeping the house clean. A proposal, and still, she wouldn't put out. Dude, give a bro some hints." Donohoe held his hands out at hip level and made a crude gyrating humping gesture. "You gotta tell me how to tap that, will ya…"

Lincoln didn't hesitate. He balled his hand into a tight fist and threw all his weight into a hard punch aimed directly at Andrew Donohoe's nose. The crunch was undeniably satisfying.

Donohoe stepped back, eyes wide and hand covering a gushing spurt of blood. "Fucking hell? What the fuck, dude?" He wiped at the spatters on his shirt and bent his head back to keep more blood from getting on his clothing. "Jesus-fuck. What was that for? Dude, you are *so* going to pay for this."

As soon as his fist connected with Donohoe's nose, Lincoln regretted it. He should have walked away. Taken the higher ground and let Donohoe reveal himself to be the asshole he really was. Instead, he'd lost it and let his anger win. He stuck out his hand, reaching immediately for Donohoe to apologize.

Before he could say anything, Opal appeared out of nowhere, slipping a supporting arm under Donohoe. "Lincoln? What the hell are you doing?" She tossed a look toward the ballroom and made a face. "Andrew, come on. Let's get some ice on that."

"Opal, I...I'm sorry. He...I..." Lincoln was at a loss for words.

Opal's eyebrows compressed into a stern formidable line. "Go back inside. Play with some puppies. I'll take care of this. Just...go back in. Now, before anyone else notices."

Lincoln watched as Opal wrapped an arm around Andrew Donohoe's waist and led him away. Her soft voice calming Andrew might as well be a dagger in Lincoln's heart.

Chapter 18

$\mathcal{O}$pal brought Andrew to a side room that wasn't being used. She only knew about it because the banquet manager had sent her a comprehensive floor plan. Andrew had his nose in the air to staunch the flow of blood, but there was still a steady flow dripping down his hand.

When would these people grow up? They were supposed to be professionals, the whole damn lot of them. And yet, here she was, cleaning up another round of imbecilic behavior. This time from two grown men acting like their testicles just dropped.

"Andrew?" The deep voice resounded faintly in the hallway.

"Don't let my dad see me like this. You gotta shut the door."

"Fine. I have to get some first aid. Just stay where you are," she said.

Opal had barely closed the door, thinking she'd bribe one of the banquet workers for a clean white button-down shirt, when she ran into Jack Donohoe.

"Is he in there? What's he done now?"

"What makes you think Andrew's done anything?"

He rolled back on his heels slightly and tipped his head. Peering over his glasses, he regarded her as if she had just told him monsters lived under her bead. "I have the uncanny ability to know when my son has had too much to drink. Usually a shitstorm follows."

Opal surreptitiously glanced at the closed door.

"There's the tell," Jack said, clapping his hands before he walked into the room. "Son, what... what in the hell happened? Jesus Christ, son, you're getting blood all over the carpet."

"That son of a bitch Pierce hit me."

Opal came back into the room and shut the door.

"I'm not sure I want to know what you said to make him slug you." Jack grasped Andrew's chin and moved his face right and then left, inspecting it with a cool detachment. "Does it hurt?"

Opal could clearly see that Andrew was in pain, but he wouldn't admit it to his dad. Jack Donohoe was a hard-ass. Images of a young Andrew flipped through her mind as she imagined exactly how difficult it must have been growing up as Jack Donohoe's son. The man was hard, raw, and unforgiving. She almost went over to Andrew to comfort and defend him, but she stayed put.

"Nothing. It's nothing, Dad."

"Andrew. It's *not* nothing. This isn't fixing a ticket. This isn't paying off a cop. This is major business. I asked you to steer clear of the booze." Jack dropped his hand and wiped his fingers against his pants, a snarl of disgust curling his lips.

"I only had a drink...or two."

"*One weekend.* You couldn't do it for one weekend. What's it gonna be this time, Andrew? We going to Florida again?" Andrew looked at Opal, his eyes wide, his mouth slightly open.

"Come on, Dad. It wasn't that serious." He glanced towards Opal, hope brightening his eyes. "Look. Opal's here. She's going to take care of this. She knows how to take care of everything."

Opal smiled, tentatively, uncomfortable with this exchange. She should have left when she had the chance, and now all eyes were on her. "I was going to go," she said, "find some supplies. First aid. Get Andrew a new shirt."

"It's her boss that's the fucking problem. He's the one that decked me."

Jack's ice blue eyes bored into her. "Did you see it, Opal?"

Opal kept her expression neutral. "Link did hit him. But I didn't hear what had happened between them." Opal knew Link, though, and she knew he wouldn't hit someone unless it was serious. *I thought I knew him, but not after this morning.* Either way, her job was to make sure the deal didn't fall apart because of strong emotions getting in the way. Opal backed toward the door. "I'll get some ice and gauze and a new shirt."

"Wait a minute, Ms. Opal. You should hear this. And you too, Andrew."

"Dad, before you say anything, I want you to know that I've asked Opal something." He turned towards her. "You always know how to take care of a situation. You always know how to make things so wrong go so right. I need your help, Opal. I meant what I said earlier. You're the ying to my yang. Will you help me? Will you be my wife?"

Jack seemed to be watching her very carefully.

"I...Andrew...your nose! It's bleeding again. Hold it tighter, I'm going to go get some things to help and a fresh shirt. If anything's going to get us out of here without alerting the press, then you need to follow my lead. Both of you," she said, looking pointedly between

Andrew and Jack. "Can I trust you two to be gentlemen and do as I say?"

"Yes ma'am."

"Good. Now, sit tight. Nobody leaves this room."

She backed to the door, and once she stepped out, she closed it thankfully. *Hell no* she didn't want to help Andrew. She was already overextended to the one man she believed in: Link. She needed to find a male worker about Andrew's size and get the first aid kit from the banquet manager. Most of the people had disbursed, but a handful of people stayed to pet the puppies. A few of the press photographers were there, looking for some vanity shots, probably hoping for an act of God so they could hit a bonus payout. She didn't see Link. Carleen was sitting at the table now, conversing with the governor of Nevada. She didn't see Gretchen. Gordy and Yukika were gone as well. Most people were flying back that evening, so she could only hope that no one else was going to cause any drama.

Opal stopped a young man and told him she was in charge of the banquet and needed to ask him something which required discretion. He nodded and when she got him to a private enough spot, close enough to an exit that he could walk through, she showed him a hundred-dollar bill and asked for his shirt. He requested two hundred and a promise that she inform his boss that his departure was required. She agreed, and they exchanged goods. He gave her his name and his shirt, and she gave him cash. She found the manager in the hallway leading to the kitchen, kept her promise to the waiter and asked the manager for the first aid kit and some ice.

When she returned to the room, both Andrew and Jack stood tall, looking as if they couldn't decide if they should hide or hit someone. Jack's face was red, as if he'd been yelling. He turned towards the door, the look of pure fight in his eyes.

"It's just me," she said, doing nothing to hide the weariness in her voice. She was getting tired of these men who couldn't keep it together.

Andrew sunk back down into his chair, shoulders slumped.

Opal draped the shirt over a chair and opened the first aid kit. She spread the contents out on a table and found the largest gauze pad she could. She rolled it in half and pressed the cotton side against Andrew's nose. He tilted his head back and closed his eyes. "Hold that in place."

Andrew's hand swayed as he reached up to do as she told him. "You are soooo beautiful, Opal. I love you, soooo much."

His eyes were round and large, looking up at her like an adoring puppy.

She ripped open a packet of gel cleaner and wiped his cheek and neck clean of blood.

"Ouch," he said.

When he was clean, she handed Andrew the replacement shirt while looking directly at Jack. "You owe me two hundred bucks for that shirt."

"Maybe you *can* play poker, Ms. Opal," he said, grinning amiably. His color had come back to normal, and he looked almost relaxed.

"Damn straight I can. Don't make any hasty decisions about how this affects our earlier business. Especially you, Andrew." She put her hand on his arm. "I know you're pissed. You want to find a way to ruin Link."

Andrew closed his eyes.

"I suppose that's your own choice, Andrew. But, hey, look at me please." He opened his eyes to meet hers. "If you ruin him, you ruin me. Just wait until we have a chance to talk next week. Give it some time."

"I can do that. *For you,*" he said, half-smiling.

"Jack."

"Opal."

She turned and was out of that room as fast as she could go without running. She didn't stop until she got to her room.

～

OPAL OPENED the door between her and Link's room. His side was closed, but she knocked tentatively. No answer. He was probably still downstairs with the puppies. She packed as quickly as humanly possible.

The intensity of the previous night's activity had faded, but the lingering smell of their love-making, so sweet and, now, so over, made her want to gag. But they had to talk. They would talk. They had to figure out how to move forward, professionally and personally.

Her phone buzzed a text notification. Gretchen sent her a picture of Gordy, Andrew, and Yukika having a drink.

Gretchen: We need to talk. I'm headed to the airport. I need deets or I'm submitting *now*.

Opal: I've got something for you. I'm headed to the airport in fifteen. Let's meet in DC after flight?

Gretchen: You on the American red eye? We can meet for breakfast at 11am. Skydome Restaurant. Pentagon City, in the Doubletree Hotel.

Opal: I'll be there, unless flight delayed.

Her flight, along with the rest of the team, got into DC that night. That would give her time to call Kenny and schedule an emergency meeting tomorrow morning before going to see Gretchen. She needed all the help she could get to make sure this complicated mess didn't end up on DCBlogAboutTown or any other blog for that matter.

She'd checked under the bed and in the sheets, finding nothing. She had an unsettled feeling that she was leaving something behind, that she had forgotten something, but she knew there was nothing. Opal walked out of the hotel room and let the door close behind her. Everything she needed was in her suitcase or in her purse.

Except Lincoln wasn't with her.

Opal's phone rang. Kenny Marshall's face flashed on the screen.

"I heard you were in some trouble?" he said.

"How the hell?"

"Don't ask. Tell me everything."

Her lips pinched together. There was no way Opal would tell him anything beyond what could be proven —the singing, the kiss on stage. Even though she was mad at Lincoln, they had still shared something intimate and special. Whether or not she had sex with Lincoln was not something for Kenny to 'fix.' Her sex life was private, and she intended to keep it that way.

But getting Gretchen off her and Lincoln's back was paramount. And there, she started to gush, and didn't stop until she reached the airport.

Chapter 19

*L*incoln had to make things right. When he got back to his room, he discovered Opal had gone off to the airport ahead of him.

"Opal texted me. She wanted to take an earlier flight out," Carleen said as they climbed into the taxi on the way to the airport. "But she just texted me to let me know she couldn't get on one."

As soon as they were through security, Lincoln headed straight to the lounge, hoping to find Opal. She sat alone in a corner, her back to the wall, her luggage on the seat next to her.

Lincoln made to move it and sit down, but she held up a hand. "No. Leave it."

"Opal. We need to talk. I have to explain..."

"Do *not* even talk to me right now," she said, interrupting him. "Yes. We need to talk, but it isn't happening until we are home and we are alone. This is not the time or place."

"We're pretty much alone," Lincoln said.

"Not really," she said, waving Carleen over with a smile. She shifted her luggage and offered Carleen the seat she had denied him. And then she left the lounge.

When they boarded the plane, Opal asked Carleen to sit in the middle so she could be on the aisle, and Lincoln lost any hope of talking to her during the flight. There was no way talking over Carleen would work. Opal had her ear buds in and so did Carleen. He spent the whole flight home feeling like a kid who was being punished without any chance at fixing things. All he wanted was to scoop her up in his arms and beg her forgiveness for being an idiot.

Carleen acted as physical barrier between them, a thick book propped up on her tray table nearly the entire flight. Whenever Lincoln moved as if to try to talk to Opal, Carleen gave him the stink eye. Opal was right. It wasn't the time or place to work things through.

After they landed, Opal grabbed her things and slipped by most of the standing-rush. By the time Link had wrangled his suitcase out of the overhead bin and made it down the gangway, Opal was nowhere in sight.

He got home at just a quarter past one and filled his electric kettle with water. Some chamomile tea would help calm his nerves. He had been restless during the flight, trying to check in on Opal, knowing that she was so close. With Carleen between them, he had not been able to relax at all. He listened to messages and unpacked. A text message from Opal lit up his phone, and his heart raced.

Maybe she was finally ready to talk. The phone wasn't ideal, but it was better than nothing. Maybe he could go over to her apartment. It was then he realized he had no idea where Opal lived. It struck him as profoundly odd that, in all the time she'd worked for him, he had never had any reason to go to her house, and the fact that he didn't even know where she lived highlighted how little he knew about her. She had mentioned her apartment before, but nothing about roommates or where the apartment might be. Was she in town? In Arlington? He had no idea what her daily commute was like.

Opal: Kenny is on board. 8:oo am strategy meeting. Your place.

Lincoln: Can we talk. Tonight? About us?

Opal: I'm tired and too angry to be rational. Go to bed. We can talk tomorrow.

Lincoln had to respect her need for distance. She had always been a straight shooter, and for him to have accused her of playing games had been way off base. His misguided sense of fear substituted his better judgment. He'd just spent the most amazing night ever with the woman he loved, and then turned around and accused her of the worst. He'd have to make it up to her somehow, and if she needed time and space? He'd give it to her. Whatever and however long it would take. Opal was worth waiting for.

Lincoln switched into the sweats he usually lounged around in and decided against tea. He wanted a mug of hot milk with nutmeg, cinnamon, and vanilla. It had been one hell of a day. Had it really just been ten hours ago that he had punched Donohoe? His fingers throbbed with a renewed pain as he flexed them. There wasn't any deep injury, just the surface skin and maybe his pride. He held his hand up to the light for inspection and grimaced at the purple green tinge around the knuckles. *Great.*

He'd lost it over Andrew Donohoe, of all people. He hoped he hadn't destroyed SUNFLOWER. *All that work. All that political maneuvering.* If it came to that, they would have to figure something out. Wallowing in his own stupidity wouldn't do him any good, but it sure felt good. Lincoln flopped onto the sofa and kicked his feet up. And, sure as hell, he wasn't going to sleep well after all of this. Lincoln started to count the tiles on his ceiling in the hope of finding sleep when the doorbell rang. Someone had gotten past the front desk of his apartment and was at his actual door.

Was it Opal? Had she changed her mind? Lincoln's heart soared. She'd come over to clear things up tonight. Lincoln bolted off the sofa and lunged for the door, swinging it open wide, grinning ear to ear.

Andrew Donohoe was at the door with his swollen nose and the flesh under his eyes already edging from red into a dark violet. Link looked past him, unable to believe it was Donohoe and not Opal. He didn't bother hiding his disappointment. The guy was going to need a thick layer of makeup to cover that up. Link shouldn't be proud of himself, but there was a hint of satisfaction that came over him. Even though he wanted to slam the door shut, he had to do the right thing.

"Look, man, I'm sorry about hitting you."

He sniffed hard and grimaced—it looked as though merely breathing caused him pain. "You sure as hell *will* be." Donohoe pointed a finger at Lincoln, landing it on the center of his chest. A strong whiff of fresh booze rode along with the words. Donohoe swung his arms back and straight down, as if he were trying to hold himself back from hitting Lincoln. Or was he having trouble keeping himself upright? Link wasn't sure. He tilted his head, waiting for whatever else Donohoe had come to say.

"You think that whole meeting in Las Vegas was set in stone? Think again, buddy. You remember those concessions we made? Well, you can forget them. All of them. We're going to have to go back and re-work the whole deal and in our favor. Got that? There's clauses in the documents. Guess you forgot to read everything we sent you, huh?"

Lincoln couldn't tell if Andrew was bluffing or if he was even going to remember this little tête-à-tête. "Fine. Let's set up a meeting for next week."

"Did you just say fine?" Andrew asked, suddenly bleary-eyed and unfocused. "Okay, then." He placed both hands on the doorsill to keep himself from falling.

Link slipped on a pair of shoes from near his door and put Andrew's arm around his shoulder. Donohoe could barely hold himself up, and how he managed to slip by front desk security was a miracle. He'd make sure to talk to them. "You're not driving, are you?"

"Driver's out front," he slurred, almost saying the sentence in one long word.

Lincoln opened the back door of the sleek Mercedes and helped Andrew inside. Andrew collapsed into a heap against the seat as Lincoln met his eyes. "Call me on Monday. Better yet, come to my office."

The driver got out of the car and hurried around. "Take him home. Even if he tells you to go somewhere else. I'll make sure you don't get in trouble for ignoring him."

The driver eyed Andrew and nodded. "Yes, sir, Congressman. I tried to talk him out of coming, but he insisted."

"Take him home." Lincoln shut the car door and went back inside.

After a restless sleep, Lincoln rose a full two hours before the meeting. He went shopping at the twenty-four hour convenience store located in the apartment building for overpriced breakfast items like eggs, bacon, and toast. He had just put the coffee on to brew and slid the bacon in the oven when the door buzzed.

Carleen, Opal and Kenny were all waiting together. Kenny held a tray overflowing with baked goods on them.

Carleen tipped her head up to sniff the air as they entered. "Oh, good. You have bacon and coffee going. We need something to balance the carbs."

"What can I say? My new beau is adept at baking."

"Oh, I'm not complaining," Carleen said. "I need more than the sugar in my system."

Lincoln took the plate and centered it on the table, removing the plastic wrap. Sweet cinnamon, toasted pecans, and a whiff of vanilla wafted upward. "Damn...that smells delicious. I've got orange juice, grapefruit. Coffee is almost ready. Bacon is ten minutes out, and I'm taking egg orders. Scrambled? Fried? Poached? I can do them all."

"You are so *helpful*, Lincoln," said Opal.

"*Sarcasm* isn't helpful." Carleen glared at Opal. "Link, you're overthinking. Scrambled for everyone."

Carleen filled up coffee cups and deposited them on the table.

Opal and Carleen sat on one side of the table, Kenny on the other. It didn't take long for Link to crack open a dozen eggs and cook them. He added chopped chives, salt and pepper as they solidified in the pan. Link placed the food in the middle and tried to catch Opal's attention, but her eyes were distant.

"Anyone want a muffin?" Kenny clapped his hands together. "Okay. Opal filled me in over the phone, but I want to make sure we're all on the same page. Just in case a detail slipped through the cracks."

"We're here to deal with the shit-storm brewing with Gretchen Hughes and her lovely blog. We need a plan to mitigate the damage her releasing various photos might cause."

Kenny put a yellow legal pad on the table. "Let me see if I got this right. Your intern is dating Harrison Rousseau. He and Gordy Carpenter, the infamous lobbyist at Ellis and Levin Associates, got into a fight at a bar. Opal managed to get Gretchen to hold off on that with the promise of something better, more political, less social as I understand."

"That's right so far," said Opal.

"Second, you invited Gretchen to Vegas to make good on that promise. She then follows the two of you to a karaoke party, even though you were wearing disguises." Kenny pulled out his phone and swiped his thumb across the screen a few times. "I have the photos Gretchen sent to Opal here, she forwarded them to me last night. I have to say, Opal, you look super cute, love the top. And Lincoln, who knew you could rock a cowboy hat and facial hair. Not many can pull it off, but you..."

"Kenny," Carleen said, interrupting him. "Can we see them?"

"Sure." He handed the phone to Carleen. "The reason I digress is because if we need to repurpose the photo with another headline, we may be able to do so. The important photo is the one of you two kissing on stage."

Carleen was about to take a sip of coffee and she practically dropped the cup after hearing that.

Link saw her try to catch Opal's eyes and he looked at her too, but she avoided both of them and blushed. "Yes."

"Is it possible that the photo of you kissing can be spun as a pair of doppelgängers? Or is it obvious it is the two of you to anyone else?"

Carleen leaned forward, her head in her hands, hunched over her plate. "I can't believe this. Of all things. Kissing in public? Even in costume that was... reckless." After a long moment, she raised her head and met Lincoln's eyes. "Kissing a *staff member*? In public? How could you?"

Opal stiffened. "Can we work on solving the problem? We have to get Gretchen to back down."

"Right. Back to the business at hand," Kenny said. "This third photo is of Gordy, Yukika and Andrew. Gordy, who we all know is a grade-A piece of work and is a slave to oil and gas, *just happens* to be hanging with Yukika Mathews and Andrew Donohoe. That is definitely going to be raising questions."

He drew four rectangles on the page and made quick caricatures of the major players in each photo. He considered the pad for a moment. "I'm going to assume that you had some other intention at the fundraiser. The Service Dogs of America isn't well-known to pull national level press, but it is good enough to work as a cover. I need to know why you were in Vegas. Not the dog and pony show about the banquet, either. The real reason."

Kenny had easily figured out that the players were all meeting for reasons other than the fundraiser. This meant he'd have to issue a full release sooner than planned. Carleen and Opal both looked at Link, then, clearly waiting for him to make the call. He sighed and laid out the basics of the SUNFLOWER program for Kenny.

When he was done, Kenny laced his fingers together and rested his chin on his fingers. He had drawn a picture of a flower in the center of the four photographs. "Well, this pretty much sucks. Let's get to the last bit, then, shall we? Can you explain to me why the fuck you hit Andrew Donohoe?"

The room fell silent as everyone looked at Link. But he only had eyes for Opal. Hers met his, but they were cool and closed off. He didn't want to come across as peevish or jealous, but how could he do that without explaining what a dick Donohoe had been at the bar? And none of them knew about Andrew's visit the night before.

"I shouldn't have hit him. I lost it...he pissed me off. He was asking me for advice on how to get Opal to sleep with him. He was upset that he'd spent so much money on dates without getting very far." He couldn't bring himself to say the actual words Donohoe had used or describe the interaction further. It was all too gross. "But that's not everything. There's more."

Kenny tilted his head back and groaned. "Out with it."

Link filled them in on Donohoe's late night visit the previous evening. "So," he said, "when he insinuated that Opal was an idiot for not sleeping with him, I hit him. But that costs us. I probably borked up SUNFLOWER."

"At least Gretchen didn't get a photo of you slugging Andrew," Opal said. She still refused to make eye contact with him, and was focused on Kenny instead.

"There's a bright side to everything, eh?" Carleen said, shaking her head. "And I suppose Andrew is going to be black and blue for a couple weeks? Someone is going to ask him how he got a busted nose."

Kenny thumped his pen against the pad of paper and closed his eyes. He held his free hand out over the table, a calming, "be quiet for a minute" gesture. He tilted his head toward a shoulder while his face contorted as he considered the options. His fingers curled into a fist, and his index finger shot upward, pointing to the ceiling and his eyes popped open.

"Okay. One of the biggest considerations here is

Gretchen. She's been around for a long time, and I know her pretty well too. She is all about becoming legit. She's tired of being dismissed as nothing but a society columnist, even when she's breaking some pretty exciting and hot drama."

"Honestly," Carleen said, "the photo of Gordy and Harrison in the bar fight is pretty much out of date."

"In PR, no one cares. And Gretchen knows that. The photo could be three years old, it wouldn't matter. She'd post the photo without a date. Does she know about the kissing game everyone was playing?" Kenny asked.

Everyone sat in stunned silence for a moment.

"Kat O'Malley told me because of an issue with a possible client. Turned out to be a non-issue, and also, you know me, discretion is my currency. Zip zip."

"Gretchen doesn't know about the game; at least, she hasn't brought it up," Opal said.

"One spin is to let Gretchen have the boys fighting, but, honestly, knowing Gretchen, I don't think she'll go for it. Not when she has a picture of Link and Opal kissing. And all these other pictures that, with the wrong headline, could be a political nightmare."

Carleen crossed her arms. "It doesn't make the congressman look good at any level."

Kenny shrugged. "DC is full of shenanigans and crazier things than that. It's not about the action. It's about the perceived message. However, we are not going to give Gretchen one iota of anything we don't have to."

Lincoln slammed his hands onto the table. "I think we should have her release our karaoke kiss."

Kenny and Carleen looked at him in stunned silence.

"What?" Opal asked, her jaw dropping.

Lincoln focused on Opal. "I love you. I do want to marry you, they weren't just words of a song." He sat upright and rubbed his hands together. "As a matter of fact, I want the whole world to know it. No more hiding it. Not from me, not from anyone."

Opal turned her focus to Lincoln and fire flickered in her eyes. "First Andrew and now *you*? Marriage is serious. Marriage should be asked on one knee in front of the Eiffel Tower. Marriage is not a solution to a problem." She turned away from Lincoln and towards Kenny. "He treats me like *I'm* his fixer, like he has no responsibility for his own god damn actions. I clean up his messes. I took care of Andrew after he hit him."

Lincoln edged past the pain and hurt to address what she had said. "I don't need you as my fixer. I love you. I want you at my side as my wife."

"Why? So I can fix things for you on a permanent basis? What the hell, Link?"

Kenny bobbed his head from side to side. "Hold on

a minute. Gretchen's forte has always been reporting on the inner lives and drama, not the political maneuvering behind the scenes. We could build a Camelot story. Big wedding. Have Gretchen follow you around for dress shopping, lots of photos of rings, china settings, all the old-fashioned romantic stuff."

Link could see it. Opal as the new Jackie Kennedy at his side—beautiful, smart, loyal.

"Are you fucking kidding me? That's the stupidest thing I've ever heard." Opal stood, spreading her fingers wide and holding her hands at the side of her head. "Are either of you listening to anything? I'm not having any of it. I am not getting married to solve your fucking PR problem."

Lincoln's breath was taken away. When Opal was impassioned about something, she was stunning. "I'm sorry," he said immediately. "What would you have us do?"

Opal spread her palms flat and leaned into the table, towering over them all. "Here's what's going to happen. I am going to print out Madeline's latest release and take it with me to edit just before my meeting with Gretchen this afternoon. I am going to tell Gretchen that she is to not look in the top-secret folder on the table while I go to the bathroom so she does exactly that. After I return from the bathroom, I will tell her that the photograph she got of Gordy,

Yukika, and Andrew is the only photograph that meets her career goals."

Lincoln listened carefully, not wanting to misstep again and gave Opal's idea full consideration. He caught her gaze. "The real dilemma is, do we give Gretchen the truth about 'us' or do we give her the political angle?"

"Exactly," Opal said.

"Opal," Carleen said, "if Gretchen is serious about getting out of the drama-blogging game, this will do it. Are you sure that's what she wants? Are you sure she won't backstab us?"

"It's something she's told me dozens of times. She's been waiting for the right story. If she breaks this, she'll have a good chance at getting a job at WaPo. If she backstabs me, she'll never get another chance like that again."

"Is that going to cause problems for SUNFLOWER?" asked Kenny.

"No more than hitting Andrew has," said Opal, glaring at Lincoln.

"What about Andrew? Are you going to keep seeing him?" asked Carleen. "We have to consider that as part of the PR story."

"I...I don't know," stuttered Opal. She looked at Link. "Maybe. I have to think about it. But first, let's get Gretchen focused on SUNFLOWER instead of all this drama."

"I meant what I said. I want to marry you, Opal."

"I. Can't. Even." Opal returned her focus on Kenny. "I am going to work on making sure Gretchen has what she needs for this story to break in our favor. This marriage nonsense...no one will believe it. It sounds like a bad cover to hide something." And then she turned to Lincoln and met his eyes. "And I will never marry you under those circumstances."

She pointed to a drawing on Kenny's legal pad. "We need to get SUNFLOWER out there before it's trashed and rumors become truth. I will call Yukika and August to explain the proposed release schedule. Gretchen is going to break SUNFLOWER the moment you introduce it. Ahead of the other press. We want to make sure popular opinion is high regarding this project we have all worked on for over a year. I will also fix this thing with Andrew Donohoe. I know how to calm him down and get him back on the plan."

Lincoln's throat tightened and he clenched his fists under the table. He hadn't had the chance to tell Opal what a foul creature Donohoe had been, how he had spoken of her like a piece of meat to be grabbed just because he'd spent thousands of dollars on her.

"Andrew Donohoe is a monster. What exactly are you proposing to do?"

Opal responded to Kenny as if he had asked the question instead of Link. "Andrew isn't so bad. At least when he asked me to marry him, we were alone on a beautiful helicopter, on a date going to the Grand Canyon."

Her phone beeped and she checked the screen, then held it up to the group. "Speak of the devil."

Opal spun around and stormed out of the apartment, slamming the door behind her.

Lincoln sat there stunned, her words ringing in his ears and a dagger in his heart.

Chapter 20

Opal stormed through the door and down the hallway away from Link's apartment. She smashed the elevator button. She almost took the stairs, but was so frothing mad at the moment, she knew she'd probably trip and fall and break her neck. She indignantly pressed the down button a few more times. *How dare he!* She turned to look back and make sure that he hadn't followed her, but the hallway was empty and devoid of sound. *What was wrong with men?* Did they think she was put on this earth to put up with their stupid crap and fix all their problems? They were grown men. The elevator doors opened. Thankfully, it was empty.

She pressed the lobby button and leaned up against the wall. The last three days had been insane. First, there had been the helicopter ride to the Grand

Canyon, which sounded more amazing than it actually was. She'd been loathe to tell anyone about it. Her mom would predictably say 'what an amazing date.' If Opal told anyone the truth, how she felt, they'd chastise her for being ungrateful. Madeline might be the only person who could sympathize since she'd rhapsodized about more amazing dates than a silly ride to the Grand Canyon.

Madeline was also the reason all of this had started. The stupid game. The kissing. The girls acting like hormonal teenagers. And now, Opal had to meet with Gretchen. Opal stomped all the way to the closest Metro and got on the right line. Fortunately, there was a seat available even though the car was packed with tourists. She opened up her phone and then a note app. There she reviewed some notes she had written down after talking to Kenny and on the plane home. Notes that she had written while Lincoln was two seats away from her on the plane.

She closed her eyes for a moment. At first, when she thought about Lincoln, all the good memories came back, like a montage in a film. His smile, looking dapper in a suit, Lincoln in his costume, Lincoln naked, his smell, his taste, his touch, and the montage finally ended with the words: *Am I just another pawn?*

Her heart raced, her face felt flushed, her stomach tightened. With a deep breath, she pushed it all aside.

She wasn't some kind of fluttering white swan, she had work to do. If she was to deal with Gretchen in an appropriate and professional manner, she couldn't show up with makeup running down her face and her political acumen in the emotional toilet. Instead, she let the joy, sadness, and anger focus her. Her target was Gretchen. Her goal was to launch SUNFLOWER in the best light possible. In order to achieve her goal successfully, she had to make sure that Gretchen felt like a professional journalist.

Opal rushed into the office and printed off the latest version of the press release for SUNFLOWER and the draft legislation after adding a date to the press release. It would have to be done by Wednesday. There was no way they could contain something this big any faster than that. Besides, if Gretchen had snapped a photo of Yukika Mathews cozying up to Gordy Carpenter, who else might have done the same? Gretchen was a known quantity. But there might be any other number of people taking pictures—tourists, general lookie-loos. There was no way to control them. Opal used a red pen to make a few notes and high-lights, hoping to draw Gretchen's attention to key points that looked particularly favorable to the congressman.

Opal rushed back to the metro with the documents in a folder marked "top secret" nestled in next to her computer. She got off the at the Crystal City Metro and used Google maps to show her the walking path to the hotel. Gretchen was seated in the restaurant, halfway through a coffee that the waitress was refilling. She was on her phone, scrolling, looking like a professional journalist.

Keep telling yourself that.

"Hi Gretchen. Glad to see you made it back safely."

She groaned and set her phone down. "Those red eyes are a killer. I hope to never take one again."

"You might have to, especially if you are on Lincoln Pierce's press junket. Lot's of red eyes to take, following him around the country as he campaigns."

"That's right. You already promised me that. Thanks for Vegas, by the way. Love all the fun stuff I found there. So many possibilities."

Opal ignored the veiled threat. "And I'm pretty proud of you for sourcing out the real story. Now, what we need to do in order to validate you as a proper political journalist is to focus on what matters."

Gretchen leaned back and looked her up and down. She added a bit of cream to her coffee, and then took a careful sip. "I see. But that means I'll have to give something up."

"Smart girl. You've played this game before."

"Let's cut to the chase."

"I'd like to. I haven't got all day, and neither do you."

"If I drop the fight picture, Harrison the environmental lawyer currently working for Lincoln, and Gordy, a lobbyist for oil and gas concerns, then I can keep the picture of you and the congressman."

"Instead of that, why don't you ask me about the picture of Gordy, Yukika, and Andrew? That sort of question might lead to uncovering something of real interest."

"I'd have to give up both the men fighting and the honorable congressman snogging a staff member picture?"

"If you want to be taken seriously as a journalist, then publishing these social stories, will only cement your reputation as a social blogger. However..." Opal swiped through the pictures. Link and Kendra. Andrew, Yukika, and August. "These people? All together? What do you think they were doing there?"

"I see," Gretchen said, trying not to let the revelation change her expression. Opal could see her working hard to maintain a straight face, and she did fairly well, but not good enough.

Don't sell if it— it's already sold.

This time, Opal waved the waitress down and asked her to bring a pot of hot water with lemon. She was already too keyed up on caffeine, and the last thing she needed was a case of the shakes. She met Gretchen's eyes, and they locked.

The waitress came by with the water and offered Gretchen a refill, but she put her hand over the cup. Opal could hear her take measured breaths. The waitress left. Plates clattered in the background, phone notifications beeped randomly. The waitress returned with a plate of toast and eggs that she deposited in front of Gretchen, and still they didn't break eye contact.

Opal swallowed hard and picked up her phone, getting ready to leave.

"This means we have to trust each other."

"I need the photos destroyed."

"They will get destroyed once I am firmly on the press junket. I'm not stupid."

"What you are...is smart. Politically smart."

"Damn straight. How long have we known each other, Opal?"

"Long enough to know that we can trust each other. You know I wouldn't commit political suicide. Not at this stage of the game."

"That's what I thought," Gretchen said. "I'll stick with the policy story, but I want exclusives, additional photos. The inside story."

"You got it. And don't share these photos with anyone. I'll know if you do."

A flash of distrust crossed over Gretchen's face, but she covered it with stoicism. "When do you want to do this?"

"We're going to introduce a new bill in forty-eight hours. The moment we do that, you can publish the story."

"No deal," Gretchen said. "I want to break the story *before* you introduce the bill."

"What? No way is that happening," Opal said, feigning outrage. She had expected exactly this ploy from Gretchen. Gretchen had fallen right into her trap. Opal sat back, pretending to think about it.

Gretchen pursed her lips. "Give me the deets now, so I can write the story and push publish the minute Pierce opens his mouth on the floor. Or, I push publish on a whole different story today." She held up her hands like an announcer reading a headline. "'Congressman Pierce and Top Aide Frolicking in Vegas.'"

Opal considered asking Gretchen to be reasonable. To be a friend for once. Maybe telling her the truth would be enough to keep her from publishing the photo of her and Link kissing. Why did he have to go off and hit Andrew? Why would he ask her to marry him in front of everyone like that? As if marrying her would be the best way to handle things.

And here she was, once again, Opal The Fixer. Handling things. It was too much. She dismissed the idea of confessing it all to Gretchen. Why should she admit to Gretchen that she had no idea what was really going on between her and Lincoln? Telling the other woman about their fight or their vulnerabilities was too much to bear. No. Opal would hand over SUNFLOWER as planned.

"You drive a hard bargain," she said. "You get the details, and I let you know when Lincoln is about to introduce the bill."

"The moment," Gretchen corrected.

"One more thing," Opal said, holding up a finger.

Gretchen's face soured. "Conditions? You think you have the right to put on conditions?"

"Yeah. I think you'll agree when you have the whole picture," Opal said with confidence. "You have to put this in a positive light. This is Lincoln's chance to shine and show off to the American people what he can do. It will launch him into the national spotlight, and it has to be a bright, happy shiny one. Not like the exposé you did on his office two years ago. Understand?"

"And if I don't think I can do that? What if I think this super-secret legislation is crap? Are you trying to hush the free press?"

Opal rolled her eyes. "You can't go from being a social blogger to a top reporter without compromise."

"I won't make any promises," Gretchen said. "It

wouldn't be ethical to promise a positive spin on something I don't even know about."

Opal stood and gathered her things, making as if to leave. Her heart pounded with the bluff she was about to pull. "Fine. You know what? I think I can find a way to spin the kiss for our benefit. And that fight with Gordy and Harrison? You know what a crock of shit that is. You go ahead, Gretchen. Post the pics of me kissing Link and enjoy the two days of fame it will bring you before you're once again forgotten along with all the other paparazzi."

She spun away, praying Gretchen would stop her. One step. Two. And Gretchen was calling her back. *Just like that.*

"Calm down, Opal. Geez. You didn't have to get all bent out of shape. You can't blame a girl for trying."

Opal slipped back into her seat. "So, positive spin?"

"Deal," Gretchen said, reaching her hand across the table.

"Deal," Opal said, shaking it. She took a sip of her hot water and set it down on the table. "I've got to go to the bathroom. Make sure no one looks in my bag, will you? There's some pretty top-secret stuff in there."

Opal left her bag with the folder she'd prepared on the way over containing the latest press release on SUNFLOWER. The rough draft had put the date of release on Wednesday morning, the day Lincoln was scheduled to introduce the bill. Madeline's plan was to post the release at the same time Lincoln was introducing the bill. Gretchen would have to pick up that detail on her own.

Opal hid herself from view around the corner and watched as Gretchen casually opened her bag and riffled through it. She pulled out the folder, laid it on the table and took snaps of the press release. She flipped through the rough draft of the legislation, snapping only four photos. From this distance, Opal couldn't see what pages she took greater interest in. After Gretchen had done the deed, Opal returned to the table.

Gretchen stood, gathering her own things to her.

Opal slung her bag over her shoulder. "Thanks for watching that for me."

Gretchen's face had turned solemn. "No problem, Opal."

"I've got to go back to the office to finalize the paperwork."

Gretchen met Opal's eyes with a softness Opal hadn't expected. She leaned in close to Opal so no one could hear her. "Thank you, Opal. Really. You're doing me a solid on this one. I won't publish a word until Lincoln steps into the chamber. And that positive spin thing? No need to spin it at all. This is amazing."

Chapter 21

After Opal stormed out and everyone else had left, Lincoln sat in his apartment, stunned and immobile for a few hours. All he could think about was Andrew and Opal. Andrew had bragged about how he'd spent thousands of dollars on her without any payout. Link hadn't believed him when he had said he had proposed to Opal. Now, it looks like he'd been telling the truth. At least Andrew and Opal hadn't gotten into bed yet. What had Opal told Donohoe? Surely she wouldn't have been considering Donohoe's proposal while they were singing Karaoke and then making love.

Was she over at Donohoe's apartment now, *calming him down?* The very thought of the two of them alone made Lincoln want to punch him all over again. The way that asshole had spoken about her? He clenched his fingers into a tight fist. Fresh pain from his bruised knuckles radiated through his hand. That had been careless. As much as he wanted to beat the living daylights out of the other man again, he needed to be calm, to approach Andrew with a plan in place.

Lincoln got antsy in his apartment, so he went for a walk, hoping to clear his head. All he wanted to do was go to Opal and talk to her. Clear the air. He was pretty sure that she hadn't heard or believed what he'd said about Donohoe. He had tried to spell it out for her, but that had turned disastrous. He would not hurt or humiliate Opal like that in front of everyone.

Link walked in what he thought was an aimless pattern, lost in agony over what to do, until he found himself in front of the Four Seasons in Georgetown—Donohoe's hotel. It would be better if he went home. Stayed away.

He went into the bar to get a drink, to wallow in his misery while giving Opal the time she needed. The next day was a work day; maybe she'd be able to talk to him by then. Let him explain things. She was a reasonable woman who would forgive him for being a jerk. But she had to know that Donohoe was not the man for her. Even if she hated him for telling her the truth, he could save her from a life with a man like that. But at what expense? Would she ever forgive him if he laid it all out for her?

Link ordered a Scotch at the bar. As it was delivered, Andrew Donohoe slid into the seat next to him. He had half expected this, hadn't he?

"What are you doing here, Pierce?" Donohoe asked. "You come looking for me?"

Lincoln pointed at his glass to order another for Andrew, but the other man stopped the order. "Just a Coke today. Thanks, Mike."

"I happened to be in the neighborhood," Lincoln said.

"Sure. Whatever. Why're you here, Link? I can't imagine you came all this way just to have a Scotch in my hotel bar."

Lincoln wasn't about to admit that he'd been drawn there by some weird magnetic pull. Some sense he had to set things right. "You see Opal today?"

Andrew's lips twitched. "No. What makes you ask?"

"She said she was going to check in with you. That's all."

"And here you are instead."

Lincoln swirled the ice in his glass around, cooling the amber liquid inside. "We have a schedule on our project. I want to make sure that's on. That there won't be any complications."

The bartender slid Donohoe his Coke. He took a

sip of it, breathed out as if he were drinking fine whiskey. "Damn, that is a fine sugar high."

Lincoln couldn't find it in him to laugh. "You had enough of the hard stuff last night?"

Donohoe's face stiffened. "So, I *was* at your place last night?"

Lincoln slowly met the other man's eyes. "You don't remember?"

Donohoe shrugged. "Everything after I got on my jet to head back here is...lacking."

If Donohoe didn't remember what he'd said, there was some small chance Lincoln could salvage the situation. "You came to my place. You were pretty upset about me hitting you. I apologized profusely, you told me not to worry about it and you left."

Donohoe laughed and clapped Lincoln on his back. "Yeah, that sounds just like me. Don't think so, *buddy*, but nice try." He sipped at his Coke again and made a face. "Fuck this horseshit. Mike, toss some rum in, will ya? Might as well make it worth my while."

"A man can hope," Lincoln said.

"Look," Andrew said, "here's the thing. I want this deal to go through. And, honestly, I'm pretty happy with it. My dad's living in a different generation and doesn't get that I'm gonna be the one in charge. I might not remember the details from last night, but I can guarantee you I wasn't laughing off the fact you gave me a broken nose. I'm not wed to any of it, though. Our project, I mean. There're lots of ways to make money."

The word *wed* sent ripples of angst through Lincoln, and he sensed what might be coming next.

"What I am wed to? More like, *who* I'd like to be wed to is that sweet filly of a woman. Opal. She is my heart's desire. That's what I want."

"She's an amazing woman," Link said neutrally. He hid one hand under the counter, squeezing it into a tight fist. It had felt pretty good to punch Andrew in the face before, it would feel just as good a second time. Except all of DC would know about it. There would be no hiding it in this crowded bar.

"I think, if my mind were pre-occupied on something else, this whole SUNFLOWER business would be off my mind. Know what I mean?"

"When did you propose to her?" Lincoln asked. "She didn't say."

"Oh, so she didn't give you the details?"

"In passing," Lincoln said, hoping to score a small victory.

Andrew huffed. "First time? We were flying over the Grand Canyon at sunset. Second time, well. That was about ten minutes after you slugged me. She was holding my head against her bosom, comforting me."

"Well, we have a problem, then," Link said. "I can't, in good conscience, vouch for you to Opal."

Donohoe turned to look at him full on. His eyes widened and then narrowed on Link, dawning comprehension sliding across his face. "Why not? Oh, shit. You're in love with her, too?" Andrew tilted his head back and laughed, garnering plenty of attention from other patrons. "Well, that explains a lot."

"Yeah, what of it?"

"Dude, I totally don't blame you. She's fantastic. And makes it easier to understand why you hit me."

"I'd like to think I would have hit you like that no matter who you were talking about."

"I get it. I do." Andrew pushed his unfinished drink away. "I'm an ass when I'm drunk. I shouldn't have talked to you about her like that. She deserves better."

Lincoln couldn't agree more. Opal definitely deserved better than Andrew Donohoe, but was he that much better? Link had hit the other man. He had asked her to marry him in a room full of people as a political expedience.

"Andrew, I want to apologize for mixing personal with the business. I shouldn't have let it get to me."

"That's all well and good, but you hit me. And now? Now you get to pay for that. Here's the deal,

Lincoln," Donohoe turned so that he faced Lincoln full on.

Lincoln squared his shoulders and faced the other man. "Deal?"

Donohoe smiled slowly, his eyes lighting up like a man who'd just been dealt a royal flush. "The deal is this. You deliver me Opal. Help me win the girl of my dreams. Tell her how amazing I am, that I'm a great guy. She'd be lucky to have me. And you'll back off. Or I completely tank your precious little project. I made sure to add provisions into the paperwork. That you signed off on. Not only can I do it, I can legally do it."

"You're insane. You can't make bargains like that when it comes to people's lives."

Donohoe laughed. "You are naïve, Pierce. You do it all the time. Every political act you do is a bargain. And it affects people's lives."

Lincoln swallowed hard. It was unlikely he would find anything else so perfect to launch his national political career. It wasn't just giving up Opal, though, it was handing her over to another man. *No way.* There was no way he could do that to her, even if it meant throwing his political dreams down the toilet.

"Fuck you," Lincoln said. "I will never help you win Opal. *No. Fucking. Way.*"

Donohoe put a hand on Lincoln's shoulder and squeezed. "You know, I'm going to give you some time to think about it. It's been a long day and you've had something to drink. Perhaps you aren't understanding the ramifications."

"Fuck off." Lincoln shrugged his shoulder free of Donohoe's touch.

Donohoe put his hand right back on Lincoln's shoulder and leaned in close to his ear. "There's a lot more at stake here than a skirt, Pierce. Don't be rash. You've wanted to be president your whole life; would you really give up that kind of power for a woman?"

"No deal." He pushed past Donohoe to escape the bar before he lost it. He was pretty sure he wouldn't stop with a single punch to the face if he got started.

"Forty-eight hours, Pierce," Donohoe shouted at him from behind. "Forty-eight hours."

Lincoln refused to respond and pushed through to the street in front of the hotel. What was he going to do now? His first instinct was to call Opal. Ask her what to do, but that was impossible. Go to Opal with this ludicrous story? Would she even believe it if she told him that Donohoe had tried to bribe him?

No way could he expect Opal to fix this. Nor did he want to. He'd have to find a way to stop Donohoe from tanking SUNFLOWER and stealing Opal's heart on his own. He prayed he wasn't too late for either.

Chapter 22

Opal sat at her desk in the office late Monday, trying to figure out all the complex emotions running through her. She took a sip of her diet soda and watched while a perfectly good maple leaf fluttered to the ground and settled onto the grass. The morning sun was reaching its zenith as she began working through the paperwork of SUNFLOWER. The program would be announced by Congressman Lincoln Pierce in two days. And despite all that could have derailed the project, they had been able to pull it off—she was even able to get Gretchen in on the deal.

She'd rather be working with Gretchen than being at odds with each other. It made for a better work environment, anyway. Opal didn't trust Gretchen, but at least they were racing the same horse now. Things were working out—finally. She wanted to rest on her laurels, but that wouldn't be a smart idea until SUNFLOWER was a done deal. Until it was live, there were no guarantees. Everything seemed to be lining up right. Except one last thing—that unresolved issue with her and Lincoln. She was better off forgetting that insanely wonderful time with Lincoln in Vegas. They weren't really right for each other. It was just a song.

But Andrew? Was he right for her? She couldn't say with certainty that he was.

Madeline Asher came into the office. They gave each other a short wave, and Madeline headed to her desk, which was directly behind Opal. Her phone rang; it was Andrew.

"Hey," she said, "I was just thinking about you."

"Hey yourself. I know you are a very busy woman, but I am dying here. I need to see you."

"Oh?" It was nice to feel needed just for herself. Not because she had to fix something, or take care of something, but because he simply wanted to be with her.

"Absolutely. I have to see you tonight. I won't take 'no' for an answer."

"Maybe I'm busy."

"So here's the deal. I'm going to come pick you up, and we are going to walk there."

"I haven't said 'yes' yet."

"There's no Mercedes. There's no helicopter. It's just me."

"That sounds intriguing."

"I'll be at your place at seven thirty. I promise you'll love this date. Oh, I almost forgot. Dress casual, jeans and whatnot."

After she hung up the phone, she was lost in her own thoughts, smiling, adjusting her shirt, getting ready to start typing up an email when she felt a presence behind her and jumped. "Oh Madeline. It's you."

"That was Andrew Donohoe, right?"

"So what if it was?"

"Look, Opal. I have to warn you about him. Steer clear of him. He's bad news."

"I know exactly what he's like. I've read People."

"All the articles I sent to you? They weren't just for research. Why are you flirting with fire?"

"He's not *that guy* in person."

"He hires a dating consultant to help craft perfect dates. All of this is a show. He'll get you in bed and then buh-bye baby."

"He's not like that." She immediately dismissed Madeline's unwelcome advice.

"Have you slept with him?"

"None of your damn business."

"No. You haven't. Otherwise he wouldn't be here."

"Do you have a point, Madeline?" Opal clenched

her jaw. She was in the midst of solving all her problems. Her meddling coworker was adding them back.

"Don't go out with him, Opal. I know we don't have the best relationship, but I don't want to see you get hurt. I have a friend, a few friends actually, who dated him."

Opal wasn't interested. She didn't want to hear about his past. She had gotten to know him on a personal level at first, which turned romantic. She probably knew him better than Madeline's friend—and knowing him would make all the difference. He was a good guy, even if his past was a little flaky.

"Okay, fine. You don't believe me? Did he do the helicopter date yet?"

Helicopter date? Madeline said this as if it were *a thing.* Had it been? Had it been *just a thing* Andrew did to impress women? Opal didn't respond. Instead, she tapped her pen on the desk. She wanted this conversation with Madeline to end.

"You're a tough card to read sometimes, Opal. Please, please listen to me when I tell you that there is something wrong with that man. He's bad news."

"None of this is your business, Madeline."

"You're right. It's um...well, I learned a lot the last couple weeks. With Ewan. I can't explain it, but I see things differently than I used to. I want you to know

I'm sorry for coming up with the game. That was stupid of me."

Opal dropped her pen. That was the last thing she had ever imagined happening was that Madeline would apologize. Maybe she ought to listen to her about Andrew. Maybe she was saying it out of concern. Madeline had seemed different lately, quieter. Usually after a weekend, she'd tell stories of her shenanigans and all the boys she was dating, but these last few days were very unlike her. She was a lot calmer than her usual self. But Opal didn't have time to keep up with Madeline's social life, nor did she want to now.

"I can tell when my words aren't wanted." Madeline shrugged while she put on a light jacket. "Take care, Opal. I'm outta here for lunch. Ring me if you want me to pick anything up for you."

After Madeline left, Opal leaned back in her chair. Madeline was wrong. She was still going to go out with Andrew. Andrew was a good guy. But still, it wouldn't hurt to careful, to watch him a little.

OPAL'S CLOSET was a myriad of memories. There was a skirt she wore when she got her first job. A special scarf her mom got for her. A pair of pink ballet shoes that she had worn as a kid. She chose a pair of jeans that were comfortable and looked great on her, but they weren't super dressy, at least not DC dressy, so she pulled them out and tossed it onto the bed. Andrew had said to dress casual so she was going to. She chose a top that dressed up her jeans, just in case he took her to a place that required a different dress code. Opal fixed her hair and did her makeup. She checked her watch; she hated it when people were late, and it was right on the dot, seven thirty.

There was a knock on the door.

Punctual. Not bad.

She opened the door, and she didn't even recognize him. He wore jeans and a Nationals t-shirt, with a Nationals ball cap. The look was good on him. And he had a very American boy-next-door look to him with a tiny bit of stubble. He smelled good too, but he'd gone a little heavy on the cologne.

"Opal," he said, stepping over the threshold. He kissed her on the cheek as a greeting. "You ready?"

"No wine before dinner?"

"Nope. I'm going old school. We're headed out to one of my favorite joints in Arlington."

"Arlington? You've actually been outside DC? Besides going to Dulles?"

"Why, yes, I have. I have traveled far and wide. Come on. Let's hop the Metro."

"No one will ever believe that Andrew Donohoe and I took the actual Metro. You going to be okay mingling with the little people?"

"Don't be silly. Let's go."

They headed out on the Metro and crossed over the river. Madeline had to be wrong. Their conversation flowed easily, and he was fun to be around. She could see how a woman could fall for him.

They got off the train and walked up the street to what could only be classified as a dive bar. The sign was broken, so she wasn't even sure what the name was. Inside, it smelled like stale beer and a good time. People were dancing on the floor to Springsteen and crowded into every nook and cranny. He led her through the crowd, making sure that he didn't lose her by looking back and checking on her, curling his fingers around hers.

And somehow, somebody was leaving just as they were arriving. Andrew leapt towards the table, along with two other people, and he barely claimed it before they could. He pulled a second stool right next to his and wiped it off for her. *Knee to knee. Shoulder to shoulder. Head to ohh...* His lips would be so close—though the last time they kissed it was zingfree. Zingless? Non-zinging? He had all the right moves, just none of the feels. She'd give him another chance, thinking it might be due to circumstance. Maybe he could be a good kisser. She ought to at least try one more time.

"I wish you could sit on my lap," Andrew said with a hard, little laugh.

Opal pulled back.

"Hey, whoa, Opal. I was just kidding. There's the waitress." He held up his hand, waving her over.

She acknowledged him, but her hands were full of drinks. It would be a while before she could come over. A look of anger passed over Andrew's face, but he caught Opal looking at him, and he changed it fast to a super smile.

"Maybe we should go to the bar?"

"Great idea," he said. "I'll run up. You want a Shock Top? You seem like you might like that."

"They sell decent beer here? I thought it would be Miller Lite only," she said, laughing. "Yes, Shock Top is fine. Nothing dark. And nothing too hoppy."

"I'll be back," he said, slipping through the crowd.

While she waited for Andrew, she checked her messages. There were several that she'd been cc'd on between Kenny, Link, and Carleen to finalize the floor presentation of the SUNFLOWER bill. She saw one from Gretchen asking for a specific date and time for her interview with Lincoln. She responded that she would find out the specific times and let her know as soon as she did. These last twenty-four hours, Lincoln had shown himself to be quite proficient at his job. Instead of handing everything off to her, he was assessing issues, deciding on resolutions, and acting on them.

She really liked this side of him.

If she was to be honest, it was more than like.

I hope I marry you. That kiss. The way he held her. His body moving against hers. The perfect way they fit together. Those orgasms.

Her breath came in short. Her heart thumped hard. She wanted to be in Lincoln's arms again.

She closed her eyes. It was better for everyone if she didn't pursue a relationship with him. Everyone was better off if she were with Andrew. *But what about Madeline's warning?* Andrew's reputation was that he *could* be kind of a jerk. She wasn't sure if she believed what Lincoln had told her about Donohoe; she didn't know if he was saying hurtful things out of jealousy or god knows what.

All of the things she'd read about Donohoe paled in comparison to the way he treated her in person. Wasn't her very real, personal experience, what mattered? Disgruntled exes spouting off to blogs and magazines weren't the most reliable source of information. Even though there were a few things about him that bothered her, overall, he wasn't a bad man.

Andrew returned from the bar carrying two beers

in frosted glasses. "Hey, thanks for coming out with me again. I wasn't sure if you would, after what happened in Vegas."

"What did happen in Vegas, anyway? What were you guys talking about?"

"Well, I shouldn't tell you," he said, pausing for effect. He let out a sigh and clasped his hands in front of him on the small table. "And normally, I wouldn't go there, but...I think you should know."

Opal was paying attention now.

"I told Link that he had to grow up."

"That's what you said?" She was shocked to hear him say something so personal. "What else did you say?"

"Look, he's going to make a great president some-day. And he has to be focused on his political agenda, and making sure all the stars align and all that. But, I told him I didn't think he was treating his staff well."

"So he decked you?"

"We talked about you specifically."

"You did what? *Me?*"

"I told him he should treat you better. Anyway, I wanted to make sure that he understood that it's a team effort to make it to the presidency."

"Okay. Um. Thank you," she said, unsure of whether or not to believe Link's version of events or his. "I need some time to think about that."

"Sure. I get it," Andrew said. "The reason I'm telling you is actually pretty selfish." He took her hand in his and focused on it, stroking the palm first, and then turning it over, rubbing her pinky. "I haven't been like this with anyone, Opal. You bring something out in me. If you didn't know already, I have a bad rep with women. But you? You're the only person who has ever gotten me, seen past my weaknesses and foibles."

Andrew dropped her hands and rubbed the top of her thigh. "I have to have you. You belong in my life. I won't take a 'no' from you."

Someone bumped into Opal and she nearly dropped her glass. The connection with Andrew was gone.

"Opal?" he said, trying to reestablish the bond between them.

She met his eyes.

He leaned in to kiss her. It started as a sweet, not quite chaste kiss, but then he tried to stick his tongue in her mouth. It was too much and she wasn't a public kisser.

She pulled back just enough, and he ended the kiss with a sweet peck on her lips.

"I guess now's as good a time as ever to apologize for asking you to marry me in front of my dad. I just...I was overcome. And I knew you would take care of everything."

Opal didn't say anything in return. She didn't want to be the one to *take care of everything*. In a relationship, she wanted a two-way street. She wanted a guy to give as much as she gave.

"I guess," she said, motioning toward the dance floor where half a dozen couples grooved to the music. "Maybe we should dance?"

He ignored her, and plowed on. "I have fallen for you, Opal Meyers. I think we should be exclusive, just you and me."

Opal was turned silent by the suggestion. Everything about it felt wrong, and yet she couldn't bring herself to tell him no outright. She wasn't certain about him being the one for her, but she also wasn't sure he wasn't. She searched for something to say as she gulped at her beer for cover.

"It's all right," he said, holding up a hand. "We don't have to. Not yet. Maybe I'm rushing you. Tell me about this upcoming recital? I want to hear all about it."

Glad to change the subject, Opal visibly relaxed. She dropped her shoulders and started talking about the girls and two boys, and how far they'd come. That she was so glad to be able to help those less fortunate. She saw Andrew's eyes flicker to someone in the crowd. She turned to look and saw that someone was taking a picture of them. She looked back to Andrew.

He had a strange sort of smile, like he couldn't help but like to be the center of attention, but then it disappeared when he made eye contact with her.

"We've got to go, Opal, I think the press has found me." He put his hat back on and lowered it over his eyes. Someone in the crowd pulled up a proper press camera and took a shot of him. The crowd turned to see who it was. Someone recognized him and shouted his name.

People clamored towards them. Andrew grabbed Opal's hand and bolted for the exit. He expertly led her through the crowd and out the door. They started running down the street, and, when she looked back, there was only a cameraman on foot taking shots of them running.

As soon as they felt safe, away from the bar and the crushing feeling of everyone coming towards them, he stopped. He put his hands on her cheeks and kissed her hard. Her heart was beating from the run and she was out of breath.

The kiss was filled with all the right moves—the right amount of gentleness, a tiny bit of tongue, a little gentle probing—but nothing about it spoke to love. She pulled away and brushed her hand against his cheek. But there was a lot she needed to think about. The fight between Link and Andrew and what it meant to her. Really, what it came down to was she just didn't know how she felt about Andrew. Or Lincoln, for that matter, and she wanted time to process everything.

"Andrew. I hate to do this, but I have to go home before I do something I regret."

"You won't regret this, I promise."

Opal smiled at him. "I'm going home. I'm just not ready."

"Sure you're ready," he said, putting his arms around her. "You were born ready."

"Aw, that's sweet, Andrew," Opal said, giving him a kiss on the cheek, "but I'm going home. Alone." She said the last word pointedly so he couldn't possibly argue. "Let's talk after SUNFLOWER. It's only a few days away."

"Okay. Fine. Anything you say," Andrew said, pulling her in closer. "Anything I can say to change your mind?"

"No. Tonight was fantastic. I had a good time, even with being chased by a mob."

"Me too. I'm going to call my driver. Wait with me?"

Opal nodded as he dropped his arms and called. He stepped away from her, putting a bit of distance between them. Was this some sort of statement, or was he only calling for a ride?

Chapter 23

*L*incoln Ulysses Pierce stood in the shade of the Lincoln Memorial contemplating the marble statue of the man whose name he bore. His parents had chosen both his first and middle names with purpose and raised him with certain expectations. All his life, his parents had told him he could grow up to be president one day if he worked hard enough, if he applied himself, if he had the vision. He had done all of that. Got good grades. Stayed out of trouble. Taken the military route with honors. Everything was about getting to the top. Now what?

The original impetus behind SUNFLOWER had been from the right place—a desire to change policy to preserve the planet for the children who were still in diapers or not even born yet. The legacy it would create for him personally hadn't been part of that first inkling, but it had morphed into a promise. Make SUNFLOWER work, and the world would notice. People would notice and love him for it. They would vote for him and his vision of healing a wounded nation. For Lincoln, SUNFLOWER was the first seedling in an entire garden of beautiful ideas that could change the world for the better.

In less than twenty-four hours, SUNFLOWER would be out in the world. Lincoln wasn't naïve enough to think there would be no opposition. But any nay-sayers would come across as uneducated. The new plan was going to be a rain maker: new jobs in areas of manufacturing depression and funding for trade schools, new sales. New profit. And it would only grow from there. Bi-partisan support would be there because they saw the benefit of positively impacting bottom line economics. But none of that mattered without money. Without Donohoe, what would happen to SUNFLOWER?

Lincoln had learned long ago that the only thing that it really took to make a project work was lots of money. And Donohoe Industries was behind it all. Andrew Donohoe's threat to tank the whole thing was very real. Was Lincoln's own happiness more important than that of being the sponsor of world-changing legislation? SUNFLOWER had the power to transform life on this planet, so wasn't it selfish of him to not give up his hopeless, romantic dreams about Opal?

He stopped short. No. He couldn't even consider handing her over to Andrew Donohoe like she was some piece of meat. She was a woman with her own agency, and what a woman she was. Even if he caved to Donohoe's demands, would Opal still choose that awful man?

Maybe. In the short term. But how long would it be before Donohoe's true colors showed themselves? Would Opal see it before getting hurt by him?

And yet, giving up on SUNFLOWER meant giving up on all his dreams. The light shifted, and the stone Lincoln glowed a rich orange in the early morning light. It was almost as if the statue came to life and tilted its head as if to say, "You stand before me with small questions? If you want to be honorable, then be honorable."

Link shook his head and blinked. The glow remained across the enigmatic marble smile. There had to be a way to salvage the situation. He couldn't call Opal and talk to her. He couldn't expect Opal to fix everything. As if on cue, Kenny Marshall called him to check in.

"Your timing is exquisite," Link said.

"I just got done with my morning run with Kat,

and I had this urge to call you. Weird. So, what's going on?"

Lincoln didn't want to tell Kenny about Donohoe's threat over Opal. It would come across wrong and not do Opal any favors. "I messed up. Big time. I should never have hit Andrew Donohoe. But he's threatening to do something major to tank SUNFLOWER tonight. I need to think through the options."

"I'm your man, Lincoln," Kenny said.

Lincoln walked away from the small cluster of tourists at the monument as he and Kenny spoke. He made his way along the reflecting pool to the Washington Monument, ducking in and around the tourist and runners. He was still talking to Kenny, but he needed to walk. He needed to be amongst the monuments that created the center of power in DC. As if they gave him the power to do the right thing. He crossed Constitution Avenue and headed into the Ellipse.

As he walked, he and Kenny had formed a plan for dealing with Andrew Donohoe. Lincoln ended up in front of the White House.

Link said goodbye to Kenny and gave his full attention to the place he'd like to call home some day. It wasn't a big building; people who had never seen it often thought it would be larger seeing it in person. He had been inside the Oval Office a few times, and once, when he was on a top committee, been alone with the president. He sat on the famed couch. They talked for seven minutes and forty-eight seconds.

The first time Lincoln had ever been to visit DC, his family had come to this very location, to picnic on the expansive Ellipse in front of the White House. So much had changed since then. The security had been completely different. People hadn't been so afraid of everything.

Lincoln stood in front of the place he desperately wanted to call home. If he was lucky, he'd be there a full eight years someday. It would only work if Opal were with him, by his side in both work and love. There were obstacles in that path. Certainly, someone would paint him as power-hungry and his opponents would call him out on dating an employee. But he had a plan now, and if it worked, everything else would fall into place.

And, if he had to, he'd choose Opal over the White House.

No matter where they were, he wanted them to be together.

He turned his back on the White House and called her.

She answered right away. Link couldn't tell from the background sound where she might be.

"Opal, I am so sorry. I wanted to do this in person,

but I had to tell you right away. I am sorry for asking you to marry me in front of everyone, as if it was a way to solve a problem. That was horrible of me. You deserve so much better. You deserve romance. I shouldn't have asked you like that."

He took a breath and hurried before she could respond. "I love you, Opal. I wanted to tell you this in person, not over the phone, but I couldn't wait for you to hear it from me, now. Before..."

"Before what, Lincoln?" she asked.

"Look, things might go horribly wrong between now and tomorrow. I'm trying to fix things, no, I *am* fixing things on my own. I want you to know that I love you, and, no matter what happens with SUNFLOWER, I love you."

The words felt so right. "I love you. I love you, I LOVE YOU." Nothing he'd ever said had ever been truer. He thrust his arms out wide and tilted his head up to the warming sun. Then he yelled at the top of his lungs, "I love Opal Meyers, world! And I want everyone to know it."

He spun around in a circle, giddy with how incredible it felt to shout it to the world.

"What are you doing? Link? Have you lost your mind?"

He regained his senses and nodded at the few people who were close enough to take notice of him.

They mirrored his joy with enthusiastic nods, bemused smiles and a few thumbs up.

He straightened his tie and put the phone back up to his ear. "I'm telling the world that I love you, Opal. I've always loved you, and I couldn't let myself see it. Until now."

"Lincoln," she said, but he interrupted her before she could say anything else.

"Opal, we make a good team. You. Me. Together? We're synergistic."

"Have you been drinking?"

"I'm drunk with love, Opal. Things are crazy right now. Tomorrow is looming. But I needed to say that. I needed you to hear it."

"I appreciate it," she said quietly. "I'm not sure how I feel... Wait. Tomorrow is looming? Did you say things might go horribly wrong? What happened? Is there something I need to fix again?"

"No. There's nothing you need to fix. I got this. I am handling Andrew Donohoe. He won't ruin SUNFLOWER. I won't let him."

"All right?" Opal sounded confused. "Why would Andrew ruin anything? We had a date last night and he didn't mention anything."

"Don't worry about it. It's nothing, okay?"

"What's going on, Lincoln? Do you not trust me?"

"That's not it. Opal, I trust you completely. Look,

I'll be in the office soon. I promise. We have a ton of work to get done before tomorrow."

"You sure you're okay?" she asked.

"Oh, I'm better than okay."

After hanging up, Lincoln shucked his jacket and hung it by a finger over his shoulder. He had a lot to do before he sprung the trap he and Kenny had planned for Andrew Donohoe. That little fucker was going down.

Chapter 24

After Link called, Opal needed to get a cup of coffee. Something about the first sip always helped her relax even if for a moment, and gave her the space to be introspective. And she needed some introspection. A warm feeling came over her. He said he loved her, he had yelled it into her ear. It was goofy. A little over the top, totally eighties romantic comedy goofy, but she loved it. She had wanted to say I love you back, but wasn't ready to admit it yet. She needed to know that his words were more than words.

Link had come into the office, but he passed everyone without saying a word and shut his office door. After telling her he loved her, Link had mentioned something that might happen to SUNFLOWER, but he wouldn't give her any details.

Was he trying to warn her about SUNFLOWER? One thing she knew for sure was that Andrew would never try to tank SUNFLOWER; they had put too much effort into making it work. Plus, if he tanked it, he'd be letting down his dad and he'd sour the business relationship with Yukika and August. There was no way he'd do that.

Chloe came to her desk and let her know that they were reviewing the final documentation and she was needed to answer a few questions. The question Chloe had was concerning a few legal concessions regarding SUNFLOWER documents that were already signed. She'd tried to call Kat and Carleen but couldn't get hold of them. She attempted to call Link a few times, even though he was less than twenty feet away behind his closed office door, but his phone went to voice mail. He did not emerge once during the afternoon.

She finished up the last of her emails and shut her computer off. It was still light outside, so she planned to walk home; she'd get some fresh air and the exercise would do her good. Opal was halfway home before she realized that she'd forgotten her phone. She'd plugged it in to recharge it and left it on her desk. She had been looking forward to getting her pajamas on, eating spaghetti for dinner, and watching a movie, preferably a classic like *An Affair to Remember*.

Turning around and retracing her steps was the last thing she wanted to do, but she needed her phone in case she needed to be somewhere fast or send an email or resolve an issue. Anyone from the office could call; Link might have something he needed her to do. She had to turn back, and decided that instead of walking home a second time, she would take a cab home. Getting through security was easy, as there was no one in line ahead of her, and the guards helped her to pass through efficiently. She walked down the hall to the office, and the door to Link's main office was slightly open. She cocked her head, positive that she had shut the door and locked it.

But maybe she hadn't.

She considered going back to security, but the bottoms of her feet hurt. It was probably nothing. She entered and walked past the secretary's desk and into the open office. There was her phone, on her desk. She opened it and was about to call an Uber when she heard voices coming from Link's private office. He was talking to someone. She didn't want to disturb him in the middle of a phone call, but she did want to talk to him. There were a few lines Chloe had found in the SUNFLOWER documentation that were bothering her and she wanted Link's opinion.

As she approached the door, she heard a second

voice. It sounded like Andrew, and he didn't sound like himself. His voice had taken on the tone of an entitled braggart. Instead of knocking on the door, she leaned in close to find out what the hell these two were up to. They both were full of vim and vigor, and if Lincoln's little premonition about things going south would happen with SUNFLOWER, it was about to happen now.

She took off her shoes and stood right behind the door. Peeking through a crack in the door into the room, she saw Andrew and Lincoln. Opal bit the inside of her lip. Link said he was handling whatever this was, and she was curious and maybe a little excited to see him take control of things.

"I don't know what kind of act you've put on in front of her, but she will see it eventually. I'm going to make sure she sees it before you hurt her."

"You're a joke, Lincoln. If you couldn't get her then, you're not going to get her now. Besides, I need Opal. She's mine."

"She doesn't belong to you, Donohoe. She doesn't belong to anyone."

"I always win. My money wins. My charm wins. And now I'm gonna make you suffer."

"How's that, Andrew? What are you going to do?"

"First, I'm gonna marry Opal. You'll never have her. She loves me and she'll love my money."

She wanted to barge into the room tell him to fuck right off and demand the two of them play ball fairly together, but she checked herself. She wanted to see how Link handled him.

"And how long will it take before you find someone else to replace your love for shiny new things?"

Opal had never heard Lincoln's voice filled with so much disdain before. All she could see through the crack in the door were Lincoln's tightly balled fists leaning into his desk. If he kept up like this, he might lose it and hit Andrew again.

"Hehe. Of course. Maybe six months. Make sure she buys into the whole fantasy. Then I'll send her shopping in Europe. By herself. Or with friends, I don't care. And I'm gonna do some of my own shopping, if you know what I mean. A man has needs."

"That's not gonna happen, Donohoe."

"Sure. And in case you don't remember what the deal was, if I don't get Opal, I'm tanking SUNFLOWER."

"Deal? There was no deal, Donohoe. You offered. I declined."

"The real problem here, Link, is that you didn't hand her over. You didn't help me. You did nothing to help my prospects. So, I'm going to recuse the Donohoe firm from SUNFLOWER. My lawyer double checked, and we are within legal standing to do so. Good fucking luck with your shit legislation."

Opal stepped back; she almost lost her footing on the slick wooden floors, but caught herself before falling. She looked to the door, afraid she might get caught. No one came busting out, but she held her breath anyway, sure they would hear her.

"For the record, I want you to know I would give up SUNFLOWER for Opal. I would even give up my run for the presidency if that's what it took. She's worth it. The last thing I'd ever do is hand over Opal to trash."

"Trash? That's it Link. I'm coming..."

"Shut up, Andrew." A third voice interrupted Andrew.

He stopped dead in his tracks and looked around the room, confused.

Link had a grin on his face like he out-fiddled the devil.

Opal couldn't place the third voice. And there were only two people in the office, unless she had missed someone. She must have. The corners were fairly dark, and she hadn't had time to thoroughly scan the room.

"Dad?" replied Andrew. "Where are you?"

"I'm on speaker phone. And I heard everything. What the hell are you trying to do, kid? We've already spent millions on infrastructure change. You looking to tank this deal?"

"Dad. You don't have the full story. Link here is trying..."

"He's trying to do the right thing by saving my bacon. I owe more to him than I do to you. What the hell is wrong with you, Andrew? You think Donohoe Industries is some play thing? Your fucking corporate wet dream?"

"Dad, come on. It's not like..."

"It is exactly like that. I'm disappointed in you, son. I'll be looking forward to your resignation letter from the COO position. If you make a good case, I'll see if we can find a position for you in Ecuador. There's a manager position open over there."

"Dad, you know I hate humidity. I don't wanna go there." Andrew had gone from frat-boy bravado to petulant whine in seconds.

Opal's stomach flipped. Andrew had come across as genuine, and she'd read him wrong. So wrong.

"Oh waah. Poor baby. Keep going and let's see how that impacts your future."

"Jesus, Dad. I'll be in the office in a few days."

"You'll be here tomorrow morning. Get your butt on that fancy plane of yours and head home."

"Yes sir," he said.

"Lincoln, thank you for looping me in on this.

We'll talk tomorrow, but you have the full support of Donohoe Industries on this project. Full speed ahead."

"Thank you, Jack. I appreciate that."

The dial tone after Jack hung up was loud in the silence of the room.

There were no more words between Andrew and Link. Opal heard footsteps approaching the door and scrambled to hide herself. Her nylons were slippery, but she made it down the darkened hall and flattened herself against the wall. No one could see her in the dark, but she had a perfect line of sight at Lincoln's door.

Andrew was in the hallway, peering into the darkness. His expression changed like he had seen something, but he shook it off.

"You haven't heard the last of me, Lincoln," Andrew said, but his threat sounded more like the parting shot at the end of a child's tantrum.

"Apparently, I have." Lincoln slammed the door in Andrew's face.

Andrew stormed off. His shoes clomped down the hallway. Opal was unsure if she needed to wait for Lincoln to leave or if she could sneak past him. Opal let out a sigh of relief, thought it might be too loud, and stared at the door again. Nothing happened. She checked to make sure her phone was on mute first before going, then walked past his office—sans shoes—

until she was safely out in the hallway of the Cannon House Office Building. She didn't dare put her shoes on until she reached the main foyer, and as she did, she turned on her phone to dial Uber. No way in hell was she walking home.

WHEN OPAL GOT HOME, the first thing she did was to go into her kitchen and start cooking. Tonight was about completely relaxing. Lincoln certainly had proved her wrong. In a good way—now that she had all the information in front of her, she knew exactly what to do.

She preheated the oven, put on a pan of water with spaghetti to boil, filled a pan with store bought sauce to warm, and started the kettle. Then she went to her bedroom and got on her favorite pajamas with little palm trees stamped all over. Back in the kitchen, she put the noodles in a bowl, poured the sauce over the top, added shredded parmesan, and put the whole thing in the oven for fifteen minutes.

On the couch, while she waited for the food to cook, she played *Words with Friends* and just completed a double word score off 'oscillate' when the phone screen showed that Andrew was calling. She was curious what he had to say and so she picked up.

"Hi Opal. It's me. Unfortunately, I had to fly home tonight. I was hoping to see you before I left, but as fate would have it, I wasn't able to."

"Why? What happened?"

"There's an emergency with the business in Ecuador. My dad needs me there to make sure everything goes smoothly."

"Oh wow. That's impressive." Opal rolled her eyes. She knew he was lying through his teeth.

"And I want you to come with me. I need you. You make everything better."

"Is there any good shopping in Ecuador? I mean, I've heard it's even difficult to get basics."

"There's plenty of shopping. I don't know what you're talking about."

The oven timer dinged.

"Andrew, I would." She paused to let him think he had her. "Actually. No. I wouldn't. I can't. I have too much going on in DC. I'm not going to Ecuador with you."

"Please, Opal. You have to. Besides, you can't stay with Lincoln. He tried to tank SUNFLOWER."

"Oh? He did? You're kidding me!" She stuck a finger down her throat in a silent *gag me* motion. "Not Lincoln! How did he do that? Why?"

"He didn't think he'd be able to get the votes for it. Didn't have the balls to go through with it."

Opal held the phone back and looked at it. The real Andrew was showing himself now. Why she didn't see it on the first date, she wasn't sure. But it didn't matter. She saw it now. "That doesn't sound like Lincoln at all."

"Obviously you don't know him as well as you think you do."

"You are so full of shit." The timer beeped at her again. "Goodbye. I have to go."

She hung up, thrilled to be done with him once and for all.

THE MORNING LINK announced SUNFLOWER was almost perfect. He spoke with conviction, but not overpowering force. His speech was commanding and fluid. Three notable congressmen from oil and coal states immediately argued against it, saying that renewables were not the wave of the future. Lincoln delved into the plans for transitioning those economies so that their constituents would receive training in the new supporting industries to replace the old ways. The immediate pushback was related to staying with what they knew; the reaction was expected. Who could blame them? They had to speak up for their people.

Ultimately, the bill was referred to committee, as expected.

Opal was ecstatic, but a little nervous. The real work getting the votes would begin to make sure the bill received an overwhelming majority. Committee work on this shouldn't take too long, unless they started to spar across the aisle. Link had been pushing his ideas since he'd been elected. The hard thing would be to assuage the fears of the naysayers and show them they'd come out winners in the long run.

Opal had a phone call with Jack scheduled in about ten minutes, so she gathered her computer bag and headed back to the office.

On the way, she ran into Lincoln headed towards her with a crew of people behind him, walking and talking at the same time. He looked so good in charge. There was a certain color to his cheeks, his steps confident. He held out his hands to her, and she took his.

"Thank you, Opal, for all the hard work you've done."

"Appreciate it, Congressman. Just so you know, you have an interview with Gretchen Hughes in five minutes. She'll be waiting for you in the office."

"Thank you, Opal. We'll catch up soon."

He started walking towards his office in discussions with the crew around him.

Opal decided to send him a text, make sure he'd be full of good energy for the interview.

Opal: I love you, Lincoln.

She watched as he stopped and the crowd following him stopped as well. He pulled up his phone, read it, and whooped with joy, his arm punching the air in victory. He spun toward her and the crowd parted. But Opal jumped into the closest open doorway before anyone could see her. She wanted him to know, but the whole world needn't know just yet.

Her to-do list for the day was finished. She had nothing left to do and didn't want to risk interrupting his interview with Gretchen, and the rest of the office was fairly empty. She had her computer bag and her phone, and was already scheduled and approved for the rest of the week off. She planned to drive up to Annapolis to visit a girlfriend with a sailboat. The plan was to anchor in somewhere around the Chesapeake Bay for some swimming and maybe fishing.

Back at home, Opal set to packing her bag. She didn't need much for one day, but needed to be back in DC by Thursday afternoon to start rehearsals for the big ballet show on Friday. There was a knock on the front door and she answered it. A delivery man was holding an outlandish bouquet of flowers for her. She signed off and he handed over a gigantic vase full of sunflowers and a manila envelope addressed to her. She stepped inside of her apartment and shut the door. *What in the world was this?* Included was a handwritten note from Andrew.

Dear Opal,
Come with me! You and I will make a great couple. I can see you as a wife and a mother. WE will have this fantastic life in Ecuador, I promise you. A mansion. A full staff. Me and you and all the life we can live. I'll send a private plane at your convenience. The second you say yes.
With love,
Andrew

Opal picked up the vase of flowers and walked three doors down to Mrs. Borges's apartment. Opal loved hearing her old stories and had asked for her opinion on several thorny events, since her knowledge was far greater than hers. But today, she wasn't coming to hear old stories. Opal knocked on her door and stood so she would be visible through the peephole.

It always took Mrs. Borge's a minute to get to the door. "To what do I owe this surprise?"

"I have a bouquet of gorgeous flowers for you, darling," Opal said and held up the vase.

"Sunflowers are my favorite," she said. "You must have impressed him."

"Ah, but he did not impress me. Had I been a femme fatale, I would have taken a different course of action."

"I see. Will you bring them in for me? I'm afraid my arms are not what they used to be."

"I would be happy to." Opal walked in and placed them on the kitchen counter. "I would love to stay, but I still have one more thing to do."

"What are you going to tell him?"

"Mrs. Borges, I am a lady. I'm going to tell him straight."

"Your momma raised you right," Mrs. Borges said, shimmying her shoulders. "Don't let those boys get the best of you."

Opal smiled but didn't say anything. Her momma was complicated, but now was not the time to get into it. "*Boys* is right. I need a man. Would you like to come over for coffee next week? I'll tell you all about it."

"Wouldn't miss it," Mrs. Borges nodded enthusiastically.

"I hate to ask, but can I borrow your car? It would be ever so helpful."

"Of course," Mrs. Borges said, swiping the keys off the counter and handing them to Opal. "She's downstairs in the usual space."

"Thanks. I'll make sure to bring her back with a full tank."

ONCE BACK IN HER APARTMENT, Opal picked up the phone and called Andrew before she lost her nerve.

He answered, "Hey, Opal. Did you get my flowers?"

"I did, Andrew. That was nice of you."

"Are you coming to Ecuador?"

"I am not."

"Why not? When can I see you again?" The petulant whine he'd used with Jack slid into his voice.

"Andrew, please stop. It's not going to work with us. I was at the office last night. No one knew I was there. Not Link, not you, not your dad." She kept her voice calm and sincere. She wasn't angry anymore, but rather grateful to have the bravery to say what she needed to say to him. Even though her heart was beating out of her ears, and frankly she was scared, it was important to her to speak up, to say the words which would provide her closure. A long time ago, she realized emotions didn't solve problems, but actions did matter.

"Did Link say something about me? Whatever he said, it's not true."

"You're a dick. Link didn't say anything about you. You sunk *your own* ship, Andrew. I can't believe I almost fell for you. Good thing your true nature came shining through."

And with that, she hung up the phone. Damn did it feel good to tell him exactly what she wanted.

Chapter 25

The interview with Gretchen was actually way more pleasant than Link could have anticipated. She asked some impressive questions and was well versed in SUNFLOWER. He would have never guessed that Gretchen would make a great political reporter. Opal had definitely called that one right.

He couldn't stop himself from looking at Opal's text every five minutes. *I love you, Lincoln.* The giddy joy that had overcome him earlier stuck with him. Carleen had set up meetings from dawn to dusk the following day, all designed to help bring other members of congress on board with the bill. By the time this thing was out of committee, there would be huge bi-partisan support. SUNFLOWER was practically a done deal.

By the time Link got home on Wednesday it was

nearly midnight. If he texted Opal now, would he wake her up? If they were living together, they would have gotten home at the same time. He liked the image of coming home to her late at night. She might be sitting on the sofa reading a book, or she might be sound asleep on the bed. If she were asleep, would he be tempted to kiss her on the cheek or watch her sleep? He wanted that more than anything. He had already waited long enough for Opal, and he couldn't wait to talk to her.

Link: Today was crazy. But thank you. Knowing you love me means everything. It fueled me through the day.

Opal: XO. Already on the boat. Out of range soon. Can't wait to see you again. Saturday?

Saturday? Lincoln had forgotten Opal had scheduled both Thursday and Friday off from work. It was going to be a long and painful two days.

Link: Until then. Text when you get back.

Opal had mentioned something about a ballet performance on Friday night. Lincoln hated that there was so much he didn't know about her private life. He found her Instagram profile and looked through her pictures, chastising himself for ever having thought Opal would have ever stooped to playing games.

It didn't take him long to find out how Opal spent a good part of her weekends. Dozens of photos of adorable little kids dressed in costumes and doing impossible ballet moves were ninety percent of what she posted. One photo of Opal helping a little girl in leg braces made his heart ache at her tenderness. He remembered the conversation they had on the rooftop deck; she had a look on her face of unbridled joy when she had told him about the class.

These photos, and everything else on her Instagram feed, would be under scrutiny the minute they announced their engagement. Lincoln had very little doubt that Opal would say no to his proposal, his real proposal, his romantic proposal, when it came. But he hadn't really considered the ramifications it would have in her private life.

Maybe he didn't have to wait two days to see her. The beginnings of a plan started to rumble in his heart. The first thing he needed to do was make sure that Opal would be protected. But it was too late to do anything right at the moment. Link climbed into bed with a plan well formed in his head. He fell asleep to images of Opal spinning in his kitchen with the lightness of a feather on a leaf.

As soon as he was awake on Thursday, he called Kenny to set up a plan to make sure Opal's privacy was handled the best way possible. To make sure her social media was cranked down to private and unassailable by hackers. To wipe the internet clean of anything that could cause Opal pain or embarrassment should it be discovered. Kenny had all the connections to make all the technical stuff go away, and Lincoln didn't really care how he did it as long as it was legal and got the job done.

Kenny would have the plan ready, but wouldn't act on it until Link had consent from Opal. First, he had to get her to agree to marry him, and then he had to help shield her from the shitstorm of press activity that would follow. He couldn't make these decisions on his own, but he could pave the way to make sure she could protect her privacy.

As far as he could tell, people hadn't been reporting on his Hallmark moment in front of the White House when he'd yelled her name at the top of his lungs. He wouldn't take that moment back, but he might have been more circumspect. He asked Kenny to put out feelers on it and to come up with a campaign to build his and Opal's story. Kenny laughed and said he'd been working on it since their Sunday meeting. Lincoln hung up feeling like there was a plan in place.

Lincoln returned to Opal's Instagram page, looking closely at every photograph and piecing together what he didn't know about her yet. After a few minutes more, he clicked around and had the contact information for the ballet school. And a few minutes after that he was talking to the director of the school. This crazy idea of his was becoming a reality.

Chapter 26

Opal was stuck on the Chesapeake Bay Bridge. *Big Shocker*. Traffic was slow in both directions. Everyone seemed to be going somewhere at once and they all converged right here. Mrs. Borges, her lovely neighbor, had let Opal borrow her 1987 silver Mercedes 560SL convertible. She wore a Givenchy silk scarf around her hair to keep it from blowing every which way, but now on the bridge she was plain hot from the beating sun and humidity creeping up on her. She turned on the air conditioner. *Ahh life in the fast lane,* she chuckled to herself.

She checked her watch and saw she would still have enough time to go home for a quick shower before the ballet dress rehearsal. Opal reviewed a mental checklist of everything she would need to make sure the rehearsal went smoothly, and texted the production assistant that she was stuck in traffic but she should be on time. Now that she was at a standstill, she had time to think.

And what did she think about the Honorable Lincoln Pierce?

If he proposed marriage to her, was she willing to quit her job and focus her efforts elsewhere? She had worked her whole life to be in this position. Everything she did was to assure she had a place in the White House. But if they were married, she wouldn't be able to work for him due to nepotism. Opal had a strong moral fiber; there was no way she wanted her work to be tainted with the scuttlebutt that it stunk of favoritism. She wanted his run to be as clean as possible.

The question lingered in her mind like the humidity on her skin; she couldn't shake it. But he wasn't going to ask her to get married. Not after she told him in no uncertain terms no way. The next logical step was creating a life for them as boyfriend and girlfriend. The words sounded so silly and romantic to her. They would either have to remain secretive about their relationship or she would have to quit in order to quell any rumors of inappropriate actions. All of the solutions led to her quitting for love.

The scarf around her head had loosened and so she took it off. Since they were at a complete stop, she removed the hairband and ran her fingers through her hair. What she would do to be free from the constraints of a public life. But if she was with Link, that was exactly what she would be committed to. Otherwise, it was best to just break it off with him. She tied her hair back into a ponytail.

For love, she'd quit her job.

She'd ask Kenny where to look for the kind of job that would help support Link's career, and she surmised it would be working for an NGO or a trade association. She had plenty of contacts in that field and would have to see what kind of positions were open. Quitting wasn't losing out on an opportunity, it was simply reframing the life she wanted.

Of course, once—if—they ever married, and he was officially running for president, she'd have a different role to play. She'd have to quit working for money to stand by his side and take on her own role as first lady. There were so many places she could make an impact. Shivers crept along her arms and back. Exciting as it was, Opal understood all too well what that could mean for her. What images had she left on the internet? What photos did classmates have of her from college?

She had never been particularly wild. Had never cavorted naked anywhere. Never done anything remotely scandalous. No, there was nothing to worry about, was there? It didn't matter, though. No matter how hard she tried, someone would twist something innocuous to fit a political agenda. What Opal needed was a thick skin. Was hers thick enough to be Lincoln Pierce's wife?

She retied the scarf, knotting it under her chin. The car in front of her crept forward and picked up to a decent speed. She was running a little late. In order to fit a shower before rehearsal, she'd have to drive to the theater.

Opal walked into the studio and gasped at the stage production of the romantic ballet Giselle. Butterflies hung from the catwalk, stoic columns the background. The lighting was soft and just perfect. It would all change, of course, during the production, but she was so happy to have this moment of finally getting to see her visualizations become a reality. The little girls ran across the stage, playing, in their full-length white tutus.

She started down to the stage, intending on meeting up with the production assistant to start working through the list of the on-stage scene require-ments. They started with the background movements, and made sure they had enough volunteers on hand to make sure the process went without a hitch, and she asked if they were all dressed in black. The PA nodded her head.

"Oh, I almost forgot to tell you, but Giselle's costume is still with the seamstress, and...well, it's awful, but she was in a car accident yesterday. She has a broken foot and her arm is in a sling. Can you go pick it up? She won't let anyone else do it. The seamstress insists that it be you and 'not some lackey' as she so succinctly put it."

"Are you kidding me?" replied Opal. "She's always so picky, but she's the best there is. It's a good thing I happened to drive today. If I'm lucky and find close parking, I should be back in an hour and a half. Two hours tops." Opal grumbled as she climbed back into the car, annoyed that she'd have to spend so much time in traffic again.

THE BALLET COSTUMES were carefully wrapped in a garment bags with the ends tied off to prevent any accidents from happening. They'd turned out immaculate, the Russian seamstress an absolute godsend, having worked in costumes her whole life and wanting to help the girls look their absolute best. If Opal ever got married, she'd thought to ask her to make the dress. *Someday*. Opal was seeing Lincoln tomorrow night. Was it presumptuous to dare hope he would propose so soon? Everything was pointing in that direction.

Once Opal was back in the studio, she noticed everything was dark. Had they quit and gone home without her? Where was everyone? Dreamy orchestra music was playing in the background. The stage curtain was pulled close.

She took a step forward and the PA touched her shoulder. "Hi, Opal," she whispered. "I'll take that. I want you to follow me." The PA led her through the seats to one that was a few rows back from the stage and a few seats away from an aisle. "Sit right there."

"Wait! What's going on?" Opal asked. She was the director, what did the PA think she was doing?

"Shhhhhh. Patience." She held a finger to her lips and grinned.

Opal figured they must have gotten everything ready for her to watch the dress rehearsal, but she needed to run through the back to make sure everyone was ready. All of a sudden, the stage lights pointed at the curtain started to brighten.

The curtain opened to the introduction of Giselle, the soft sound of strings. All ten of her lovely students were dressed up with white tutus and holding white roses. The two boys wore deep blue Nutcracker Prince jackets with the gold trim. Everyone on stage looked wonderful.

But this was not the beginning of Giselle. They made a V on the stage, and in the apex of the V was a chair next to a podium box. She was about to get up and tell the PA, but then the students did two pirouettes with a final pose and all of their arms pointed upstage. A spotlight came on, and there he was, her man, Lincoln Pierce, dressed up wearing a fancy tuxedo with tails and a top hat.

Her throat choked up and tears brimmed her eyes. The music changed to something more fast-paced. Opal's lips parted and her heart skipped a beat to the rhythm of the music. Lincoln was doing a solo of their Karaoke debut from Vegas, "Marry You" by Bruno Mars. The whole effect and the slight chill made Opal's skin break out in goosebumps.

He held up a sign saying "Listen Please."

With a microphone in hand, he sung the first verse. His tenor was strong and well-practiced this time through. No warbling, no indecision. He had the words memorized, and he kept his eyes trained on her. And when the first chorus came up, he changed the words to "I KNOW I wanna marry you." There was absolutely no doubt about it.

A series of small spotlights appeared, like a path, from him to her. The dancers followed the light all the way to her. One student handed her a rose, then a second student, and so on until all twelve dancers were in the aisle and she had an armful of white roses. She placed her nose in the bouquet and inhaled its fresh and heady scent. A young girl with Down syndrome held out her hand. Opal nearly started crying, but held back for fear if she started, she wouldn't get to see the best part. The young girl led her on stage and took the roses from her, setting them next to her. The dancers followed and returned to their places on stage.

One of the boy dancers came out and threw rose petals between Lincoln and Opal. *Such a little scamp!* He winked at Opal and she laughed.

Lincoln took off his top hat and nudged the boy aside. He bowed to Lincoln and then to Opal before disappearing into the dark with a flourish.

The girls each spun and encircled the two of them. Then each, one after another, like a wave, did an arabesque before spinning away and leaping off stage right.

The spotlight flooded the two of them, making it so the only thing Opal could see was Link. It was as if the entire world had disappeared around them, and they were the only two people on the planet.

Lincoln dropped to his knees before her and held out black velvet box.

"Opal, I want you to know how much you mean

to me."

She was so choked up with emotion words escaped her. She clutched her necklace and tried to breathe slowly.

"I can't imagine another day without you."

Opal took a moment to gain control of the emotions bubbling up inside her. This was everything she had dreamed of, and she knew what was coming next. She had to break the tension somehow. "Two days was too long?"

"Yes. Two minutes is too long. I love you. Will you marry me?" he asked, reaching for her hand.

"Lincoln," she said, placing her hand in his. "I will."

Lincoln put the ring on her finger; it was an exquisitely detailed antique ring.

She grasped his hands and pulled him towards her. "Now you better stand up here and kiss me!"

"Yes ma'am. And I'll be happy to do so for the rest of our lives!"

Clapping erupted from both wings, reminding Opal that they were there. The lighting shifted and the entire studio flooded onto the stage, gathering around them to hug Opal and look at the ring.

"This is what I want, Link," she said, nearly oblivious to the sudden chaos around them. Tears trickled down her cheeks. "This means everything to me."

Chapter 27

The next morning, Link and Opal made plans to walk in separately at work. After his proposal, she had told him in no uncertain terms that she had work to do—they still had to run through the dress rehearsal and after that, she still had crucial paperwork to finish regarding SUNFLOWER. He had left to spend the evening strategizing with Kenny on the best way to reveal his engagement. He had arranged a meeting at the start of the day with Kenny and Madeline Asher, and of course Opal.

Opal was ahead of him in the security line, and he smiled. She was going to be his wife. Soon enough, after he executed his plan with Kenny and Madeline, they'd be able to walk in together. Maybe not holding hands, but even if they did, people wouldn't bat an eye.

Link practically bounced into the office. He

greeted everyone as he entered and beckoned Opal to join him. It was still ten minutes before Kenny and Madeline were scheduled to arrive. Opal came in with her notepad in hand, her hair pinned up, and looking so damn sexy. He got up and shut the door behind her.

"Good morning, Future Wife." He pulled Opal into his arms and gazed into her gorgeous, bright blue eyes.

She kissed him on the lips. "Good morning, Future Husband. Oh wow. Kissing you here feels almost naughty."

"I am the luckiest man in the world, Mrs. Meyers-Pierce. I love you."

"And I the luckiest woman, Mr. Meyers-Pierce. I love you back."

Link released her and stood back, scooping up her hands in his. She had not worn the engagement ring to work. He rubbed at the bare spot on her finger and nodded. "I suppose that's the right way to start with this."

"I've thought about this for a long time, and the best thing for me to do is look for another job. I'm putting in my notice. Unless you need me for the two weeks, today will be my last day. Kenny's got a couple of opportunities lined up; there's a COO position opening up at one of the NGO's and I'd be remiss not to explore it. And if you can believe it, Service Dogs of America even reached out to me."

Link gave Opal a chaste kiss and went to sit down. He leaned back in his chair. He knew Opal had struggled with the decision, that she had been in politics since high school, she was a policy expert, and could navigate through the political minutiae with ease.

"Please sit," he said. She obliged.

"You know I support you. And I know how much you love being in this business. When you're ready, if you want to run for office, I'll support you completely. The most important thing I want to tell you is thank you. I know this is hard for you."

Opal stood up and came around to Lincoln. She swiveled his chair toward her. "You are very welcome, Congressman." Then she leaned in and kissed him again.

Before the engagement, he thought this kind of news would have broken his heart, but he couldn't argue with her reasoning. In fact, he was excited for what the future would bring, both professionally and personally. "I'd love to have you stay, but you'll find something perfect. Kenny and Madeline are coming in to put a plan in place to scrub whatever you want off the internet before any of this goes public."

"I can't believe your proposal didn't go viral last night. It was so..." She looked at him with an expression of love and sweetness. Her throat tightened slightly at the memory. Had he really been that romantic? "It was perfect. I can't wait until tonight."

Link stood and kissed Opal again. This time she leaned back and when her lips opened slightly.

She arched her back and moaned quietly, inviting him in.

He pulled back. "Dear God, Opal, if we keep this up, I'm going to have to take you right here in the office." Link stepped back and took a deep breath, "Tonight, dear. I promise you tonight."

"I can't wait," she said, subtly licking her top lip.

"Damn it, Opal. Stop it or I'm going to have to take you home right now."

"Tonight is a long time away, Link." Her soft, sultry voice matching the clear invitation in her eyes.

"I don't know how you do that, little vixen." He gave her a sound and solid kiss. "Now go sit over there before hell breaks loose."

"Yes sir," she said, and took a seat in front of the desk.

Link took a few breaths to calm his body and his heart. He was semi-hard and wanted to take her right there, to pull up her skirt and sink into her, to watch her head lean back in pure pleasure, but now was not the time. "Did anyone videotape the proposal last night?"

"Yes, the PA sent me a video last night. Made me cry all over again. Anyway, I got everyone involved to agree to keep it a secret—including all the moms. Everyone there understood why I asked, and they adore you. Especially after last night. So, here's hoping."

A knock on the door interrupted them. Kenny and Madeline came in and offered their congratulations. Madeline gave Opal a hug, and Kenny shook Link's hand. The group settled and discussions began about developing a timeline that would allow Opal to leave the office, set up a campaign showing them dating, and when to officially announce the engagement. If they needed, they could work in the photo from Las Vegas at some point being the catalyst for Opal leaving the congressman's employment. Madeline said, "'Suddenly discovering they were falling in love, Opal Meyers chose to leave her job to make it easier for them to date without interfering with their work.'"

After the plan was finalized, the team left. Opal blew him a kiss goodbye, and then she was gone. The rest of the day was agonizingly long, and he didn't get a chance to see her again until that evening. Opal had told him that in order for Mrs. Borges to attend the performance, she'd have to drive her there and return her home.

"But I'm all yours by nine pm," she said. "I

promise."

The performance of Giselle was wonderful and he made sure everyone received a bouquet of white roses while on stage. For Opal, he chose a bouquet of red roses.

After the production, Opal kissed Link and let him know that she'd be over in about an hour. He kissed her hand as they parted and confirmed their date for the following evening. "I hope you'll be okay with homemade spaghetti and a movie at my place."

Opal nodded and kissed him goodbye. "I can't wait."

LINK STOPPED at the store and bought focaccia, garlic, green beans, and a tiramisu from the upscale grocer. When Link got home, he put on the spaghetti sauce into his Instant Pot. Damn right he was proud of his purchase. He fixed himself a whiskey before he got to work. First, he set out pillar candles on all the side tables and lit them for the perfect romantic ambience. Then he set the table with his grandmother's best china and crystal, silver candelabra, and flowers he picked up at the market. The linens he chose covered the glass table and softened the man-cave effect somewhat. He wanted tonight to be perfect.

He buzzed Opal in. He'd have to get her permanent access to the place soon.

As the elevator door opened, he greeted her with a hug and a kiss. She wore a soft cotton blouse with a pair of worn jeans and flip flops.

"Funny, isn't it?" she asked.

"What is?"

"We're engaged and this is our first official date."

"Nope. Karaoke night was our first date."

"That was not a date," she said. "That was..." she paused for a moment. "It was fantastic, but I wouldn't technically call it a date."

He laughed, then draped his arm around her shoulders as they walked to his apartment. It felt so natural, so right. She went ahead of him into the apartment and stopped as she took it in.

"All these candles. Fine china? Oh, Link, it's so romantic."

"Only the best for you."

Opal stepped into the kitchen and bent her head over the sauce pot. She closed her eyes and inhaled. "This smells amazing."

"I was thinking we'd eat, then watch a movie. *Desk Set* or *African Queen?*"

"*Casablanca?*"

"Maybe. I saw it just last week."

"So did I. That's funny. Two peas..."

"...in a pod," he said, finishing her sentence. "Let's see how it goes after dinner?"

"Sure," Opal leaned against a counter as he worked, sipping at a glass of syrah. Link couldn't believe he had the whole rest of his life to spend evenings like this with Opal.

When the spaghetti was finished, he dished up a plate for her. She poured a wine for herself and a whiskey for him. They sat down to the meal and talked about their day. Made some general plans for the wedding. He wanted to keep the political end minimal, she wanted small.

After dinner, Opal said, "Let's save dessert for later. I can't eat another bite right now."

He took her hand and led her into the living room. "Come into my man cave, dear."

She giggled and shook her head, "Oh dear. I hope you don't mind a few changes."

"I'd love anything you suggest. Except no pillows. I can't stand couch pillows."

"Come on, Link. One pillow?"

"Oh fine."

"Two?"

"Don't push it," he said, and brought her into his arms for a kiss. They settled on the couch and after a few minutes of discussion, decided on *Casablanca* for their movie. Opal snuggled into his side on the sofa.

He rested his chin on her head. As the movie started, he shifted so he could kiss her. He grasped her face with both hands, his thumbs tracing her sweet lips.

Opal ran her hands around his waist and up his back, her fingers digging into his shoulder blades. "Oh, Link. It feels like forever."

"Ever since I met you, I had to hold back, not give in."

"You knew for that long?"

She kissed him fiercely, parted her lips and invited him in. Their tongues swirled around each other, taking the measure of each other, ignoring the movie that played out before them. He stood up and picked her up off the couch. She put her arms around his neck and he walked back to his bedroom.

Once there, he laid her on the bed. She sat up on her elbows. "I'll be right back," he said and left to go get the pillar candles that were still burning on the dining room table. When he returned, he set them on his dresser. The curtains were closed and the lights off.

"I want to undress you," he said. "I want to see you."

"I want that too," she replied, still on the bed.

He took her hand and said, "Stand up."

She did as he asked. Link hooked his fingers into the waistband of the yoga pants and started to pull them down. Opal wiggled her hips so the fabric could move past her. He kissed her belly. Then he stood tall and lifted her shirt over her head. Once the shirt reached her hands, she took it off from there. He stood back and let himself take her all in. Her curly hair and how he couldn't wait to smell the tea tree oil shampoo she used. The look in her eyes that spoke of love and promises of love. Her soft breasts encased in a lacy bra. Her nipples already hard, expectant. She wore matching panties made of the same lacy fabric.

"Now it's your turn, Link. Take your pants off," she said.

He pulled down the sweats he'd been wearing and then took off his shirt.

"But leave your boxers on. I want to take those off."

He approached her. He was hard already, his penis aching to get out. He ran his hands down the sides of her ribs, and she put her arms around his neck. She lifted her chin to him and he kissed her, this time without abandon, letting himself take her. He cradled the back of her head, letting his fingers intertwine in her hair. She responded by running her hands down his back, cupping his bottom, pressing him to her.

He wanted to touch her, all of her, and they ended up against the wall. He pinned her hands there with one hand and pulled down a bra cup, pulling her breast out, his fingers circling the areola, pinching the nipple. She leaned back with pleasure, moaning for more. He took the nipple in his mouth, sucking it hard. Without releasing her nipple, he let go of his other hand and pulled down the other bra cup and squeezed her breast. The combination made him crazy, the softness of her breast in one hand and the hardness of her nipple in his mouth made his dick feel like it was about to explode.

He pulled back and lifted her, bringing her to the bed. He stood before her.

She hooked her fingers into his boxers and pulled them down. His rigid hardness stood proud before her. She took it in her hands and pulled it gently towards her. She put the tip of it into her mouth, and her tongue swirled around the head, dipping into the hole. He leaned back in ecstasy, "Opal." She encapsulated it between her warm fingers, moving up and down, she started to suck on only the tip.

The feeling was intense, sending ripples of pleasure up his body, but not enough to send him over the edge. "I want you," he said.

She started to take off her bra and he stopped her. "Let me." He sat next to her on the bed, and she turned so that her back was facing her. With a broad caress of her back, he finally landed on the clasp and undid it easily. He reached from behind and let his hands cup her breasts, pulling her body towards her. She leaned her head on his shoulder and sighed.

He turned her towards him and motioned to the middle of the bed. She moved to the center and lifted her knees, spreading her legs for him. He couldn't resist the invitation and pushed her knees apart, then with his hand, he circled her. Her pussy was hot and throbbing. Juices were seeping down. He pinched her clitoris and rubbed back and forth against it.

"Oh Lincoln, I need you."

He slipped three fingers into her and she opened her eyes, watching him. He loved that cloudy look of desire on her, and moved his hand back and forth. Her head dropped back and she moaned. He moved faster, egging her on, watching her hips move against his hand, taking pleasure from him, giving him hers.

As he watched her, and watched as his hand moving back and forth inside her, he was amazed at how much pleasure they could derive from each other, and something changed in him. A protective nature that he'd never felt before settled inside him. He had to taste her, to have her in his mouth. He removed his fingers and heard her cry out in anguish. He waited for her to look at him. And then he took his fingers and put them in his mouth, slowly sucking the juices off them.

Her mouth dropped open and desire flooded him. He moved between her legs and pushed them apart, as wide as then would go. With his fingers, he spread out her pussy in front of him. The labia purple, the folds slick with her juices, her opening convulsing with desire. He plowed his face right into her, lapping and licking all that he could; selfishly, he wanted everything she could give him. His tongue swirled around her clitoris, hard and throbbing, begging for release. He crested her clitoris with one hand while his tongue rammed into her. She clenched and unclenched, her hips moved back and forth to meet his thrusts.

"Oh god, Lincoln, take me. Fuck me."

He pulled back from her and there was that little cry again. "Yes, Mrs. Meyers-Pierce. Your wish is my command."

He got on his knees in front of her and pushed her knees up against her so that her pussy was open to him. He leaned forward and his penis was at the edge of her, just inside. She struggled against him, angling her hips, trying to get him inside her, but he held off. "Opal," he said, "look at me."

She opened her eyes and met his.

"I love you. I love the way you taste. I love the way you feel right now. I love you." He leaned forward and pushed her knees towards her body, which caused her to open to him even further. With their eyes met, he sunk himself into her wet hot folds until he was completely inside her. "You and I are one."

He kissed her lips, and she bit his bottom lip. She

put her arms behind him and pressed him into her further, "Deeper. Come into me deeper." He pushed against her with everything he had, knowing that he wouldn't hurt her. Her eyes widened as she took him all of him in, past the root of his penis. "Oh Link. I love you."

He slowly pulled back and then came into her again hard and full and as deep as he could.

"Take me. Take all of me," she said, and leaned her head back. He started pounding into her, letting go of everything, letting her take all of him, and she accepted, moving to take her own gratification as well. His eyes closed. She contracted around him, pulled him in, connected them together. Like being on a roller coaster, he felt the switch of his body, and he was about to come. She met his every move, convulsing around his hardness, pulling at him, squeezing him tight. She'd never let go and so he did, he let it all go and suddenly his body stopped and he felt the explosion come out of him and straight into her. He collapsed on top of her, both of them breathing heavy. Her legs fell to the side. He kissed her face, her neck, her breast. "I love you, Opal Meyers-Pierce."

"I love you too, Link," she responded. And they lay like that, together, connected body and spirit, two peas in a pod.

Epilogue

One year to the day after Lincoln proposed, he stood in front of the mirror and adjusted the medals on his dress whites. The last few days had been hectic, to say the least. He took in a deep breath, closed his eyes, and counted to ten. Two hands landed on his shoulders, shaking him back into the room.

"Lincoln, you look damn handsome, son. Your mom and I couldn't be prouder of you. Opal is more than we'd ever hoped for in a wife for you."

He hugged his father and released him.

Kenny popped his head into the room. "Ten minutes, people. Ten minutes." He eyed Lincoln and gave him the thumbs up before disappearing again.

It was only ten minutes until he would finally get to put the ring on Opal's finger and kiss her as his wife. Soon they would be Lincoln and Opal Meyers-Pierce.

He had agreed that both of them should change their names, that the notion of a woman relinquishing her identity in favor of her husband was outdated. He didn't care if he lost name recognition. What mattered was Opal.

In ten minutes, he would get to see her in her wedding dress.

"You ready, Link?" It was Sammy, his best man. He would have forgone any further groomsmen, but Opal had insisted on having six bridesmaids and it would have looked very unbalanced if he hadn't invited in more friends. And the best part was they had enough Naval officers in his wedding party to do the arch of sabers ceremony.

And, he had to admit, the party the night before had been quite the reunion for his office staff. Chloe Cassell had served as an intern for the entire year while attending law school. She'd graduated and had agreed to come on staff full time. She and Harrison Rousseau were living together in an apartment in Dupont Circle. They hadn't tied the knot yet, but they had announced their engagement at a party a couple weeks earlier.

Katherine O'Malley had slipped into Carleen's position shortly after SUNFLOWER broke. As an office manager, she sometimes terrified him, but she was good at the job. She'd shocked everyone with an elopement in Hawaii while there for a friend's wedding.

Madeline Asher had quit right before Thanksgiving the year before. Her father's vineyard had burned down during the devastating California fire season, and she'd moved back home to help him rebuild the business. Of all the women in the office, he assumed Madeline would have ended up with a wealthy man like Andrew Donohoe, but instead, word was she had a boyfriend who was actually a well-respected fundraiser in the NGO community.

It had been a while since he'd seen Lizbeth Crandall, too, though she'd resurfaced after months in China on an undercover assignment. She was so pregnant at the moment, Lincoln wasn't sure she could make it down the aisle. When he joked about it with Opal she laughed. "I think it would be cool for a baby to be born at our wedding, but maybe she can hold off until we cut the cake."

Eleanor Winslow's departure a couple months prior had been a blow to the office, but Lincoln couldn't argue with her reasoning. The seating chart app she had written for banquet managers was already being used in thousands of hotels. She had royalties flowing in, and she was already creating another program to expand her business.

Cheyenne LeFleur was now Cheyenne Moore.

She and Xander had both come, each with a baby in a front pack. The three-month-old twins were like night and day, one blond like their mom, one dark like their dad. Cheyenne and her restaurant partners were catering the reception, so she was there for double duty. She had plenty of people who could help out with the catering; besides managing a babe in arms, she was simply making sure that everything was done perfectly. Xander would have no shortage of people willing to help him with the babies during the ceremony.

Sammy pressed on Link's shoulders. "You ready? It's time."

Large bouquets of peonies with elaborate satin bows hung along every pew. The United States Naval Academy chapel was sweet with their scent. Lincoln closed his eyes for a moment, locking in every sensation so he'd remember it for the rest of his life. The groomsmen had finished seating the other guests. Lincoln offered his arms to his mother and father and walked them down the aisle. He hugged and kissed both of them before they took their seats.

Standing at the altar of the church, Lincoln made eye contact and nodded at many of the guests. There were plenty of important people here, but he'd studiously avoided inviting anyone who would require a secret service escort.

The groomsmen and bridesmaids had lined up along the outside, ready for the big event when he took his place up near the minister. The string quartet lit into Pachelbel's Canon for the wedding party processional. He waited patiently for each couple to come down the aisle and turn to their respective sides. The last pairing of groomsmen and bridesmaid took their position at the altar.

This was it.

The music shifted and the organist played the most familiar chords on the planet, the Wedding March. This was the moment he'd been waiting for nearly his whole life.

Opal rounded the corner on her mother's arm. He felt complete calm and complete chaos in that single moment.

Here comes the bride. My lady. My love.

Lincoln beheld a majestic jewel before him. Opal's hair was in an elegant up-do. Simple. A ballerina's bun with tiny pearls decorating it throughout. Her veil was attached to her hair with a simple tiara of champagne gold and pearls to match the colors of her dress. The lacy sheath dress hugged her body with exquisite precision. Opal had said she hired a Russian seamstress to make the dress, and it had been worth every single penny.

Lincoln basked in her beauty, hardly able to

believe how lucky he was that this goddess of a woman was walking down the aisle to be his wife.

Lincoln had wanted a more formal wedding. Opal had wanted to keep it small and not invite the entire US Congress. In the end, they decided to have the wedding ceremony at the Naval Academy and then a reception among the flowers and a gorgeous view overlooking the Chesapeake Bay for her. She was ecstatic that they worked it out and both of them were happy.

The US Naval Academy chapel commanded respect. She was glad to have her wedding here, the grandiosity of the architecture adding to the feeling that something monumental was about to happen. Opal scanned the crowd as she hovered at the entrance to the chapel; she felt as if someone had taken all of the air out of her.

There was so much love and kindness in everyone's eyes as they stood and turned to watch her. Her mom was with her, and they were linked arm in arm. An overwhelming desire to cry came over her. The aisle end caps were decorated with blooming peonies. And the best part of it, there was Link at the altar waiting for her. Once she made eye contact with him, the need to cry passed. She didn't feel overwhelmed. She felt confident and beautiful. The knowledge that she was marrying the love of her life, the right man for her, with this audience filled with friends and family members as their witnesses was empowering.

Standing at the edge of her new life, waiting for her cue to begin the short march to her dream, instead of closing her eyes, she opened them wide, ready to accept her new role, ready to step into a new life that was hers for the taking. All she had to do was take that first step. Her mom looked to her with a question in her eyes with raised eyebrows. A classical mom look. *Everything okay?* Opal nodded.

Her mom patted the pin on she wore on her dress. It was a miniature picture of Opal's father. He had died when she was thirteen from cancer, but they both kept his memory alive. "You know he's watching you, right?"

"I know, Mom. I still have you to watch over me too."

"I love you, and I am so happy for you." She leaned in to kiss her on the cheek. "You ready?"

"I am." Opal said, taking a deep breath and exhaling slowly.

The girls from her ballet class were dressed up in their ballet costumes, and they walked down the aisle, tossing petals onto the floor. Some of the girls couldn't help it and were dancing down the aisle causing the audience to buzz with warm sounds. When they got to the altar, they moved to her side. Everyone looked down to her expectantly. The Wedding March burst into the air.

This was it.

She looked up at Lincoln. He was standing proud and tall in his naval dress white uniform.

Damn. Hot diggity damn. He looked good. She didn't know he could look this good, though. Her man. Her soul mate. It was the first time she'd seen him in uniform. The real life of him didn't do the pictures justice.

The first step she took towards him was a little bit unsure. She was wearing heels and wasn't used to the cut of the dress, but her second step was better. She paused for a moment to measure her cadence to the marching rhythm. Her third and fourth step came naturally. She passed by all the smiling faces, and waved to those as she could. Even though they had made a conscious decision to keep the wedding small, there were still so many people. Her gaze came back to Lincoln, standing there, handsome as she'd never seen him before, sporting an expression of serene joy mixed with the giddy excitement that comes from standing in front of friends and family.

To declare their love for one another.

Carleen had advised her to take moments throughout the night to remember the event. That no matter what, she had said, it was her special day. Try to relax and enjoy everything about the day from getting dressed to getting undressed. Important advice for her since she was such a perfectionist.

They had written their own vows for each other. She had nowhere else to place the paper, since she hadn't memorized it, and tucked it into her bra. Her super special wedding bra. The bra that matched her super special wedding panties. All for Link's eyes only. She'd heard that most often, couples were too tired from the wedding to have sex, but she'd asked Lincoln if they could abstain for three months before the wedding to heighten their desire for each other the day of their wedding. She was pretty sure she knew how the night would end.

She glided down the aisle, the smell of flowers mixed with the dusty smell of stone in the Naval Academy. She waved to friends in the audience and blew a kiss to Mrs. Borges. Just before the altar, her mom stopped and gave her a kiss on the cheek. She stood in the front aisle and gave her a short nod.

Opal turned and Link had come down a few steps to meet her. He had the best smile ever, the one that said nothing else mattered. The one that said she was the one. The one that said an adventure was waiting.

She took his hand oh so willingly and returned his smile, the one that said 'Watch out world. Here we come.'

The officiant began the ceremony with all the usual *gathered here, no man asunder etc.* It went by so fast, that, before she knew it, he was looking at her expectantly to recite her vows. The vows that were in her bra. *THE VOWS WERE IN HER BRA.*

There were important people in the audience; she couldn't remember who they were because she needed to get the little slip of paper that had all the words she should have memorized out of *her bra.* She fake-yawned and ran her hand over her dress, slipping two fingers under the material and taking out the paper. There was laughter from the audience. Link's widened and his lips twitched into a bemused smile.

She shushed the crowd. They laughed even harder. Opal had a little giggle, and Link looked like he wasn't sure if he should laugh or be mortified. He turned to the crowd and shrugged his shoulder. Everyone roared. Opal and Link turned back to each other and they made eye contact, his hands gripping her free one. Once the chapel was quiet again, Opal read the words she had written.

"Dearest Link. Dearest of my heart. I give you my promise that as your wife, you shall not walk alone.

Together we move forward on a journey and explore our lives together. I love that you are caring and generous. I love that you are stand up for what you believe in. You are a man of your word. There are realities to a marriage we must all endure. You should know I am willing to provide you with comfort whenever Army plays Navy."

The raucous Navy guys took a moment to quiet down.

Lincoln leaned his head back and laughed. When he looked at her, there was that smile again. That radiant, devil may care, 'I'm the happiest man in the world' smile.

The officiant indicated that it was now Lincoln's turn to speak.

Link didn't need any paper. He was either winging it or had memorized what he wanted to say.

"Oh man. That was good, Opal. That's the thing, right there, ladies and gentlemen, why I love her so much. You always make me smile. You make me want to be a better man. You have the kindest heart of anyone I know, but you're one hell of a tough broad. Your love is my anchor; it keeps me moored in stormy waters. I promise to communicate when it's needed and without fear. I promise to value the things that make us unique and those that bond us. And like you, I know that there are realities in marriage. I promise to never ever turn the thermostat below sixty-eight degrees."

Opal smiled and couldn't help but laugh along with everyone else. She couldn't believe her absolute luck in finding someone so perfect.

After a couple of readings, Link squeezed her hands and winked, moving away. The little devil had a surprise up his sleeve. Something completely off script. Three men strode up to instruments strategically placed in the choir loft behind the pulpit. She had been introduced to them at a party for people coming in out of town the night before as Link's old band mates. The name of the band he still refused to say.

Link slipped the strap of an electric guitar over his head and they began to play. They lit into the song that had brought them together—Marry Me. She had no idea when they had found time to practice it, but they did a terrific rendition.

Link returned to her, holding out his hands. She grasped them and the officiant gave a short homily that reminded everyone in the room they were part of the support for a newly married couple. Finally, it was time for the ring exchange.

They'd chosen matching gold wedding bands, simple and without adornment. The insides were inscribed with their initials and their wedding date. The words 'with this ring I thee wed' made it feel so official. The extra weight of the gold on her finger was an anchor tethering her to Link in a permanent way.

"I proclaim you husband and wife. The groom may now kiss the bride."

Lincoln put his arms around her and dipped her slightly. Then he kissed her with a sensuous kiss on the lips.

He lifted her back up and as they took hands, she snuck one more kiss in on his lips before they turned to face their family and friends.

The crowd stood and erupted in applause as they walked down the aisle together.

AFTER MARCHING down the aisle as a newly married couple, they were swiftly guided to a side room to sign their official documents. While they did that, the guests were lined up outside the chapel and the eight members of the saber team organized themselves. All had either served with Link or been classmates with him in Annapolis.

Once all were ready, the doors from the chapel were opened and they moved to the top step. The arch team occupied the steps from the top down, spaced two steps apart each. The officiant stood behind them and made the official announcement at the top of his voice. "May I present Mr. and Mrs. Lincoln Meyers-Pierce."

Sammy gave an order and, with precision, the sabers were withdrawn from their sheaths and held upright against their shoulders. With a second order they moved their sabers in unison to almost touching their nose before lifting them high at the perfect angle, their sharp edges up to the sky.

The perfect arch of metal, their tips almost touching, was a sight to behold. Opal squealed with glee; usually she wasn't one for showmanship, but then, it had never been about her.

"Captain Lincoln Ulysses Meyers-Pierce and Opal Meyers-Pierce. We grant you our loyalty. Please proceed through the arch."

"Ready, my love?" Lincoln said to Opal.

"I'm ready," she said.

As they made to step past the first set of swords, Lincoln's firm arm guided her to not actually move as the pair lowered their sabers in front of them. One of the men said, "The right of passage is a kiss."

Link turned to Opal and kissed her.

"You didn't warn me about this part," she said.

"There's more."

The ritual was repeated with each of the arches in turn. As they made their way through, the crowd cheered them on and demanded longer kisses each time.

As they stepped past the last pair of sabers, Opal felt the light tap of one against her bottom. "Welcome to the Navy family, ma'am."

Opal looked at Link and he laughed. "I hope you don't mind, darling. It's a Naval tradition, but I did tell them to only have the last saber tap you."

How could she be mad? The Navy was a huge part of Link's life and her being part of that life was now official. Something had changed within her; she was a married woman; she would be his loyal, life-long partner.

Mrs. Borges's 1987 silver Mercedes 560SL convertible was decorated with bouquets of flowers tastefully added to the rearview windows and the bumper along with a string of cans tied to the back. He opened the door to the car and she got in. He got in next to her and started the car up with a roar, gassing the engine. The crowd clapped and whooped with glee. Opal turned to Link and kissed him.

"We're married!"

"Yes we are, love, yes we are."

And with that, he put the car in drive and they were off to celebrate their marriage.

More by Juno Chase

The DC Knights series can be read in any order, but we hope you don't miss any of them!

New to the Game—D.C. Knights Book 1

Chloe's the new intern, but she jumps into the game both feet first.

Playing For Keeps—D.C. Knights Book 2

Katherine thinks she's got things figured out until a sexy scientist tangos his way into her heart.

All In—D.C. Knights Book 3

Madeline has no problem playing games until she meets Ewan a man who knows how to treat her like a woman.

Fair and Square—D.C. Knights Book 4

Lizbeth doesn't have time for games, but she ends up in the midst of a political game no one in Congressman Pierce's office saw coming.

Only Bluffing—D.C. Knights Book 5

Eleanor Winslow and Daniel Prado are from different worlds. Will their love overcome dark histories and ancient legacies?

Game On—D.C. Knights Book 6

Cheyenne LeFleur lives on the wild side. Will Alexander Moore be able to handle her history, or will he reject her like so many before him?

For the Win—D.C. Knights Book 7 The final chapter in this series. Congressman Lincoln Pierce deserves love, too. Can he find it while maintaining his principles?

Also by Juno Chase:

ARTIFACT of BETRAYAL: an exciting romantic suspense novel

If you had to choose between saving your life or the love of your life, *who would you choose?*

Claire Townsend has it all, a great job, her own shop in Brooklyn, until one night when she loses everything. With thirteen days to pay off a dangerous loan shark, she decides to partake in a black-market smuggling operation to save her own neck.

Bruno Canul is an archeologist who works as a consultant with the FBI. He chases a suspect to Belize only to find the ex-love-of-his-life as part of the crew. He can't tell if he should trust Claire or if she's joined forces with the smuggler.

Afraid her choices will get Bruno killed, Claire tries to resist falling back in love with him. If she goes through with the smuggling scheme, she can pay off her loan, but she'd lose Bruno's love and trust *forever*. If she stands up for their love, she's a dead woman.

This adventurous romantic suspense is sure to keep you on the edge of your seat as Claire and Bruno find love in the jungle and ancient Mayan ruins of Belize.

About Juno Chase

Who said chivalry is dead? They were totally wrong! We love, love, love hot guys who are modern day knights and heroes but also know how to heat things up between the sheets.

Juno Chase is the nom de plume of two married moms who love reading and writing happy stories. We wanted to see these modern day knights celebrated in romance, so here we are. We're not a big group of people writing—there is just the two of us. We both spend lots of time reading and writing in each story to bring you the most complete, hot, and exciting stories possible.

Thank you so much for reading *New to the Game*, we hope you enjoyed reading it as much as we did writing it. If you sign up for our newsletter, you will be the first to know whenever we have a new book available.

Follow Juno Chase on your favorite social Media. We'd love to hear from you!

www.Junochase.com
juno@junochase.com

Acknowledgments

We'd like to thank a few people who helped us get this book into your lovely hands, dear readers. We are part of an amazing writing group who has listened to our ideas, helped us with plotting, and given us some straight feedback. We couldn't have done this without your energy and help-—you ladies rock! Thank you for all your reading time and thoughtful suggestions to help make the D.C. Knights series a reality.

To our intrepid beta readers. Thank you for taking the time to read and give us honest criticism. Especially to Dawn who has faithfully read everything we've handed her and keeps asking for more!

And to our families—our fabulous husbands and children who have supported us in so many different ways and picked up the pieces as needed. We love you!

www.ingramcontent.com/pod-product-compliance
Lightning Source LLC
Chambersburg PA
CBHW032205180726
48284CB00001B/199